MASSACRE AT CROW CREEK CROSSING

Pinnacle Westerns
by Spur Award Winner
CHARLES G. WEST

Hell Hath No Fury

No Justice in Hell

MASSACRE AT CROW CREEK CROSSING

CHARLES G. WEST

PINNACLE BOOKS
Kensington Publishing Corp.
www.kensingtonbooks.com

PINNACLE BOOKS are published by

Kensington Publishing Corp.
119 West 40th Street
New York, NY 10018

All Kensington titles, imprints, and distributed lines are available at special quantity discounts for bulk purchases for sales promotions, premiums, fund-raising, educational, or institutional use. Special book excerpts or customized printings can also be created to fit specific needs. For details, write or phone the office of the Kensington sales manager: Kensington Publishing Corp., 119 West 40th Street, New York, NY 10018, attn: Sales Department; phone 1-800-221-2647.

PINNACLE BOOKS and the Pinnacle logo are Reg. U.S. Pat. & TM Off.

ISBN-13: 978-0-7860-4558-7
ISBN-10: 0-7860-4558-2

First printing: November 2019

10 9 8 7 6 5 4 3 2 1

Printed in the United States of America

Electronic edition:

ISBN-13: 978-0-7860-4559-4 (e-book)
ISBN-10: 0-7860-4559-0 (e-book)

For Ronda

CHAPTER 1

Cole Bonner stood up again after having put the mortally wounded deer out of her misery. He looked back when he heard Harley Branch pushing through the willows beside the busy stream behind him.

"I swear," Harley offered, "she got farther than I thought she would." He was breathing heavily from his efforts to catch up to the deer and his younger friend. "Fine shot, though," he continued as he walked up beside Cole and peered down at the doe. "Right behind her front leg—you're gettin' pretty good with that bow. I reckon that's what you were aimin' at, tryin' for a lung shot."

Cole snorted, amused. "Hell, I was just aimin' at the deer. It just happened to hit her there."

Harley snorted in reply, knowing Cole had hit the deer exactly where he had aimed. His young friend seemed to be handy with just about any kind of weapon, so Harley had not been surprised by the short time required for him to become quite efficient with a bow. Cole had deemed it important to learn to use the weapon since money for .44 cartridges was not in great supply.

"I reckon we'll butcher it and smoke it and pack it if we've got any more room on the horses to tote it," Harley said. "If we run up on any more deer, we're liable to have to train some of 'em to use as packhorses to tote the rest of the meat." He paused to chuckle at the thought of it. "I reckon old Medicine Bear will be surprised to see us show up with all the meat we've cured—happy, too. He ain't lookin' for us to come back before spring."

"Reckon so." Cole had not planned to return to the Crow village on the Laramie River before spring, and maybe not until summer, depending on how he felt. The time he and Harley had spent in the mountains had served to entice him to push on to explore the ranges beyond the Bighorns. It was a period in his life when he needed to find a peace in his soul, and the high snowy peaks seemed to speak to him. There were things he would like to forget, and people he would always remember. The solitude of the Rocky Mountain ridges and valleys came to him as a place to heal. But as winter deepened, he realized that Harley was past the point when the mountains spoke to him. Cole owed a great deal to the short, bow-legged little man the Crow people affectionately called Thunder Mouse. Harley had come along at a time when Cole needed someone who knew the country and would stand with him when the going got rough.

Although Harley never complained about the rough dwelling they had fashioned at the bottom of a long narrow ravine, Cole decided to pull out of the snowy Bighorns and take Harley back to a warm tipi. "This oughta just about do it," he said, nodding toward the carcass. "We'll start back in the mornin'."

"Whatever you think best, partner," Harley said as casually as he could manage, still trying to disguise his eagerness to return to the Crow camp. They worked the rest of that day, smoking the largest portion of the fresh kill to preserve it, while keeping a generous amount of it to eat on the way back to the village.

On the second day of travel about a mile short of the South Fork of the Powder River, Cole pulled his horse up short when he discovered a thin column of smoke rising on the far side of a treeless ridge up ahead. He waited for Harley to pull up beside him on the low rise before commenting. "If I had to guess, I'd say that oughta be comin' from beside the river."

"I expect you're right," Harley agreed. They both studied the smoke that etched a thin dirty yellow line on the cloudy gray sky. "About right for a campfire, providing there's a sizable party campin' there," he added.

Cole was thinking the same as Harley. They had seen signs of a hunting party in the foothills, and on one occasion, had gotten close enough to identify it as Sioux. They could play it safe and swing around far enough to strike the river south of the camp and avoid it altogether. With no wish to encounter the Sioux hunters, that would be the wisest choice to make. Cole could not ignore the natural urge to take a look, however, in case it was not the hunting party's camp. Some innocent travelers might be under attack by Sioux warriors, although if that was the case, he and Harley were close enough to hear any shooting, and there was no sound of that. Also, if that was the case, it probably meant they were too late to help. It was not likely to be settlers traveling this time of year in that country, anyway—maybe a cavalry patrol that found itself outnumbered by the hostiles.

Still, Cole decided it couldn't hurt to find out who was burning what, if only to determine any threat to Harley and himself. "We might best take a look."

"I reckon," Harley agreed, knowing his friend well enough to have been certain they would all along.

The snakelike course of the river was easily traced by the trees and bushes that lined its banks as it wound its way through the open prairie on both sides. Their concern was that they would have to cross that rolling treeless plain before reaching the cover of the cottonwoods beside the river. Anyone who might be watching from the river could easily see them before they got within one hundred yards. Consequently they decided to angle off toward the east to strike the river farther downstream and then work back to the point where the smoke originated. Hindered a great deal by the string of packhorses behind each rider, they knew it would not be to their advantage to be spotted by anyone in the event they were forced to run. They planned to tie the horses in the trees when they approached the camp and proceed on foot from that point.

It took almost half an hour to reach a spot on the riverbank approximately two hundred yards short of the place from which the smoke emanated. They dismounted and Harley remained there to guard the horses while Cole made his way along the bank on foot.

"Make sure don't nobody spot you," Harley said. "We might have to leave in a hurry if that is a pack of Sioux and they come after you. I'll have a helluva time tryin' to manage this big bunch of packhorses by myself."

"I don't plan on gettin' caught," Cole assured him. "But if I do, I'll try to get off at least one round to warn you. If you hear it, don't wait for me." He didn't care much for alerting a Sioux hunting party of his and Harley's presence and losing the supply of meat they had cured to take to the Crow village, as well as the horses that were carrying it. There was also concern for the hides he was packing. He sorely needed them to trade for the ammunition and supplies he was running short of.

In spite of those concerns, however, he could not ignore the column of smoke and ride on, not knowing if someone there was in a bad situation. "I'll whistle if it's all clear."

"Just be careful," Harley reminded him once more as Cole started out along the bank of the river.

Within fifty yards of the smoke, he still heard no sounds that would indicate the presence of anyone. Another ten yards took him to the edge of a low bank of berry bushes where he got his first glimpse of the source of the dirty yellow smoke. In a small clearing near the water's edge, a typical farm wagon was still smoldering, the wagon box and its contents having been mostly consumed by the flames beneath it. He paused for a few moments, scanning the campsite carefully, then looked back at the burning wagon. To set it on fire, the Indians had simply pulled the wagon over their victims' campfire and parked it there. He scanned the campsite again to make sure, but it was obvious that no one was left in the camp, at least no one alive. Cole shifted his gaze back closer to the edge of the river when the dark shape of a body caught his eye. *Someone*, he thought, *prospector or settler, has rolled the dice and lost.* It was a shame, but it was not that rare an occurrence at a time when Sioux war parties were raiding all along the Yellowstone and its tributaries. Satisfied that there was no longer any danger, he stood up and whistled for Harley to bring the horses.

Cole walked out of the cottonwoods and went straight to the body lying near the water, paying close attention to the tracks in the light snow on the ground. By the time he reached the body, he knew it was not Indians who had attacked the unfortunate victim. There were no tracks left by unshod ponies, as there would have been had the man been killed by Indians. And there were footprints left by men in boots, not moccasins. The men who did this rode shod horses. And from what he could see, there were no more than two or three men. He turned the body over and stared down at the victim, a youngish man, possibly no more than twenty-five or thirty. Dressed in the simple garb of a farmer or prospector, his scalp had not been taken, a further indication that the evil business was conducted by white men. There were two bullet holes in his chest and a more obvious one in his forehead, that one evidently to make sure he was dead.

Cole was looking around at what remains he could find near the smoldering wagon when Harley entered the clearing, leading the horses.

"I swear . . ." Harley muttered when he saw the corpse, "some bad business here." He looked over at Cole, still close by the wagon. "Whaddaya figure?"

"Well, it wasn't Indians," Cole replied, concerned more than he had been because of the pieces of woman's clothes he'd found that had not been completely consumed by the flames. He held a scorched skirt up for Harley to see, all that was left of a gingham dress.

"I swear . . ." Harley muttered again, shaking his head slowly. "What in the world was they doin' out here in the middle of nowhere, all alone?" He looked around him as if searching for another body.

Sharing the same thought, both men began a scout of the clearing, hoping to find the woman still alive. After a thorough search, they concluded that she had been taken by the men who had killed her husband.

"They headed out this way," Harley called from the opposite end of the clearing. When Cole joined him, Harley added, "Yonder," and pointed toward a line of low hills to the southeast.

Cole studied the line of tracks that led into the river. "Might be three men, but I'd bet there was just two of 'em and the woman, and maybe two packhorses, with the woman ridin' a mule." He pointed to the smaller hoofprints mixed in with the others. He stepped up in the saddle then and forded the river to see if they had continued in the same direction once they crossed.

He returned to join Harley, shrugged, and said, "I reckon we'd best find out what happened to the woman." His comment seemed almost casual, but the picture of what the woman might be enduring was not something he could ignore. Her husband looked to be a fairly young man, causing Cole to speculate on the woman's fate. Had she been older, she would more than likely be lying dead beside her husband. "I can't waste any more time," he said to Harley. "I don't know how much head start they've got, but there ain't much daylight left before they'll be thinkin' about making camp."

Harley understood what Cole was about to say. He was thinking the same thing, so he cut him off. "That feller layin' over there is just startin' to get real stiff, so maybe they ain't got too much of a lead. I figure it'd be best if you was to go on after 'em and I'll come behind you with the horses. If they hold to that line the tracks started out on, they're pretty much headin' the same way we are. I hope I won't be that far behind you." He knew what Cole was capable of on his own and that he would just slow him down. "You just be careful you don't go ridin' into no ambush."

"Right." Cole turned the big Morgan back

toward the other side again. "It ain't gonna be a hard trail to follow," he called back over his shoulder. He hated to leave his friend with the job of protecting their horses, but in good conscience, he had no choice. He just hoped that he could find the woman before she was harmed too badly.

"I'll wait here till the horses have had a chance to drink before I start after you," Harley said. "While I'm waitin', I'll put this poor feller in the ground."

Cole waved his hand to acknowledge, then set out following the obvious trail in the light snow. Harley paused a few minutes, watching his young friend as he rode off after the men who had done this evil business. He had not mentioned it, but he was sure that memories of Cole's past had come rushing back to remind him of the tragedy that had destroyed his family—also at the hands of murderers like these he was bound to go after today. Harley could tell when the occasional memory came back to haunt his friend, but Cole never spoke of it. *Maybe time will eventually heal his sorrow*, Harley thought.

As he had told Harley, Cole had no trouble following the trail, which led to the southeast in the general direction of the little settlement of Casper. He encouraged Joe to a fast walk, and the big Morgan gelding responded willingly. Cole had planned to rest Joe at the river even though he had not shown signs of exhaustion, but he was going to have to ask a little more of him. If the men he pursued were heading to Casper, it was unlikely they planned to reach that town with a woman hostage in tow, so he could not waste any time in the chase. Maybe they would stop a little earlier than usual to make camp. That would be good for him, but might not be good for their captive. The thought increased the urgency he already felt for the woman's situation.

Malcolm Womack pulled his horse to a halt and waited for his brother to pull up beside him. He pointed to a pocket of trees a few hundred yards ahead, where a stream wound its way through a shallow valley. "That looks like a good place."

"I was startin' to wonder if you was gonna stop anytime soon," Travis said. Younger than his brother by a year and a half, he was accustomed to waiting for Malcolm when it came to making decisions— at least when their eldest brother, Troy, was not present. That was the case on this trip, Troy having elected to remain in Laramie.

Malcolm chuckled in response. "You ain't gettin' itchy, are you, brother? Hell, we ain't rode more 'n five miles from their camp." He turned in the saddle to look back at the woman on the mule behind him. "How 'bout you, Buttercup? You gettin' itchy, too?" He chuckled again at the joke he had made, amused by the lack of response from his hostage.

In mortal fear for her life, Carrie Green was not certain whether or not she might prefer death to the horror she feared was awaiting her. Her eyes downcast, she sat astride the mule that had pulled her wagon, her mind's eye still blinded by the picture of her husband's brutal slaying. Since there was no saddle and no reins, she had kept from falling off by holding on to the mule's stubby mane, her wrists firmly bound together. She wished now that she had been killed with her husband, and the thought of letting go of the mane had tempted her. But she feared a fall from the mule would only cause her more pain to add to that from the deep bruise on her face, the result of a stunning blow from Malcolm's fist. It came as a clear message of her helplessness at the hands of her abductors.

"Yonder in that sharp bend looks like the best spot," Travis suggested, the hint of excitement obvious in his voice. "There's still a good bit of daylight left. I reckon we're just gonna stop long enough to rest the horses, ain't we?" His mind was already heating up with thoughts of what he might do to pass the time while the horses were resting.

His brother's impatience caused Malcolm to chortle. "Why, hell no. We might as well camp early—give us a little time to enjoy some of that ham Buttercup and her husband brought with 'em, and maybe see if she's worth the trouble it took to take her with us. They sure as hell weren't carryin' anythin' else in that wagon worth two cents." The lecherous grin plastered on Travis's face told him it was good news to him. *Too bad ol' Troy stayed back in Laramie,* Malcolm thought. *He'd sure enough get a kick out of this.*

Travis was a little slow between the ears. It was not noticeable right off, but his lack of common sense exposed itself within a short time in any company. Malcolm was looking forward to seeing Travis's reaction to having a tussle with a respectable woman, even if it was against her will.

Malcolm grinned. That would be after he had his tussle with the unfortunate woman, of course. He laughed to himself, thinking that Travis would probably try to pay her afterward. Malcolm shook his head when another thought occurred to him. *She's a right handsome little filly. Too bad I'm gonna have to kill her before we hit town.* "Come on," he blurted. "Let's get on down there and get us a fire goin'. I'm hungry." He gave his horse a kick and started off down the rise, leading Carrie's mule.

Travis followed, leading their two packhorses, the foolish grin of anticipation still in place.

They weaved their way through the stand of pines that bordered the stream and pulled up just short of the water. Travis slid off his horse immediately, drew his knife to cut the rope binding her wrists, and rushed to pull Carrie off the mule. Kicking at him furiously, she tried to resist his efforts and for a few moments it appeared to be a draw, since he only had one free hand. Finally in frustration, he dropped the knife, grabbed her ankle, and jerked her roughly off the mule. Landing hard on the ground, she nevertheless kicked at him before sliding on her backside under the mule to escape him. The mule naturally jumped sideways to avoid the frantic woman under its belly, almost knocking Travis down in the process.

Highly entertained by his brother's clumsy attempts to subdue the terrified woman, Malcolm threw his head back and laughed. "Damned if you ain't got a strange way of courtin' a woman," he chided. "Just hold off a bit before you get all lathered up and I have to throw you in the water to cool you off. Take care of the horses first, then we'll get a fire goin', so we can get somethin' to eat. We got all night to see that the lady gets all she deserves. Don't that make more sense?"

After a moment, Travis settled down and stepped back to stand beside Malcolm. They stared down at the frightened woman for a few moments as she continued to slowly push herself away from them until she was stopped when she met with the trunk of a young cottonwood at her back.

"That's as good as any," Malcolm smirked. "Fetch me that rope," he said to Travis. When his brother stepped quickly to get the coil of rope from his saddle, Malcolm took it from him and proceeded to tie Carrie to the tree she had unintentionally selected. "There," he declared, "now you just pull yourself together and we might give you a little somethin' to eat to keep your strength up. And, Buttercup, you're gonna need it. That boy's as rank as an unbroke mustang."

Like a calf roped and tied for branding, Carrie stared up at him with eyes wide with fear. For the first time since her abduction, she spoke, pleading for mercy. "Please don't hurt me," she sobbed.

Enjoying evil satisfaction from the doomed woman's helplessness, Malcolm replied, "Why, we ain't gonna hurt you much. You might even have a good time." He left her then to contemplate the ordeal awaiting her while he went to help Travis unsaddle the horses.

A multitude of thoughts collided inside her brain, thoughts of terror and the recurring image of her husband as he lay dying, seconds before the sickening sight of the final shot to his head. Friends in Bozeman had advised against starting back to Cheyenne alone, but Robert had been determined to get back before hard winter set in. She sobbed when she thought about it, ashamed that she could think of blaming him for delivering her to this fate. She even envied him, now dead, with no suffering left to face.

From the tree where she was tied, she could see the two men thirty yards away by the side of the stream, joking and teasing each other as they un- saddled the horses and began to collect firewood to build a fire. *After they have had their way with me,* she thought, *they will kill me, just as they did Robert.* It was enough to cause the tears to flow down her cheeks again. The thought of the assault upon her body was more horrifying than the death that was sure to follow. She could think of only one way to de- prive them of their wicked pleasures. Even though she truly believed that it was a sin to kill one's self, she felt sure that God would be forgiving in this case. Resolved then to try, for she was not sure she had the strength to accomplish it, she strained to reach under her heavy skirt for the knife knocked from Travis's hand when the mule bumped him. He had evidently forgotten it in the excitement. It had fallen between her legs, and she had managed to drag it with her on her skirt tail as she had backed away from the two men.

In his hurry to make camp, Malcolm had not deemed it necessary to bind her securely to the tree since he was planning to untie her again in a matter of minutes. Consequently, Carrie was held to the tree by several loops of the rope around her upper body and her arms down to her elbows. Even though her wrists were still tied, she found she could just reach the knife by straining as hard as she could. Once she secured the handle in her hands, she drew it up to her to see if she had enough freedom to make the move necessary to plunge the blade into her breast. The question she could not answer was whether or not she could summon enough strength to force the knife into her bosom. Determined to do it, however, she hesitated a moment to ask God for forgiveness. Then she closed her eyes, and calling on all the strength she could muster, she snatched the knife toward her breast. She was immediately stunned when her arms were blocked by an unyielding force and a hand was clamped tightly over her mouth.

"Don't make a sound," a voice behind the tree ordered. Her eyes fluttered open and she could still see the two brothers down near the stream. "I've come to help you." The arm that had blocked her knife thrust was cloaked in a buckskin sleeve, leaving her to believe her rescuer was an Indian. Thinking she had been saved from one fate only to be threatened by another, she was too terrified to decide which would be worse.

As the hand covering her mouth was slowly withdrawn, she thought to scream until the voice said, "My name's Cole Bonner. I'm gonna try to get you outta here." He took the knife from her hand and cut one strand of the rope around her shoulders. When he had freed her, he pulled her back behind the tree with him.

Less fearful now, she quickly scrambled back to him, eager to do anything he ordered.

"Any minute now, they're gonna look over here and see you're gone," he said, speaking softly. "Are there just the two of 'em? Anybody else with 'em?"

She shook her head anxiously, her tears flowing freely, as she uttered, "They killed my husband! They murdered him!"

"I know," he said, doing his best to calm her as he cut the ropes binding her wrists, for she looked as if she might lose control of her emotions. "And I'm gonna try to get you somewhere safe while I take care of them. Just do what I tell you. Can you do that?"

She nodded.

"Good." He led her a few steps away, keeping the tree between them and the two, so far, unsuspecting outlaws. Pointing toward a small gap in a bank of laurel, he said, "Run just as fast as you can through that hole in the bushes. Twenty or thirty yards on the other side of 'em you oughta find my horse standin' in the trees. Wait for me there."

Before he could say more, the sharp report of a handgun rang out and a chunk of bark flew from the tree behind them at almost the same instant. It was followed in rapid succession by three more shots, each one impacting with the tree trunk.

"Go!" Cole ordered, and Carrie did not hesitate. He watched her briefly to make sure she gained the bank of bushes and disappeared beyond, then he turned his attention back to the two men inching their way toward the tree, firing wildly as they approached.

Lying flat on his belly, Cole inched up closer to the trunk of the tree, wishing they had picked a bigger tree to tie the woman to. The unfortunate cottonwood was suffering a major assault as the two brothers concentrated their fire at the foot of it. The rain of bullets made Cole reluctant to expose his head and half his body to get off a shot in return. Knowing he couldn't remain there much longer before one of their shots found him, he pulled a piece of a dead limb out from under him. With almost one movement, he tossed the limb at some bushes to his right, then quickly rolled to his left, his rifle held tightly up against his chest. There was little time to aim, but the moment's distraction caused by the limb he had thrown afforded him the opportunity for a quick shot. He pulled the trigger before the butt of the Henry was even close to his shoulder. The shot caught one of the men in the shoulder, knocking him to the ground.

"Travis!" Malcolm Womack cried out when he saw his brother fall. He dropped immediately to take cover behind a rotten log. "You all right?"

"I'm hit!" Travis answered.

"Can you move?" Malcolm asked. When Travis replied that he thought he could, Malcolm said, "Crawl back to the riverbank. I'll keep this son of a bitch busy till you get there." Seeing Travis making his way backward toward the cover of the low bank, Malcolm raised his head to take a shot at the rifleman, only to receive a face full of wood splinters when a slug from Cole's rifle tore into the rotten log. It was enough to cause him to push himself backward while keeping as flat on the ground as he could, hoping to reach the river-bank, firing in the direction of the rifle blast as he did. He dropped below the low bank just as the hammer of his pistol clicked on an empty cylinder. Using the cover of the bank, he quickly reloaded the empty cylinders. Ready to fire again, he raised up to find his adversary standing no more than fifty feet away, his rifle aimed, waiting for Malcolm to show himself.

In the next instant, the .44 slug from the Henry struck him in the center of his chest. The loaded pistol dropped from his hand as he slumped to the ground, never wondering why his brother had not shot the tall figure in buckskins as he stood unprotected, waiting to take the fatal shot.

Cole walked cautiously to the edge of the bank to make sure Malcolm wasn't playing possum. The blank, wide-eyed look of surprise frozen on Malcolm's face told him he was no longer a threat. He looked then toward the north when he heard the sound of hooves, just in time to see a horse and rider disappearing beyond the bend of the river. The thought of pursuit crossed his mind, but he discarded it. It would take too much time, and he had the woman to think about. It would be best to do what he could for her, wait for Harley to catch up, and move on. It seemed unlikely to think they'd see any more of the outlaw that had escaped. He was wounded, how badly Cole wasn't sure, although it appeared to be no more than a shoulder wound. From the way the outlaw had run off, leaving his partner with no backup, told Cole the man had no stomach for a face-off.

Beyond the bend in the river, Travis Womack urged his horse for more speed. When he had been shot and retreated to the cover of the riverbank, he had not been sure how many were in the party that attacked them. His first thought had been to get away, with only a brief concern for Malcolm, thinking it his brother's choice to run or stay. There had been no time to saddle his horse or grab his saddlebags. Before galloping away along the river, he looked back to see the one lone man, standing in the open, waiting for Malcolm to pop up from the riverbank. In mere seconds, he saw Malcolm raise up to be immediately shot down. He felt bad for his brother, but his death only served to convince him that he had been wise to run. Too bad Malcolm didn't. He would retain that vivid image of a wild man in buckskins, Indian or white, he wasn't sure.

CHAPTER 2

Tense with fright after hearing all the shooting on the other side of the thick laurel bushes, Carrie was not sure what she should do. What if the mysterious man who had come to help her was killed by the two murderers who had taken her? When the shooting finally stopped, she wondered if she should take the stranger's horse and flee. When she looked at the dark horse tied to a laurel branch, it looked so big and powerful that she questioned her ability to ride it. She was no rider by any means, having barely been able to hang on to the mule's mane to keep from falling off. Flustered by indecision, she decided not to try riding the horse and chose to hide instead. She ran farther back in the trees to find a place to hide. A deep gully that ran back toward the river seemed the best place, so she stepped down into it and huddled up against one side of it.

Pushing through the bushes again, Cole found Joe where he had tied him, but there was no sign of the woman. He called out, "Ma'am?" But there was no answer. *Surely she didn't run off,* he thought.

Maybe she just tried to find a place to hide. Thinking that to be the most probable thing, he looked around him at the ground. He couldn't help shaking his head in wonder when he looked at the obvious footprints in the thin layer of snow. He proceeded to follow them, pausing several times when they led in one direction, then back in the opposite, first right, then left. It was plain to see that the woman had run in fright, unable to find a place to hide. Finally finding a deep gully leading down to the water, she had evidently settled on it to take refuge. With the tracks in a straight line toward it, Cole stopped some distance short of the gully and called out again. "You can come outta that gully now. Ain't nobody gonna hurt you."

A few long moments passed, then finally she peeked up over the edge of the gully. Seeing him standing several yards away, patiently waiting, she sheepishly climbed up out of her hiding place, realizing she had not thought about the obvious trail she had left in the snow. Seeing him standing tall and powerful, she wondered if she could trust his intentions any more than those of the two he had just freed her from. As soon as he spoke, however, she sensed an honest quality about the man. Although dressed like a savage, he obviously was not, and she felt safe almost immediately.

"I'm real sorry about your husband, Ma'am," Cole said. "What were you doin' out in the Bighorn Valley by yourselves? Where were you headed?"

"We were on our way to Cheyenne," Carrie said. "My husband's father has a store there. We were going to try to make a new start there."

"Farmin'?" Cole guessed.

Carrie nodded.

"Where did you start out from?" Cole asked.

"The Yellowstone. About six miles from Boze-man. We had a piece of land near the river, but it was a sorry piece of land, so we decided it best to go to Cheyenne. Robert's father told him he could help in the store while he looked for some decent land to work. But now this has happened, and with Robert gone, I don't know what else to do but to go on to Cheyenne. I've got nobody to go back to in Bozeman."

"Yessum, I can see that you're in a real bind," Cole said. "I reckon if you're still wantin' to go on to Cheyenne, though, I can take you there." He had no desire to see Cheyenne again. There were too many memories in the little town that was orig-inally called Crow Creek Crossing. So many of those memories were bitter ones. But he didn't see that he had much choice, now that he had rescued this woman. He felt responsible for her, at least as far as seeing her safely to Cheyenne.

"I would certainly be beholden to you," Carrie said, although without her husband she was not sure Cheyenne was the best place for her. She had never met his parents, and she could not be cer-tain she would be welcome there now that Robert was gone. How would they react, she wondered, when a strange young woman appeared, claiming to be their daughter-in-law?

"Maybe you got family somewhere else," Cole suggested when she confessed her concerns.

"No, no family," she replied. "Robert was all the family I had."

"What's your name?"

"Carrie," she replied, Carrie Green."

"Green," Cole repeated. "Your married name?"

She nodded.

"That'd be Douglas Green then. Is that your husband's father?" He remembered the owner of the dry goods store in Cheyenne.

She nodded again.

He stroked his chin as he thought over the circumstances in which he now found himself. After a minute, during which Carrie watched him anxiously, he sighed and said, "Well, Carrie, I've had dealin's with Douglas Green and I've met Mrs. Green. They both strike me as nice folks. They'll most likely welcome you in their home. Tell you what. I'll see that you get to Cheyenne to your in-laws, but we're gonna have to make a stop at a Crow village on the way. We're packin' a right smart load of meat that'll look mighty good to those folks in that village. My partner's comin' along behind me with the packhorses, so we'll wait for him to catch up. He's seein' that your husband's body gets a decent burial. While we wait, why don't you come on back and sit by that fire those fellows started. Maybe I can fix you something to eat, if you're hungry. First I'll see if I can round up the horses they left behind."

Already, Carrie felt she was in safe hands, even though she felt as limp as a rag now that the tension in her body was reduced. "I'm not hungry right now, but I could sure use some coffee." She was trying, but it would be a while yet before she could recover from the events that just happened. And she wasn't sure she could eat, even if she had been hungry. "Thank you for taking care of Robert," she said softly.

Before Harley showed up with the packhorses, Cole had caught the sorrel that Malcolm Womack had ridden as well as their two packhorses. Carrie's mule wandered back on its own. Seeing the body before Cole had dragged it out of the clearing, Carrie identified it as the one called Malcolm. She told Cole they were brothers, and the one who had fled was Travis Womack, the youngest of three.

When Cole had stripped Malcolm's body of weapons and ammunition, he had found forty-seven dollars in his pockets and he promptly handed it to Carrie. "Ain't much in the way of makin' up for the loss of your husband," he had told her, "but if anybody's got a right to it, it oughta be you."

There was also the matter of the outlaws' packs and some clothes for Carrie, since hers, other than what she was presently wearing, had been destroyed along with everything else in her wagon. The dress she had on was torn in several places, the result of the rough handling she had suffered at the hands of the two brothers. Travis had been closer to Carrie's size than his brother, so she found some of his things that would work for her. The biggest complaint was the fact that they needed a good washing. She was resolved to endure the smell, however, the alternative being to freeze to death. Since the brothers had pulled the saddles off their horses, they were both left behind. Travis had not had the time to saddle his horse before he fled. Consequently, Carrie would no longer ride without a saddle, and she would be riding the sorrel instead of a mule.

By the time Harley arrived, Cole and Carrie were seated by the fire drinking coffee from the pot the Womack brothers had used.

"Save me a cup of that," Harley called out as he led the horses into the clearing by the stream. "We gonna be here a while?" he asked before stepping down from the saddle.

"Yeah, reckon we'd better," Cole answered. "I expect the horses need some rest. I know Joe does. I pushed him pretty hard to catch up with the lady, here."

Harley stepped down from the saddle and nodded politely to Carrie. "I'm mighty glad to see you're all right, miss." Then he looked at Cole for the story.

When Cole brought him up to date on the shoot-out, and the identity of the woman joining them, Harley had only one question. "The feller that took off, you reckon he'll be back? Looks like we've got everythin' he owns and you killed his brother, to boot."

"There's a chance, I reckon," Cole replied, "but I don't figure he'll come back for more. I put a bullet in him. I don't know how bad he's hurt, but I think he would have already been back, if he was of a mind to."

"Might not be too good an idea to stop here for the night, anyway," Harley advised, still concerned.

"Just in case that other one ain't hurt as bad as you think. Might be he'll take a notion to sneak back here." He waited for Cole's reply, but when he did no more than shrug, Harley continued. "Whaddaya say we take advantage of the hour or so of daylight we got left and push a little farther on?"

Cole shrugged again, not really worried about a visit from the wounded outlaw. He had not taken even one shot after he had been hit in the shoulder. Cole wasn't even sure if the man had waited to see his brother killed before climbing on his horse and running. But if it would make Harley more comfortable, Cole didn't object to the suggestion.

"You're right," he said. "We haven't started cookin' any food yet, so we won't even unload the horses. We oughta find some water between here and the North Platte, so we'll camp when we come to a good spot." The North Platte River was probably no more than twenty miles from where they stood. But there wasn't enough daylight left to count on making that distance, and the horses were too tired to be pushed another twenty miles that day.

After they took time to drink their coffee, they started out again, holding the horses to an easy walk. After what Cole estimated to be a distance of about eight or nine miles, they came to a small creek. He figured that was as far as he wanted to push his horse. It was almost dark, anyway, so they made their camp beside the creek.

Feeling a sudden relief, now that she was removed from the campsite where he had found her, Carrie was able to dispense with any lingering fears she might have had. For it was obvious to her that the hands she found herself in were sent by the angels and she was safe. Why the Good Lord had sent them to save her, but not her husband, was not for her to ponder. It was just one more sorrowful event in her lifetime to add to those that had preceded it. She would just give thanks for her salvation and vow to be strong in facing what the fates had in store for her. With her confidence restored, she insisted that she could take over the cooking, since they provided the food. She found that it helped take her mind off the loss of her husband when she busied herself with the mundane chore.

Harley agreed with Cole when it came to the property of the Womack brothers. Carrie should be given anything that she might sell or trade. That included the three horses and the contents of the packs. Carrie insisted that Cole certainly deserved something for rescuing her, and in the end, he settled for the weapons and ammunition. Harley was struck with admiration for the fancy Spanish-style saddle that had belonged to Malcolm Womack and immediately offered to buy it from Carrie. Cole wondered what Harley was going to use for money, but Carrie, grateful to them both, insisted that Harley should take it. She was perfectly comfortable with Travis's saddle. The fancy trimmings on the other saddle held no special interest for her, but Harley was overjoyed. He had never seen it in his means to afford a saddle so elegant with its high cantle and handsome designs embossed on the skirts and back jockey.

When they broke camp the next morning, Cole was certain that his old partner appeared to be sitting especially straight and tall in his new saddle as he led them out toward the crossing at the Platte. He looked back at Carrie, riding the sorrel, dressed almost entirely in garments owned by Travis Womack, looking more like a child in hand-me-downs than a recently widowed woman. *We ought to make quite an impression when we ride into Medicine Bear's camp,* he couldn't help thinking.

For Travis Womack, the cold cloudy morning that greeted him promised nothing but pain and hunger. His shoulder had stopped bleeding, but it was still throbbing with pain. He had nothing to eat or drink, save water from the Platte River, where he had been forced to stop for the night. Confident at least that the tall, fearsome-looking man wearing buckskins was not on his trail, he was thinking about finding something to fill his stomach. Unfortunately, his Winchester '66 rifle was still on his saddle, back on the South Fork of the Powder River. Somehow, he had managed to hold on to his pistol when he was shot, however, so he was searching the banks of the river, hoping to get a shot at a muskrat. He was not looking forward to the long ride ahead of him to Laramie to join his brother. It was sorry news he had to deliver. Troy would be furious to hear of Malcolm's death at the hand of the buckskin-clad killer. To make matters worse, Travis had been forced to return with nothing to show for their trip to Bozeman. His luck improved, however, with the arrival of two trappers at his camp.

* * *

"Well, I'll be . . ." Zeb Worley exclaimed softly to his partner as they sat on their horses on a rise near the bluffs of the river. "Whaddaya make of that?"

"Damned if I know," Smiley Bates replied. "Looks like he's lookin' for somethin' in the river."

They looked back again at the small fire near the trees beside the river. They could see a horse down near the water's edge, but there was no evidence of a saddle or bedroll, and no packhorse, either.

Smiley remarked, "Ain't much of a camp."

"He sure as hell travels light, don't he?" Zeb commented.

"Maybe he's run into some trouble somewhere, and that's the reason he ain't got nothin'," Smiley said.

They watched the movements of the lone man for a while longer as Travis made his way along the bank. Finally it struck them that he was walking a little awkwardly, almost stumbling a couple of times.

"Damned if I don't believe he's been shot," Smiley observed.

"Could be," Zeb replied. "Maybe he got caught in a bind somewhere. Sure looks like he could use a little help."

"I reckon we oughta ride on down there and see what's what," Smiley said.

"I reckon," Zeb replied, "but it wouldn't hurt to keep an eye on him, just in case." He urged his horse forward with a light pressure of his heels and the bay gelding descended the bluff at a slow walk, a packhorse trailing behind him.

Smiley followed along behind Zeb, leading a packhorse as well.

Intent upon trying to find something to eat, Travis was not aware he had visitors until his horse nickered a greeting. Startled, he turned quickly to defend himself, his pistol in hand, thinking the buckskin-clad killer had found him. But the two trappers approaching were brandishing no weapons and appeared to be peaceful enough. Travis realized that they were a sign of good luck and welcome after just having sampled a dose of the other kind. He holstered his weapon and walked up the bank to meet them.

When Travis's pistol was back in the holster, Zeb and Smiley felt no need to remain wary. They had pulled up abruptly when Travis turned to first discover them and immediately brought his pistol to bear on them. With the weapon holstered, they proceeded to approach. Close enough to confirm what they had suspected, they could plainly see that the man was favoring a wounded shoulder.

"Looks like you've had a little spell of trouble, young feller," Smiley said.

"You could say that rightly enough," Travis replied. "More 'n I figure I needed."

"Maybe it was a good thing we come along," Zeb said. "It sure 'pears you could use a little help."

"Mister, that's the God's honest truth," Travis said, doing his best to appear respectful, a trait that did not come naturally to any of the Womack men.

"We might oughta start by takin' a look at that shoulder," Zeb said. "Smiley, here, is pretty good at doctorin' bullet holes and knife wounds. Looks like you was tryin' to find somethin' to eat. While

Smiley tends to that shoulder, I'll see about fixin' you somethin'. We've got some fresh deer meat, just kilt last evenin'."

"Well, I surely do appreciate it," Travis said. "When you first rode up, I thought you were the same fellers that ambushed me." He watched while the two trappers dismounted. "Killed my brother," he went on while they took care of their horses. "Took everythin' I own, my saddle, and my rifle. I was mighty lucky to get away with my horse."

"I swear. That sure is sorry business. Set down on that there log and I'll see what that wound looks like."

While Smiley worked on Travis's bullet wound, Zeb busied himself over the fire, roasting some venison and boiling some coffee. Travis continued to create a story for them of how he and his brother were bushwhacked by outlaws, so convincingly that they began to be concerned for their own safety.

"Where 'bouts was this spot where they jumped you and your brother?" Zeb asked. "Maybe we oughta be lookin' out for ourselves. We was more worried about Injuns than a gang of outlaws."

"I don't think you've got anythin' to worry about from those fellers," Travis assured him. "That was back this side of the South Fork of the Powder, and they were travelin' toward the east."

"How you know that?" Zeb asked. "I thought you said they was hid and jumped you when you rode down to water your horses."

His question caused Travis to pause for a moment while he tried to think of an answer. "That's right, I did say that, didn't I? Well, I reckon I just figured they were headed that way. It don't matter none, anyway. They ain't nowhere around here and I ain't worried about 'em no more because I've got supplies and horses to take care of what I'm needin'."

Zeb and Smiley exchanged puzzled glances. "Where are your horses?" Zeb asked. "We didn't see but that one by the creek."

Travis chuckled, amused by their blank faces. "You rode in on 'em," he said and continued to grin at them.

A little slow to grasp the meaning of the young man's casual remark, Smiley stared in astonishment at the .44 Colt suddenly aimed at his stomach. A fraction of a second later, he recoiled with the impact of the slug as it tore into his gut. Equally slow to react, Zeb was frozen for a moment, caught with a coffeepot in his hand. He dropped the pot, turned, and ran for his horse, only to be stopped by a bullet in his back before he was halfway there. He staggered on for a few more feet before falling facedown on the ground.

Travis got up from the log he had been seated on while Smiley tended his wound. He paused to gaze at the wounded man writhing in pain on the ground. "You son of a bitch," Smiley rasped painfully.

"You done a right handy job on my shoulder," Travis said, "so I reckon the least I can do is put you outta your misery." Another shot from his .44 in Smiley's forehead silenced him forever. "That oughta do the job," Travis commented and walked unhurriedly toward Zeb to check on him. He found the unfortunate trapper mortally wounded, but still clawing at the light covering of snow in an attempt to pull himself over the ground. "I reckon I oughta tell you how tickled I am that you and your partner came along, 'cause I was in a fix," he said as he placed another round in the back of Zeb's head.

He looked around him then while he casually replaced the cartridges he had used, pleased with the good fortune that had come his way. There was still the regrettable news he was bound to report to his brother, Troy. But instead of showing up in Laramie with nothing to show for the trip to Bozeman, it would be tempered a bit with four extra horses and whatever possessions the trappers had. With that thought in mind, he went to work searching the bodies and the packs of his victims. He soon found that he had gained very little of value other than some decent hides he could sell, a couple of Civil War surplus Sharps rifles, and two .44 caliber pistols. The horses looked to be in pretty good shape, though. It was enough to permit him to return to Laramie with a modicum of pride—even if it was without his brother. "Hell," he snorted, "Malcolm oughta not been caught with his head down behind that bank, anyway." His brother's death was certainly a disappointment, but not to the extent that would cause him to feel guilt for not packing him up. To the contrary, the only emotion he felt was one of relief that he had managed to escape getting killed, himself. Add to that the good fortune that sent him Zeb and Smiley, he felt in good spirits as he set out for Laramie, leading the horses he had just acquired.

* * *

The journey to the Crow village near the confluence of the Laramie and the North Laramie Rivers would take the pack train three and a half days. During that time, Carrie developed a deep trust in the two men who had happened into her life at the precise moment she needed them. It was much too soon for her to get over the loss of her husband, but the easygoing nature of her two traveling companions, and their polite consideration toward her, made her suffering bearable. Her two rescuers appeared to be a perfect team. The older man, called Harley, was an elf-like little man, no taller than Carrie herself, although she wondered if he might not be a head taller if his legs were straight. They were so bowed that he looked as if he had come from his mother's womb ready to ride a horse. Judging by the heavy solid white beard that covered most of his ruddy face, however, she had to speculate that that event must have been many years ago.

In contrast, the younger half of the partnership was as straight and tall as a lodgepole pine. A serious man of few words, Cole Bonner made her think of a mountain lion. Dressed in animal skins, as was Harley, he was clean-shaven. His hair was worn in two braids after the style of the Crow Indians he lived with. Whereas Harley could rattle on about any subject, Cole used his words as if they were too expensive to waste. *A perfect set,* Carrie thought. Robert could rest in peace knowing that she was with them.

* * *

"Do you think we'll reach that Indian village tomorrow?" Carrie asked as she brought Harley a cup of coffee.

"Yes, Ma'am," Harley answered. "We'll be home tomorrow, all right." He chuckled and added, "Leastways, me and Cole will be home tomorrow. Crow Creek Crossin's a good eighty miles or more from there," he said, referring to Cheyenne by its original name. "You gettin' kinda anxious to get on down to your in-laws?"

She hesitated before answering. "To be honest, I'm not really looking forward to it. I've never met my late husband's folks, so I'll be a complete stranger in their home. I don't know if they'll be glad to see me or not, especially since I'll be bringing such bad news." She sat down beside the fire near him. "I might be thinking about going someplace else if I had someplace else to go to."

"Why, I'm sure they'll be tickled to meet you," Harley said, although he fully understood her apprehension. "And I know they'll wanna take care of you since their son picked you for a wife. How long was you and Robert married?"

"Not quite a year and a half," she answered with a sad smile, thinking what a short time it had been. She and her husband were still only beginning to get to know each other.

"So you two hadn't got around to havin' young'uns yet, I reckon."

"There was one. A boy, but he was stillborn," she said, looking down at her lap as if ashamed.

"We would have named him Douglas, after his grandfather."

"I declare," Harley said, "that's sure enough bad luck." For one of the few times in his life, he found himself short of words. "Well, you're young yet," he finally consoled. "You've got time to start out with somebody else. Why, the way I hear talk of Crow Creek Crossin', I mean Cheyenne, and the way it keeps growin', I expect there's a gracious plenty young men there that'd stomp all over each other to get to a pretty little gal like you."

She responded with another sad smile, causing him to declare, "I'd best go see if Cole needs any help with the horses. We gotta be ready to ride come sunup." The conversation was getting a little too uncomfortable for him, so he swigged his coffee down and got to his feet. He realized that she was sincere when she said she wasn't looking forward to meeting her husband's folks. But according to what she had told Cole and him, she had no other place to go.

Before retreating to join Cole with the horses, he offered one other suggestion. "You might wanna stay a little while in Medicine Bear's village, till you feel like ridin' on down to Cheyenne. I expect you'd be welcome for as long as you wanted to stay."

Once again, the sad smile appeared. "Maybe," she said. "I guess we'll see." In truth, she could not see any possibility that she would be comfortable in an Indian village for any length of time. The thought brought a picture to mind of savages dancing around a roaring fire, brandishing tomahawks and bows, and chanting songs with no distinguishable words. Since both of her rescuers looked like they'd be right at home in a tipi, she declined to express her opinion.

As Harley had said, they were up and in the saddle at sunup, planning to stop for breakfast when the horses needed rest. Carrie wished she felt the enthusiasm to reach the Indian village that was so evident in Harley's attitude. To the contrary, she didn't expect her experience to be as comfortable as the one she now had with just Cole and Harley. She tried to tell herself that it would at least postpone the meeting she was to have with Robert's parents. These were the thoughts troubling her when they rode through the trees to get her first glimpse at the Crow village by the river.

CHAPTER 3

Having heard the sound of loud voices outside, Yellow Calf came out of the tipi to see the cause. A small group of people, his wife among them, had gathered near the lower end of the village watching someone approaching.

Yellow Calf walked down to join his wife. "What is it?"

Moon Shadow pointed toward the cottonwoods on the other side of the river. "There, in the trees. White Wolf and Thunder Mouse return."

Yellow Calf stared at the opposite bank, and in a few seconds, the riders cleared the trees and started to cross the river. "I see them," he said. "There is someone with them, a boy maybe." His face lit up with a smile then. "The packhorses are heavily loaded. Maybe this is why they are back so soon."

"Maybe," Moon Shadow said and chuckled. "I think maybe Thunder Mouse needs to get back to his warm tipi."

Close enough to be seen clearly, Harley and Cole acknowledged the welcome greetings with a raised arm above their heads. They led their string of packhorses up from the river as more of the village's residents joined the crowd, excited to see what looked to be a welcome supply of meat and hides. After a genuine welcoming for the hunters' return, all eyes turned toward the rider with them. Dressed as she was in Travis Womack's clothing, Carrie was not at once recognized as a woman. When Harley told the people who she was, and the tragic circumstances that caused her to join them, she was warmly greeted, and Moon Shadow immediately took her under her wing.

Having never been in an Indian village before, Carrie didn't know what to expect. With no knowledge of the Crow tongue, she had to rely on Moon Shadow's limited English, but she soon learned that the patient Crow woman knew enough of the language to communicate adequately. And Moon Shadow's hospitality was much like what she would expect to receive in any neighbor's home, the conical shape of the dwelling the only difference. In fact, after her most recent time spent in a wagon or sleeping at a campsite with no shelter, the accommodations seemed almost luxurious. She was ashamed to admit to herself how wrong her preconceived notion had been. When she offered Moon Shadow money for taking her in, the Crow woman refused it, telling her that she would need that money if she was going to Cheyenne. "We will eat the meat Thunder Mouse and White Wolf have brought," Moon Shadow said. "When it gets low, we will send them to hunt again."

"You are most kind," Carrie said, sensing a

genuine compassion for her. Still feeling a certain amount of dread of the reception she might receive from Douglas and Martha Green in Cheyenne, she was almost tempted to remain in the Crow village for as long as they would have her. Her common sense told her that was unrealistic thinking, however, for she was too long accustomed to the white man's town. And, besides, what would she do to become a useful part of the village? Although she had just arrived, already she was struck by the realization that there were no young people in evidence. The little village was seemingly made up of older people. It occurred to her then that the village depended upon Cole and Harley to keep them living as they had always lived, instead of having to go to the reservation. She gained even more respect for her two guardians.

Since Carrie didn't seem anxious to get on her way to meet her in-laws, Cole decided to delay the trip to Cheyenne for a few days. He needed to sell the hides he had kept for himself, and maybe trade the firearms he had collected when he'd rescued Carrie. It was a forty-mile ride to Fort Laramie and a trading post where he preferred to make his trades, so that would take him a couple of days. There was a trading post about halfway between the village and Cheyenne, located on the Chugwater Creek at a place called Iron Mountain. That would have been right on the way to Cheyenne, but Cole felt that Raymond Potter, the owner, was not a fair man to deal with.

Harley was content to stay in the village and keep an eye on Carrie while Cole was gone. That would, in fact, require very little effort on his part, since Carrie was going to stay in Moon Shadow's tipi. Harley had a tipi of his own in the camp and Moon Shadow would no doubt see to his needs as well. She had been for some time, at least ever since he began to winter with Medicine Bear's village, and that was almost seven years now. Harley was looked upon as an uncle or cousin and was highly thought of in the camp. His Crow name, Thunder Mouse, was given to him by Yellow Calf because of his short stature and his boisterous nature. It was a name that Harley tolerated, although he would have preferred a more heroic name, like the name Walking Owl had bestowed upon Cole. The old medicine man had given Cole the name of White Wolf because of a dream Cole related in which a white wolf had come to him. As for Cole, he had been with the Crow people long enough to feel each time he returned to the small village was much like coming home.

Before leaving for Fort Laramie, he asked Carrie if there was anything she needed from the trading post. "I could surely use a hairbrush, if they have one," she replied. "I can give you some of that money to pay for it."

"Like Moon Shadow told you," he said. "You'd best hang onto that money. I'm gonna be tradin' a lot of hides and guns, and I expect I'll be able to talk them into throwin' a hairbrush in as part of the deal—that is, if they have hairbrushes."

It was late in the afternoon when Cole approached the bend in the Platte River where Murphy's Store was located. Standing apart from the cottonwoods that lined the river at this point, it was built of solid log construction, much like a fort. And in less peaceful times, it had served as a fort against attacks from Sioux Indians, one of which resulted in the loss of the barn. A new barn stood only a few yards from the burned timbers of the original, and Cole could see about a dozen horses in the corral. Like his store, Ian Murphy was built of strong fiber as well and over the years had gained a reputation as a fair man, whether trading with white man or red. Consequently, his store was a favorite with trappers and hunters, law-abiding and otherwise. He carried a good stock of basic supplies and whiskey by the jar, but he didn't sell whiskey by the drink. He had always maintained that he ran a store and not a saloon. Cole had traded with Murphy before and had always been satisfied with the trade.

He paused for a moment before nudging Joe with his heels, and the big Morgan dutifully entered the shallow water and started across. Cole guided him away from a couple of deep holes he remembered from before to save his packhorse from struggling with its heavy load of hides. There were no other horses tied at the hitching rail in front, but Cole knew that didn't mean there were no customers there, for Murphy had a couple of rooms to rent upstairs. It was not unusual to find travelors stopping there for more than one day.

"Cole Bonner," Murphy greeted him at once when he walked in the door. "I was beginnin' to think you'd gone under. Is your partner with you?"

"How do, Murphy?" Cole responded. "No, Harley

stayed back in Medicine Bear's village with his feet to the fire."

"I can't say as I blame him," Murphy said with a chuckle. "It's gettin' cold pretty quick this year. You lookin' to trade some hides?"

"Matter of fact," Cole replied. "You can take a look at 'em. I think they're pretty good quality, maybe prime for deer. We got most of 'em up in the high mountains where it's already pretty cold, so they had already thickened up. I got one bearskin that's a dandy."

"Well, let's take a look," Murphy said and started to follow Cole out the door. He was stopped by a loud voice near the back of the room.

"Hey, where you goin', Murphy? Are we gonna have to wait all night to get some supper?" This came from a table where three men were seated, working on a jar of corn whiskey.

"Hold your horses, Yarborough," Murphy replied. "She ain't got no magic beans back there." He looked at Cole. "Hold on just a minute, Cole, let me see if Bessie's about done with the cookin'."

"Go ahead," Cole said, "I'll go outside and untie those hides."

Murphy went to the kitchen to hurry Bessie, which did not go well with the cantankerous cook, and she told him as much. On his way back, he paused long enough to tell the men at the table that supper was on its way. The three men were not among Murphy's favorite customers, and his usual policy was to placate them in hopes they would get their business with him done as quickly as possible. The leader of the three, Flint Yarborough, was a vicious scoundrel. Of that, Murphy had no doubt, but Yarborough was capable of civil behavior when it suited him. The two outlaws who rode with him, however, were as rough-cut as the hewn logs of Murphy's trading post. Of the two, Red Swann was the handiest with a .44 six-shooter, while Tiny Weaver was a brute of enormous proportions housing a pea-size brain. It had been some time since the three outlaws had occasion to stop at Murphy's. According to what Yarborough had told him, they had spent the past six months in Missouri, and were now heading to Laramie.

Outside, Murphy inspected the hides, making notes on a paper sack, as Cole pulled them off his packhorse. When he pulled the last one, Murphy said, "You were right, they're in pretty good shape. Let's go back inside and I'll figure up a bid for the whole load, includin' the bearskin."

Back inside, Murphy glanced first to see if his three other customers had their supper yet, and when he saw that they did, he went directly to the counter to figure how much credit he was willing to offer for the hides. Cole never haggled with him over the value of his hides, having always found him fair, so a figure was quickly agreed upon, and Cole started calling off a list of supplies he needed. "Before I use up all my credit, I'd best see about one important item," he said. "Any chance you've got a hairbrush for sale?"

"A hairbrush?" Murphy echoed, not sure he knew what Cole meant. When Cole nodded, Murphy asked, "Like a lady's hairbrush?"

"Yep," Cole answered, "a lady's hairbrush."

"I thought you were talkin' about a horse brush

or a currycomb," Murphy said. "As a matter of fact, I do have a hairbrush, and I'll be glad to sell it to you. Tell you the truth, I didn't expect to ever have anybody lookin' for one. I ordered it for a fellow owns a farm about twelve miles east of here, wanted it for his wife—took six months before I ever got it. When it did get here, it was a set of two brushes. Fellow didn't want but one of 'em, so I reckon I've been savin' the other one for you."

"Well, that'll sure save me from disappointin' a lady back in Medicine Bear's village," Cole said. He went on to finish up his trading with a large sack of coffee for Moon Shadow. "Now, I'd like to try whatever Bessie cooked up for supper before I go." He had eaten her cooking before and it wasn't bad, so he thought he might as well chance it again.

"Good idea," Murphy said. "I'll join you." He went into the kitchen to tell Bessie while Cole carried his purchases out to tie on his packhorse. When Cole came back inside, he found Murphy sitting at the other small table near the back of the room waiting for him. "Bessie'll be out in a minute."

Overhearing, Yarborough interrupted, "Tell her to bring that coffeepot around again."

"Yeah, and some more of this slop she calls stew," the brute named Tiny blurted, much to Red's amusement.

Murphy ignored their remarks, being certain that Bessie could hear their requests, and content to let her handle their complaints, if there were any. In a few moments, the feisty Indian woman came from the kitchen with a coffeepot and two cups for Murphy and Cole. She set them down on the table and filled them before going to the other table to refill Yarborough's cup. The other two cups were still full, since Red and Tiny were still working on the jar of whiskey. Then she turned back to Murphy. "I bring your supper now."

"Don't forget to bring me more stew," Tiny ordered.

"I bring you more stew, I charge you for two suppers," she said.

"The hell you will," Tiny responded, then looked toward Murphy. "You let that damn Injun talk to your customers like that?"

"I ain't got nothin' to do with it," Murphy said. "That's her business, cookin' for customers. Best to just eat your supper and let her be." He looked at Cole and winked. "You get on her bad side and she's liable to put somethin' in your supper that'll keep you runnin' to the outhouse all night."

"She does, and it'll be the last time she does it," Red spoke up. "I ain't got much use for Injuns, anyway," he glared at Cole then, "or white men that dress up like Injuns."

With no interest in getting involved in a fight with a half-drunken gunman, Cole chose to ignore the remark obviously meant to challenge him. He was glad to see Bessie arrive at that moment with two plates of stew for him and Murphy. Murphy was glad as well. "Here we are," he announced as Bessie set the plates down. "Time to quit talkin' and start eatin'."

Red was not ready to let it go, however, having judged Cole's lack of response as a sign of cowardice. Like most bullies, that was enough to egg him on. "Wonder if he unties them pigtails when he brushes his hair with his new hairbrush?" he said, plenty loud enough to be heard.

Eager to encourage him, Tiny was quick to comment. "I bet he does. And maybe he's got some of them ribbons he uses to make his hair real pretty, so he looks more like a squaw."

Murphy shot a quick look at Cole, concerned now that Yarborough and his partners were intent upon making some real trouble. "Maybe it'd be best if you just go ahead and get outta here before this gets out of hand," he whispered softly.

"I reckon you're right," Cole replied, making no attempt to keep from being overheard. "I'll be leavin' right away, but not till after I finish this plate of stew Bessie cooked. It looks too good to waste."

His response served to amuse Flint Yarborough. "Looks to me like this fellow ain't that easy to rile up, Red. I reckon he ain't heard about your reputation."

"Come on, Yarborough," Murphy said, "there ain't no call for trouble. Everything's been goin' all right, ain't it? You and your boys have been treated right since you got here yesterday. Right? Cole, here, don't want no trouble. Right, Cole?"

"That's a fact," Cole said and took a large bite out of a biscuit. "I didn't come here lookin' for trouble. I just wanted to trade for some supplies and buy some supper."

"And brush your hair with your pretty little hairbrush," Red snarled.

"You just can't let it go, can you?" Cole said, his

patience running out. With one quick motion, he whipped the Henry rifle up from the floor where it had been resting beside his chair. To the complete surprise of all four of the men seated there, he cranked a cartridge into the chamber and leveled the rifle directly at Red. The reaction of the three at the other table was predictable, with all three pushing their chairs back in an effort to get to their weapons. In Tiny's case, it resulted in the huge man's chair going over backward to land him on the floor. "The first one that draws a weapon gets this first shot, so who wants it?" It was warning enough to freeze all three.

There was a moment of silence before Yarborough thought to challenge him. "You've got the jump on us, but there's three of us, and I guarantee you that if you pull that trigger, any one of us is quick enough to shoot you before you can crank another round in that rifle."

"I can't argue with that," Cole said. "So as long as you gave me a guarantee, I'll give you one. The first one of you that draws, I guarantee you're gonna be the first one dead." He shifted his rifle to aim directly at Yarborough.

Yarborough slowly broke out a wry smile. "I reckon you're holdin' the winnin' hand on this deal. Don't nobody draw a weapon," he ordered. "We were just havin' a little fun, anyway. No hard feelin's. Tiny, get up from there and finish your supper."

"Fine," Cole said, "no hard feelin's. I'll just finish this plate of stew, then I'll leave you fellows to enjoy your evenin'. Think nothin' of this rifle still restin' on the table. It just gives me a feelin' of comfort while I'm eatin'." He continued to eat without wasting any more time, while watching the scowling face of Red Swann. Tiny, simple soul that he was, shrugged it off and attacked his supper again. When he had finished, Cole took the last gulp of his coffee, then carefully got up from the table while still covering Yarborough with his rifle. He left some money on the table for his supper, then backed slowly toward the door.

Still smiling as if genuinely amused, Yarborough watched his retreat. "Maybe we'll see you again sometime," he said when Cole reached the door.

Once he got outside, Cole wasted no time climbing in the saddle while keeping an eye on the door. He wheeled Joe away from the rail and gave him his heels. The big Morgan seemed to know he wanted a quick departure. Relieved when there were no gunshots to follow him as he crossed back over the river, he left Murphy's Store at a lope in the fading light of day. He decided to put a few miles between him and the store before making camp, allowing for the possibility that his trouble with the three outlaws was not over.

Behind him, Yarborough stopped Red when he got up as soon as the door closed. "Let him be," Yarborough said. "You open that door and you'll get a .44 slug in your belly."

"I ain't lettin' that son of a bitch get away with that," Red fumed, still smoldering at the ease with which Cole had gotten away. "I ain't backin' down to no half-breed Injun."

"Hell, Red, forget about it," Tiny said. Even he could see there was no need to go riding off in the approaching darkness, maybe to ride into a hot ambush.

"You know he's gonna stop somewhere pretty quick for the night," Red insisted.

"Maybe, maybe not," Yarborough said. "He's already had his supper. Depends on his horses. If they ain't tired, he might ride half the night. I say to hell with him. You've let him get under your skin. I ain't worried about him. I'm just wantin' to get down to Laramie." Red sat down at the table again, but the longer he sat there, the madder he got, and before several minutes had passed, he was on his feet again. "You ain't gonna forget it, are you?" Yarborough asked.

"No, I ain't gonna forget it," Red replied. "I told you that." He stood glaring at his two partners, waiting for their response. When he got it, it only served to make him madder.

"Don't look at me," Yarborough said. "I don't care enough about that half-breed to go to the trouble of runnin' him down tonight. You need to cool off before you talk yourself into walkin' into an ambush." He looked at Tiny, who seemed to find Red's anger amusing. "Maybe Tiny'll go after him with you." Tiny shook his head, still grinning at Red's frustration. Determined to show them both that he made no idle threats, Red took a long swig from the jar of whiskey, set the empty jar down hard on the table, and marched out the door.

Spurred on equally by his need to settle with Cole and his desire to make his two partners eat their words, Red hurried to the corral to get his horse saddled. Confident that if he could determine which way Cole rode out, he could likely pick up his trail. There were several trails leading to Murphy's Store. It was only a matter of finding the one Cole took, and that was not a problem because Murphy's hired hand, Jack Peters, was loading some hay into the hayloft from a flatbed wagon. "Hey," Red hailed him, "feller just rode outta here leadin' a packhorse, which way'd he go?"

"Him?" Jack answered. "He lef'out on the river trail, yonder way." He turned and pointed to a trail that ultimately led to the North Laramie River.

Red didn't bother to reply to him and turned his horse toward the trail he indicated at a lope. Unconcerned about overworking his horse, he held the sorrel to that steady gait. He was confident that he would be riding faster than the man he chased and would catch up to him before he had to worry about resting his horse. The trail was easy enough to follow, even in the rapidly growing darkness that descended upon the open prairie away from the river. He had not ridden an hour when he saw the dark outline of trees ahead to indicate a stream or a creek. A few moments later, he reined the sorrel back to a fast walk when he caught a glimpse of a fire in a stand of pines. *Ha, he didn't get far before he made camp*, he thought. Still about a mile from the trees, he felt confident that he couldn't be seen out on the dark prairie, even if Cole was watching for him. But there was no sense in being reckless and riding right into a welcome from the Henry rifle, as Yarborough had

suggested. *I ain't that dumb,* he thought and turned
the sorrel's head to angle off of the trail he had
been following.

When he reached a point he figured to be about
one hundred yards upstream from the point where
he saw the fire, he turned his horse to ride into the
trees. Once in the protection of the trees, he dismounted and tied the horse to a low tree limb.
Then he drew the Winchester '66 from his saddle
sling and cranked a round into the chamber.
Ready then, he set out through the trees on foot,
following the winding creek back toward the campfire. When he came to a spot where the trees were
a little less dense, he could see the fire, maybe fifty
yards away, and the figure of the man sitting beside
it. His horses were beyond the camp, maybe thirty
yards, he figured. *Now I'll show you how to sneak up
on an Injun,* he told himself, confident he had
caught his prey off guard. Before he moved in any
closer, he paused to consider the possibility that he
might be walking into a trap. It was an old trick to
roll up a blanket or two to look like a man sleeping, but there was nothing like that near the campfire. Instead, he could see a man sitting next to the
fire, and his back was turned toward him. More
certain than ever, Red pulled his Winchester up to
rest against his shoulder and took dead aim at
the center of the man's back. Before pulling the
trigger, he hesitated a moment to consider waiting
until he got closer to see the fear in the man's face
when he discovered what was happening. It was
just a moment, however, because he decided it best
to shoot him down before he knew he was being

stalked. He squeezed the trigger and smiled when the .44 slug struck a point that looked to be centered between the shoulder blades. The man keeled over, his body twisting violently, facedown, telling Red it was a kill shot. He moved forward quickly then to make sure his target was not going to get up.

Remaining cautious, Red moved up behind his victim, his rifle reloaded and ready to fire again, if necessary, but there was no sign of life. He pushed through the last bunch of small bushes that stood between him and his target, then stopped, confused. It appeared that the man's head had come off and rolled into the fire! "What tha. . . ." Red blurted when he discovered the body to be two medium-sized links of a dead log, with a blanket draped around them. His panic lasted for no more than a split second when he turned just in time to receive the full force of the butt of the Henry rifle jammed into his face. Dropped, as if he had been shot, he was rendered senseless as he lay sprawled on his back, helpless to defend himself.

Wasting no time, Cole grabbed his ankles and flipped him over on his belly. Then he pulled his hands behind his back and tied his wrists together. He relieved him of his gun belt and pulled his boots off. "I oughta kill you for puttin' a hole in my blanket," he said as he stood over him. "But I'm just gonna charge you one horse, your guns, and a pair of boots. Now that oughta make you and me even, so I don't expect to see you again." He wasn't sure Red understood what he was saying; he was still looking pretty confused. So he decided to waste no more time. He pulled his blanket off the rotting links of logs and shook it out before using it to carry his newly confiscated firearms and boots to the willows where his horses were waiting. He took another look at the prone form of Red Swann as he rode past the campfire and went back to find Red's horse tied to a tree limb. Tying the sorrel's reins to a short lead from his packhorse, he rode for a couple of miles before stopping to transfer his bag of weapons and boots to Red's horse.

The entire incident had turned out differently than he had anticipated. After his little confrontation with the three outlaws at Murphy's Store, he figured he was not through with them. Fully prepared to take on the three of them, he set up his fake camp, knowing they would be out to kill him and he was bound to stop them if he could. When only the hothead, Red, showed up, he decided to send him back to his friends with sore feet, knowing the humiliation would be worse punishment than death for someone like him. The thing to do now was to hide his trail as well as he could, in case they did decide to come after him.

Cole's plan worked as well as he had hoped. Red laid there by the fire, too groggy to realize what had happened to him until the fire had almost died out. When he finally came to his senses, enough to appreciate the terrible pain he was in, he tried to get up, only then aware that his hands were tied behind his back. There followed a struggle, but he finally got to his feet, aware then that his nose was shattered and there was nothing he could do to stop the bleeding. Wondering if he was going to be able to untie his hands, he started back through the trees to get his horse, not sure he was going to be able to climb on it when he found him. It was then he realized his boots were missing when he stepped on a sharp root protruding from the ground. When he reached the place where he had tied his horse, he discovered the sorrel was gone, and the full impact of his humiliating disaster caused him to roar out his anger and frustration. Faced with the mortifying return to face Yarborough and Tiny, he would have chosen not to return at all, had he any other option. With a raging hatred for the man dressed like an Indian, he did the only thing he could and started walking back to Murphy's. It was only a few miles, but in his stocking feet on the cold hard ground, it seemed like many more.

It was Jack Peters who spotted a man walking up from the river. Thinking at first that he looked a little strange, almost limping. He then realized that he walked with his hands behind his back. When he realized it was Red, he climbed down from the hayloft to meet him. "Good Lord in heaven!" Jack exclaimed when he walked up to him. "Did you get throwed?" It was an obvious question, since he came back without his horse.

"No, I didn't get throwed," Red fumed. "Cut me loose!" Jack pulled out his pocketknife and went to work on the rope around his wrists, waiting anxiously for the explanation, but Red didn't offer one. Jack had sense enough not to ask. When Red's hands were free, Jack stepped back and watched him head for the store, noticing then that he had no boots on, which probably contributed to the limp he had when he came walking up from the river.

Inside the store, the conversation between the three men standing at the counter suddenly stopped cold when Red walked in the door. Yarborough almost laughed, but even he was cautious about making any remarks. It was Tiny who blurted, "Dang, Red, what the hell happened to you? You look like you run into the side of the barn." When Red just glared at him in answer, Tiny asked, "Did you catch up with that feller?"

When Red still did not speak, Yarborough said, "Yeah, he caught up with him." He shook his head slowly, thinking about the man called Cole Bonner. "And it looks like he's gonna need some doctorin'. That nose looks like it's broke." He looked at Murphy, who was still struck speechless, staring at Red. "Murphy, does that woman of yours still do a little patchwork?"

"Yeah," he answered. "Bessie does some doctorin'. I'll get her."

Standing in the middle of the room still smoldering while they stared at him, Red finally spoke. Looking at Yarborough, he said, "We're goin' after that son of a bitch."

Yarborough realized that what he said in response might cause some real trouble between him and Red, but he knew it was important that he called the shots. As calmly as he could affect, he said, "No, Red, we're not. It's in our best interest to get on down to Laramie like we planned."

"Damn it, Flint," Red exclaimed. "The son of a bitch ambushed me, stole my horse, my guns, even my boots! We've got to go after him!"

"I tried to tell you to leave that man be," Yarborough replied, talking calmly, like a father counseling a wayward son. "The best thing for us right now is to get on down to Laramie. There ain't nothin' worth foolin' with in this part of the territory, and there sure ain't no sense in ridin' off in the prairie after some half-wild Injun lover." He paused to gauge Red's reaction to his advice before continuing. "Me and Tiny are headin' out for Laramie in the mornin'. You get your nose fixed up, and you'd best come with us." He felt confident that Red would swallow his pride and come along.

Late afternoon the following day saw the tipis of Medicine Bear's village come into view. At the sight of the village, Cole nudged Joe into an easy lope, guiding him toward Yellow Calf and several of the other men who had paused to watch him. Yellow Calf called to Harley as soon as he saw that it was Cole approaching. By the time Cole pulled up, Harley, Moon Shadow, and Carrie were standing with Yellow Calf and the others, waiting for him. "Well, you got back when you said you would," Harley greeted him. "Did Murphy treat you right? Those were prime hides you took up there."

"Yep," Cole answered. "He gave us a pretty fair price, just like he usually does." He started pulling some of the supplies off the packhorse to give Moon Shadow. Then he reached inside his saddlebag, pulled the hairbrush out, and held it up for Carrie to see. "Only one like it this side of the Platte," he announced, "and the only one Ian Murphy had." Her reaction upon seeing it was worth the trip to fetch it.

"Well, it sure surprises me that Murphy had one," Harley remarked. "I wouldn'ta thought he'd have anybody lookin' for one. Run into any trouble?"

"Nope, nothin' to speak of," Cole answered.

"So I guess we'll be starting out for Cheyenne tomorrow," Carrie said. The absence of enthusiasm in her tone caused Cole to question her eagerness to go.

"Tomorrow or the next day," Cole replied, "whatever you wanna do."

Close to the time Cole rode to Fort Laramie, Travis Womack pulled up at the stable in the town of Laramie, some ninety to one hundred miles away. The owner of the stable, a balding man named Grover Taylor, walked out to meet him.

"Womack," Grover greeted him indifferently, "Ain't seen you in town for a spell. You been away?"

"Up toward Montana country," Travis answered, equally stoic. "My brother been in today?"

"As a matter of fact," Grover answered, "that's his gray yonder in the corral."

Travis nodded in response, relieved to hear that Troy was in town. His first stop had been at the run-down shack he and his two brothers had been living in on a fork of the Laramie River about a dozen miles west of town. But Troy was not there, nor was there any sign he had been there for some time, causing Travis to fear he had left the territory. "I reckon he's stayin' somewhere in town."

"I expect so," Grover said, not really interested in Troy's whereabouts. "You lookin' to board those horses?"

"Yeah," Travis replied, "at least till I find out what my brother's gonna do. I expect I'll find him at the Bucket of Blood this time of day, probably in a card game with Big Steve Long and the boys."

Grover cocked his head at that remark. "I doubt that." Then when Travis responded with a questioning expression, he said, "You have been outta town for a long time, ain'tcha?" When Travis still wore a blank face, Grover enlightened him. "The folks around here finally had enough of your friend, Big Steve Long, with his killin' and robbin'. There's a new county sheriff now, Nathaniel Boswell. He got up a vigilance committee, and they marched into the Bucket of Blood a couple of weeks ago and arrested Long and those two half brothers of his—took 'em out and hanged 'em."

The news stunned Travis for a moment. He and his brothers had come to Laramie to ride with Big Steve Long. Long had been the town sheriff, and as such, he'd ridden roughshod over the town and everything around it. He and his two half brothers, Con and Ace Moyer, owned the Bucket of Blood saloon.

Where does that leave Troy and me, Travis wondered. Finally, he asked, "But you saw Troy in here this mornin', right?"

"Yeah, he was in here," Grover answered. "He's been stayin' in town for about a week now. I was kinda surprised he was still here, after Boswell cleaned out Long and his friends." He could almost see Travis's mind turning over the news he had been surprised with. *And Lord willing, maybe we'll see the last of you, your brothers, and the rest of your kind around here*, he thought. "I'll take care of your horses for you. You gonna take those packs off of 'em?"

"Yeah, reckon I'd better," Travis replied, then changed his mind. "No, I'm gonna take 'em with me. I'll be back after I find Troy." He decided it best to make sure Troy was all right before leaving his horses. Up to the point when he and Malcolm had left to head for Bozeman, he and his brothers were guilty only of being friendly with Long and the Moyers. Troy might have done something to make them unwelcome since then. It would be best to find out in case he might have to make a quick departure.

Travis took a quick precautionary look up and down the short street on either side of the Bucket of Blood before stepping inside the door. As soon as he entered the noisy establishment, he looked toward the bar. Fred Wiggins was tending bar as usual. Travis scanned the barroom, which was about half empty, until he spotted his brother sitting alone at a back corner table, a bottle before him. Relieved to have found him sitting peacefully, Travis made straight for the table.

When he heard the sound of hurried footsteps coming toward his table, Troy glanced up, surprised to see his brother. "Travis!" he blurted. "When did you get back?" He looked around. "Where's Malcolm?"

"Malcolm's dead, Troy," Travis replied. "We ran into some trouble."

Stunned, Troy looked around him quickly as if afraid someone might hear. "Set down and keep your voice down." He waited for Travis to slide into the chair across from him before noticing the wad of bandage under his coat. "You been shot?"

Travis nodded vigorously in response.

"And you say Malcolm's dead? Who shot him? What kinda trouble did you run into?" His eyes narrowed and deep frown lines creased his forehead. "Who shot Malcolm?" he repeated.

"I don't know who he was," Travis replied. "But I got a look at him before he shot me and I had to run for it. I was lucky to get away."

"Was he a lawman, one of those damn deputy marshals?"

"No, he sure as hell wasn't no lawman," Travis replied. "He's a wild-lookin' son of a bitch—Injun or half-breed—I don't know which." He went on to tell Troy the circumstances that had caused the loss of their brother's life, leaving out the part about his running for it without waiting to help Malcolm.

"He's a dead man," Troy growled. "He's gotta pay for this. Nobody kills one of my brothers and gets away with it." Cutting his gaze sharply around to focus on Travis, he muttered, "And you couldn't do nothin' about it?" It was a question, but could also serve as an accusation.

"That's a fact," Travis replied at once. "When I got hit, it knocked me flat. My whole arm went dead on me. I couldn't even raise my hand for a while there. Malcolm told me to pull myself back below the bank where we could stand him off. I hadn't even caught sight of the son of a bitch by then, but I finally managed to get back below the bank and I saw him out in the open. Tall jasper, looked like an Injun, only I don't think he was— just wearin' buckskins. He was standing with a rifle just waitin' for one of us to show our heads above the bank. Malcolm raised up before I could holler at him. I didn't really have no choice. I couldn't raise up to shoot, and I was already bad hurt, so I was lucky to get away without gettin' killed, myself."

Troy, still trying to get over hearing that Malcolm was dead, tried to picture the scene Travis described, unable to understand why Travis had to run. He decided to give him the benefit of the doubt, since he had suffered a wound in the attack. "What did this jasper jump you for, anyway?"

"I don't know," Travis said. "Mighta been because of the woman."

"You had a woman with you?" Troy asked. "Where'd you pick up a woman?"

"We warn't gonna keep her." Travis went on to relate their attack upon the couple in the wagon and the taking of the woman. "I didn't wanna take her with us," he lied, "but Malcolm, he got all sweet on her, and that's what slowed us down. I don't like sayin' it, but if Malcolm hadn't wanted to make early camp so he could be with that woman, that son of a bitch woulda never caught up with us." He went on to tell Troy how they had been surprised by the Indian, or half-breed, whatever he was, when they had stopped to make camp.

Troy listened attentively until Fred interrupted

when he brought over an extra glass so Travis could help his brother empty the bottle.

"Sounds to me like you two were mighty careless to let somebody sneak up on you like that," Troy concluded after Fred returned to the bar. Still puzzled over the reason for the attack, Troy asked, "Why did he jump you? Was he after the woman?"

Travis just shrugged and shook his head.

"You know where to find this feller?" Troy continued. "'Cause he's gonna have to answer to me for killin' Malcolm, and that's a fact. You know where to find him?"

"I ain't got no idea," Travis said.

"Damn," Troy muttered, still making an effort to keep his voice low. After thinking about it for another moment, he switched to another subject and said, "Well, we've got to make ourselves scarce around this town." When Travis asked why, Troy began to tell him about the hanging of Big Steve Long and Ace and Con Moyer.

"I heard about it," Travis said. "The feller down at the stable told me." He glanced over at the bar where Fred Wiggins was rinsing some shot glasses and placing them on a tray to dry. "Who owns the Bucket of Blood now? Fred?"

"Don't nobody own it. The vigilance committee says it wants it shut down. The only reason Fred's still here is because he talked 'em into letting him stay till he runs outta whiskey and supplies, then he's gone. I've been stayin' here for about a week, but they're gonna close it down. That's why we'd best move on to another town," Troy said with more than a hint of impatience for his brother's lack of common sense. "It ain't healthy for any friends of Big Steve's around here no more. And, after that hangin', I don't like the way people have been eyeballin' me ever' time I walk out on the street. They've got that vigilance committee started up. The town's tryin' to get respectable. It's a good thing you got here when you did, 'cause I was fixin' to move on to another town to wait out the winter."

"Well, I'll be damned if I ever saw this happenin'," Travis uttered. "I never thought they'd hang Big Steve. Hell, he was the sheriff." He let that sink in for a few moments, feeling a cautious urge to look around him at the other customers in the saloon, lest they suddenly rise up together and come at him and his brother. "Where was you thinkin' 'bout headin'?"

"I figured I'd ride down to Cheyenne," Troy said.

"Cheyenne?" Travis asked. "Any particular reason? Everybody left that town when the railroad moved up here to Laramie. It's most likely dried up by now."

"That ain't what I hear," Troy said. "Matter of fact, the town's got a lot bigger since all the railroad workers and the people that follow 'em left. Might be the best place for us to hole up till spring. Leastways, we oughta look it over."

"You know they got up a vigilance committee down there, too," Travis reminded him. "We heard about it, you remember. Called theirselves the Gunny Sack Gang. They're the ones that run Slade Corbett outta Cheyenne."

"I know it," Troy insisted. "But they don't know us. We ain't ever been in Cheyenne. All I know is we'd best get ourselves outta Laramie. Those vigilantes will be watchin' anybody who was friends with Big Steve Long and the Moyer boys. Cheyenne ain't that far from here, and I don't figure on leavin' the territory before I settle the score with that son of a bitch that killed Malcolm."

"I reckon you're right," Travis conceded, even though he didn't know who the man was who shot Malcolm, or where he was heading. It seemed pretty good odds that they would never find him. His appearance left Travis with the impression that he must live with some tribe of Indians.

"Let's get outta here," Troy said.

They got up from the table, Troy grabbed the bottle, and they stopped at the bar on their way out. Troy paid Fred Wiggins for the bottle and followed Travis out the door. He found him standing at the hitching rail by his horse.

Confused by the other horses tied at the rail, Troy asked, "Are those your horses?" He pointed toward the four next to Travis's bay gelding, one with a saddle, one without, and two carrying packs.

"Yep," Travis answered, then went on to explain the circumstances that caused him to lose their packhorses and return with different ones. "It was hard luck gettin' jumped by that bushwhacker. I lost my saddle and Malcolm's horse and that fancy saddle of his. But all my luck wasn't bad, 'cause two fellers came along at the right time. So I ended up with a pretty good swap."

Troy, by that time, was already giving the horses a closer examination. "Well, you mighta made a swap, but I think you mighta come up with the short end of it. That one horse looks pretty good, but them packhorses and that other 'n don't look like they coulda stood up to the two you and Malcolm rode off with." He shook his head slowly and continued. "And you sure-God got skunked on the saddles. Both of them two saddles ain't worth the one you rode, and they sure as hell ain't worth that Mexican saddle of Malcolm's. I reckon I shouldn'ta let you two ride up to Bozeman without me to keep you outta trouble."

That was the reaction Travis had anticipated from his older brother, and one he was prepared to defend against. "Hell, wouldn'ta made any difference if you'da been with us or not. He was on us before we had a chance to set up our camp. You'd best be glad you weren't with us. You might be dead, too. It was just a miracle I got away."

Troy didn't reply for a few long moments while he studied his brother's face. He couldn't deny a faint suspicion that things didn't happen exactly as Travis told it, and his brother didn't want to admit that he had run without trying to fight. When he finally spoke, it was with a hint of sarcasm in his tone. "You didn't make much of a trade when you gave up your Winchester for them Sharps ridin' on the saddles, either."

"I ain't sayin' we wasn't hit with some hard luck," Travis responded. "I'm just sayin' I didn't come away empty-handed. Besides, that Sharps is a fine rifle, might be better 'n my Winchester at huntin' buffalo."

"You figure on huntin' a lot of buffalo, do ya?" Troy asked, still sarcastic. When Travis declined to reply, Troy said, "Come on, let's go pick up my horse. We'll sell off what we don't need and get the hell outta this town. I wanna meet the son of a bitch who's a big enough grizzly bear to kill Malcolm and send you runnin' for me."

"That ain't the way it was. I told you," Travis protested again.

"Where *you* goin'?" Cole asked, somewhat surprised when Harley led his horse up to the tipi where he had just saddled Carrie's horse and was in the process of adjusting the packs on his packhorse.

"Where do you think?" Harley replied. "Goin' to take Carrie to Cheyenne."

Completely surprised, Cole said, "I figured you'd wanna stay here. Hell, I thought you were in a hurry to get back home, so you could warm those old bones of yours by the fire."

"Well, you thought wrong," Harley said. "I was just ready to leave them mountains after we got more meat and hides than we could carry without killin' our horses." He was not willing to admit that Cole was correct in his assumption. He had been missing the comfort of a warm tipi, and he had intended to stay in the Crow camp while Cole took Carrie to Cheyenne.

Over the last year or so, however, he had gotten accustomed to being the tall white warrior's right-hand man. Consequently, when it came time for Cole to ride off without him, he didn't like the thought of being left behind. Father Time was creeping up on him. He realized that. It happened to all men, but he also suddenly realized that he wasn't ready to remain in camp and sit by the fire, waiting out the slow death so many men accepted.

Besides, he told himself, *I think I'd kinda miss riding with my partner.* "You need me to make sure you don't get lost on your way down there to Crow Creek," he japed.

"I reckon that is a possibility," Cole came back. He was pleased that Harley had decided to accompany him. He could use his help in handling the extra horses. About to direct a few more sarcastic comments Harley's way, he was interrupted by the arrival of Moon Shadow and Carrie. "Well, you look like a proper Absáalooke maiden," Cole said to her. "I don't think anybody will take you for a boy now."

Carrie answered with a smile, extended her arms to each side, then slowly turned a complete circle so they could admire the doeskin garment Moon Shadow had sewn for her. She was obviously pleased to be rid of Travis Womack's clothes. "I tried to pay Moon Shadow for my dress, but she would not accept my money."

Moon Shadow shook her head. "I tell her she need that money. Spend it quick in that town."

"I expect you might be right," Cole said, thinking of the forty-seven dollars he had given her. "Maybe we can do some tradin' with Leon Bloodworth at the stable when we get there and get you a little more money for those two packhorses. He's always interested in buyin' horses. Then you could get rid of that fellow's coat, too."

"And maybe that mule, too," Harley added, "if it keeps taggin' along behind them packhorses." Without encouragement, the mule had followed along behind them, all the way from the camp where they had found Carrie. He would be interested to see if the mule was content to stay with the Indian ponies or would continue to follow the packhorses from the Crow camp.

Cole turned his attention back to Carrie. "I expect we'd best get started. It's a good two days' ride to Cheyenne, and we're startin' out a little later than I had planned." He cupped his hands together to provide a step for her and lifted her up into the saddle. Yellow Calf, who had come out by then, joined with his wife to wish them a safe journey. Carrie expressed her appreciation to them both and received an invitation to come back any time. Had Cole been paying a little closer attention, he might have noticed a trace of sadness in Carrie's face that hinted of a reluctance to leave the gentle Crow woman.

With the late start, Cole decided that it might be necessary to spend two nights on the trail instead of the one he had originally planned. Had it been only Harley and him, he would probably have pushed on into the night, but every time he thought to look at Carrie to see how she was doing, she looked as if she was having a hard time of it. When they made their first stop to rest the horses, she was obviously very stiff, in spite of now having a saddle. And he could see that she was making a big effort not to show the effects of her ride.

When she saw Harley gathering wood for a fire, she asked Cole, "Are we going to eat now? Do you want me to slice some meat to fry?"

"No, ma'am," Cole replied. "We'll just have a little coffee. We won't be here long. Just gonna rest the horses for a spell, then we'll ride on down till we strike the Chugwater. That ain't but ten more miles from here, and it's a better place to camp for the night. Think you can make that all right?"

"Oh, certainly," she quickly answered. "Whatever you want to do is fine with me."

"I thought it might be gettin' a little hard on you. I mean, you not bein' used to so much ridin'. I expect you musta been plum-nigh wore out from that ride to Medicine Bear's village, and now maybe this trip to Cheyenne might be tirin' you out some more."

"No, no," she insisted. "I'm doing just fine."

"Good," he said. "It might be easier on you if you can relax a little bit more. You look like you're kinda stiff, like you're tryin' to stand up straight in the saddle. That sorrel you're ridin' has got a nice easy gait, but you're fightin' him. If you relax and let your body move with the horse's body, you'll be a whole lot more comfortable."

She realized right away that her attempts to hide her discomfort had not been convincing. There was no sense in trying to fool them, and she had only tried because she didn't want to appear to be so much trouble. "I'll try," she said. "It seems like the horse and I have totally opposite motions. Every time I go up, the horse goes down, and when I go down, the horse goes up. My bottom is so sore," she finally confessed, "and my back feels like it's broken in three places. I'm so stiff I can hardly move."

They both laughed.

"When we get goin' again, just relax and try to move with the horse's gait, and pretty soon you'll get where you can go to sleep in the saddle."

"I don't know," she said, and rubbed her bottom for emphasis. "I hope you're right."

"What are you two laughin' at?" Harley asked when he walked over to join them.

"Carrie's bottom's sore," Cole said with a rare chuckle.

Harley paused for a moment, unaccustomed to much humor from his partner. "I ain't surprised," he finally declared. "She's settin' so stiff in the saddle, it's a wonder her back ain't broke." He stared at them, astonished, when his comment caused them both to laugh again.

"I'll get some coffee started," Carrie said, and went at once to the stream to fill the coffeepot. Since the horrible death of her husband, it was the first time she had felt at ease enough to allow herself a healthy chuckle. She was aware of how fortunate she had been to have crossed paths with Cole and Harley, and she realized how easily she had come to feel safe in their company. Instead of the comfort she might have felt in knowing she would be safely taken to Cheyenne, however, it brought a dread of leaving them. *It certainly isn't the first twist my life has taken,* she thought, as her mind recalled the unlikely events that led her to the rolling plain in Wyoming Territory.

CHAPTER 4

They rode the length of the main street in Cheyenne, heading toward the stables at the far end.

"This place is growing like a boil," Harley declared as they walked the horses slowly past a saloon that was not there the last time he and Cole had been in town. "The Cowboy's Rest," he read aloud. "Maybe we oughta pay 'em a visit after we get Carrie settled. I ain't no cowboy, but I could use some rest."

He looked at Cole for his reaction, but his tall friend was evidently lost in thoughts of his own as he gazed up the street toward the hotel. It was not difficult to guess what those thoughts might be. For his young friend's sake, Harley hoped they had been away from Cheyenne long enough for Cole to forget about the bad things that had happened there and only remember the good folks they had known.

When Cole finally spoke, he directed his question to Carrie. "This is Douglas Green's dry goods store. You sure you don't wanna go there first?" He reined Joe to a stop in front of the store and waited for Carrie to pull up alongside.

She caught up to him, being careful to guide her horse so as to have Cole between her and the store. "No," she said. "Let's go on down to the stable. I'd like to take a minute to run a brush through my hair before I meet Mr. and Mrs. Green for the first time. With this dress I've got on, I'm afraid they'll think I'm an Indian."

Overhearing, Harley blurted, "What's wrong with your hair? Hell, ain't nothin' wrong with your hair. I doubt they'd care if there was." He looked back and forth from Carrie to Cole, but neither answered him. He shrugged when Cole simply nudged Joe with his heels and the big Morgan started up again.

"Cole Bonner," Leon Bloodworth greeted them as he walked out of the stable to meet the riders. "I ain't seen you in I don't know when. Harley, I see you're still kickin'." He grinned as he tipped his hat to Carrie. "Who's this you got with you?" Without waiting for an answer, he said, "Ma'am, most likely nobody's told you, but you're ridin' in mighty questionable company." He chuckled loudly in appreciation of his humor.

"I swear, Leon," Harley answered him. "I can see you ain't got no smarter since we was last in here. Pay him no mind," he said to Carrie. "He don't know how to act in a lady's presence."

"You musta struck it rich since you left here," Leon commented when he took a good look at Harley's new saddle. "That's a mighty fancy rig for a fanny poor as yours."

"Might be a little too high class to park in a

run-down stable like your'n, come to think of it," Harley fired back.

Ignoring the usual japing between Harley and Leon, Cole stepped down and went to help Carrie dismount. "This is Carrie Green," he said to Leon. "She was married to Douglas Green's son, and she's come to deliver the sorry news that her husband was killed by bushwhackers on their way from Bozeman."

All joking aside, Leon turned respectful at once. "Leon Bloodworth, ma'am, I'm right sorry to hear about your husband." He shook his head slowly. "I know that's a sorry piece of news to have to bring to Douglas and Martha."

"Mr. Bloodworth," Carrie responded politely.

When she said no more than that, Leon looked at Cole and asked, "You wantin' to board these horses? You thinkin' about stayin' in town for a while?"

"Yeah, maybe for a night or two, I reckon," Cole answered. "At least for me and Harley's horses. Carrie, here, will most likely be stayin' with her in-laws, but she'll be interested in sellin' those two that belong to her and the mule, too." He nodded toward the two packhorses. "Maybe more, I don't know if she's decided to keep that sorrel she's ridin' or not. I reckon you're still buyin' and sellin' horses. But right now, I think she wants to tidy up a little before she sees her in-laws, maybe in your outhouse or kitchen." He glanced at Carrie for confirmation. She nodded in reply.

Leon, already appraising the two packhorses, paused before responding. He was obviously caught off guard by the lady's request. "I'm interested in talkin' trade, always am," he stuttered. "But I don't know if my outhouse is any kind of place for a lady like yourself to freshen up. I don't usually have no visitors usin' the outhouse. I don't use it, myself, half the time." His sudden look of panic faded when a thought occurred to him. "Best thing for you would be to go to the hotel. They've got a nice ladies' wash-room right behind the dinin' room. That'd suit you a whole lot better 'n my stable." Confident again, he looked at Harley and shook his head. "I ain't sur-prised you didn't think of that."

"I reckon I should have," Cole said. "That would be better." In truth, he had thought of that, but he had assumed Carrie would want to go to Green's general store right away, even before she saw to her horses. He had not been planning to visit the hotel dining room, even though he knew he would enjoy one of the fine meals Maggie Whitehouse pro-vided. *But,* he told himself, *I'm probably silly to stay away. Mary Lou Cagle probably no longer works there since she married Gordon Luck.* Gordon would most likely want his wife to stay home and cook for him.

"That sounds like the best thing to do," Carrie said, convinced that the condition of his outhouse might even be worse that he described.

"I'll take care of your animals for you, ma'am," Leon said. "Water 'em and feed 'em, and when you get ready, we'll talk about sellin' 'em."

"Just so you know," Cole told him, "it'll be me you'll be doin' the tradin' with. We'll walk up to the hotel with Miss Green and leave our horses tied up here. We'll leave the saddles on 'em till we decide if we're gonna stay in town tonight." He was not looking at Carrie, else he might have caught the momentary look of panic in her eyes.

The disappointment in Leon's face was too difficult to hide, but he tried to make light of it. "Well, I swear, Cole, you know I'd be as fair to her as I would to you or Harley."

"Ha!" Harley snorted and turned to accompany Cole and Carrie up the street.

Sheriff John Henry Black stood leaning against the front desk of the hotel, talking to the owner, Arthur Campbell, when Carrie and her two escorts walked in. He stood aside politely when she came to the desk. Both Black and Campbell eyed the woman openly, curious to hear what she had in mind.

"Can I help you, ma'am?" Campbell asked, too absorbed in scrutinizing the young woman dressed in deerskins to give full notice to the two men accompanying her.

"She's lookin' to clean herself up a little," Harley answered for her. "She's been in the saddle for a few days gettin' here, and she'd like to use your washroom."

"I'll pay for it, if there's a charge," Cole said.

"Harley?" Campbell blurted, surprised when he glanced in the little man's direction. He shifted his gaze immediately to the tall man behind him. "Cole Bonner! I declare, I didn't even know that was you, wearing those buckskins. Your lady friend had all my attention, I guess."

He gestured to John Henry Black, who had shifted his interest immediately to the two men, strangers to him. "Say howdy to Sheriff Black," Campbell said. "It took us a while to find a good man for the sheriff's job after Jim Thompson was gunned down right in front of the Cowboy's Rest. Then John Henry, here, came riding in from Kansas one day and took it on. Sheriff, this is Cole Bonner. He's the fellow we told you about. Without Cole's help, Slade Corbett and his gang mighta run all the honest folks outta town."

"I heard about you," Black said as he continued to study the formidable young man standing before him. "Seems like every time you came to town somebody got killed." He smiled then and extended his hand.

Cole shook it. "Pleased to meet you. I hope that ain't gonna happen this time." He nodded toward Harley and said, "This is Harley Branch."

"Now, introduce me to your lady friend," Campbell said.

"This is Carrie Green," Cole said. "She's come to stay with Douglas Green and his wife." He went on then to tell them the sad circumstances that brought Carrie to Cheyenne to meet her mother- and father-in-law. "She lost everything she owned," Cole concluded. "That's why she's wearin' that Indian getup."

Carrie, having stood silent up to that point while all four men looked at her as if she was a mare at a horse auction, spoke for the first time. "If I can, I'd like to clean up a little before I go to meet the Greens."

Realizing she had been practically ignored while they learned why she happened to be there, Arthur Campbell replied at once. "Why of course you can, ma'am, and it won't be no charge to you at all. I'll get someone to help you." He came out from behind the desk and went to the door that led to a hallway, then to another door that led to the dining room. When he returned, he said, "One of Maggie's girls who works in the dining room will be glad to take you in hand."

Cole exchanged glances with Harley, each wondering how far their obligation went in delivering Carrie to Cheyenne. Neither made any comment, but both decided independently that the job wouldn't be over until they handed her over to her in-laws.

In the next moment, the door to the hallway opened and in walked Mary Lou Cagle. She froze when she saw Cole. Equally stunned, he could not speak at once, but after a few seconds, he forced himself to recover.

She was the first to speak. "Cole Bonner." She said his name softly, as if beholding a mysterious legend. Then in a voice more fitting to her usual confidence, she added, "If that is you in that Indian getup."

"Hello, Mary Lou," Cole managed to reply.

"It's been quite a while since you left Cheyenne," Mary Lou said as she studied the change in his appearance—buckskins and long Indian-style hair. Realizing she was staring, she shifted her gaze immediately toward Carrie, dressed in buckskin clothing as well, with a heavy blanket wrapped around her shoulders. "Is this lady with you?"

"I reckon so," Cole sputtered, unable to think of any other answer.

Mary Lou gave Carrie a quick looking over, but before she could address her, Arthur Campbell said, "This young lady just got to town, and she's had a bad time of it before Cole and Harley found her. How 'bout showing her where she can freshen up?"

"Why, sure," Mary Lou replied. "I'd be glad to. Come on, honey, and I'll take you to the washroom." She stepped back and held the door for Carrie.

When the door closed behind them, Cole glanced at Harley, inhaled deeply, and shook his head. "I didn't expect to see Mary Lou still workin' in the dinin' room. I'm kinda surprised Gordon Luck lets her."

"Me, too," Harley said.

Campbell shrugged, realizing there was no reason to think they would know. "Mary Lou never married Gordon." When he received a quick look of surprise from each of the two, he added, "Mary Lou called it off."

"Did she say why?" Cole asked at once.

"Said it would just have been a big mistake, is what she told Maggie," Campbell said. "Gordon didn't take it too well. But, like I told him, it was better than getting married, then finding out a little ways down the road that she wanted out." Campbell cocked his head to one side and chuckled as he recalled. "Gordon stands in good with the Lord, so he finally decided that musta been the way God prefers it."

"Reckon so," Cole said, remembering then that Gordon Luck ran a sawmill, but also served as the

pastor of the church. He glanced at Harley, who
was eyeing him, a wide grin beaming through
the heavy brush that covered a large portion of
his face.

"That ain't the first time Mary Lou's had a
chance to get married," Campbell continued. "She
was married once, a long time ago, and I reckon
she figures once was enough for her."

"Wouldn't blame her," Harley said. "Could be
she's holdin' out for the right man to come along."
He cocked an eye at his partner, but Cole made no
response, his mind still grappling with the unexpected development.

"Water for that tub is in these buckets," Mary
Lou said, trying not to be obvious as she appraised
Carrie. "All you have to do is put it on the stove
and heat it up." She pointed to the little potbellied
stove in the corner of the small room. "Are you
wanting to take a tub bath?" she asked as an afterthought.

"I wasn't going to," Carrie replied. "I was just
planning to freshen up a little and run a brush
through my hair. But since everything is so handy,
I think a bath might be a good idea."

Mary Lou knew that she should leave without
asking any more questions, but she found that she
was just irritated enough to pry. "Have you known
Cole very long?"

"Only a little over a week," Carrie answered.
Seeing the surprised expression on Mary Lou's
face, it struck her then that the question had held
more than casual interest. "I owe my life to Cole

Bonner," she said, then went on to tell Mary Lou about the loss of her husband and the circumstances that had led her to this town with a hastily sewn dress made from animal hides her only garment. "The only dress of my own was torn so badly that I threw it in the fire when Moon Shadow gave me this one."

When she fully realized the tragedy Carrie had recently endured, and the part that Cole had played in it, Mary Lou felt her cheeks flush with the shameful thoughts she had assumed. She quickly tried to atone for the cool reception she had offered the poor woman who had just seen her husband murdered. "I'm so very sorry to hear about your husband," she said. "If there is anything I can do to help you, please don't hesitate to let me know. Douglas and Martha Green are kind, decent folks, and I know they will welcome you into their home."

"I fear they will think Robert married an Indian woman," Carrie said. "But it was either this, or meet them for the first time wearing the clothes of one of the men who murdered their son."

"Maybe I can help you with that," Mary Lou volunteered, now eager to be of assistance to the unfortunate young widow. "We look pretty much the same size. Maybe I'm a little bigger. I'll go get you one of my dresses to wear until you have a chance to get some new clothes."

"Oh, that would be so kind of you," Carrie exclaimed. "I don't know how I can repay you." She hesitated then added, "And Cole and Harley for all their kindness."

"Think nothing of it," Mary Lou said. "I'm glad

we can help." With a more positive attitude, she
left then to fetch a suitable dress from her room.
"You go on now and get to your bath, and I'll be
back with some clothes for you." She quickly
picked up one of the buckets of water and placed
it on the stove, then went out the door.

Before going to her room, Mary Lou went back
into the kitchen to tell Maggie Whitehouse what
she was doing. "I know it's almost time to serve
supper, but I need to help that poor woman get
ready to meet her in-laws for the first time."

"Beulah and I can handle it till you get back,"
Maggie assured her. "You better not take too long,
though, if she wants to catch Martha at the store.
You know, she goes home early to fix Douglas's
supper." She favored her with a mischievous smile
and asked, "So Cole Bonner just showed up at the
hotel and brought a woman with him, huh?"

"Bite your tongue," Mary Lou scolded. "I told
you what that poor woman just went through. You
oughta be ashamed." She felt no desire to confess
that her initial reaction to seeing Cole again, and
with another woman, was one of pure jealousy. She
had turned down an offer of marriage to a promi-
nent businessman because of her inability to rid
her mind of Cole Bonner. And then to see him
return after a year of roaming the wild mountains
like an Indian—with a young woman, no less—she
felt ready to strangle him.

Reminding herself that she needed to catch
Martha Green before she went home, Mary Lou
left to hurry Carrie along and help her get dressed.

* * *

At first glance, the men still talking at the front desk thought Mary Lou had bumped into another woman on her way back from the kitchen.

Harley was the first to express his surprise. "Well, I'll be . . ." he exclaimed, searching for the right words. "If you ain't pretty as a picture. I didn't know that was you at first."

"Harley's right," Cole said. "You look real nice, Carrie. Mr. and Mrs. Green will be mighty proud to meet you." His gaze drifted to focus on Mary Lou and found her eyes focused on him. He quickly looked away.

Carrie could not help blushing with the attention paid to her and tried to make light of it. "I declare, I musta looked pretty bad before." She could not tell them that she was almost trembling inside with the uncertainty of meeting her in-laws. For, without her husband, she was not confident that they would welcome her. She was a stranger to them and might be a constant reminder that he had been murdered. Once again she wondered if she was making the right decision in coming. Maybe she would have felt more welcome had she stayed with Moon Shadow and Yellow Calf.

It was too late to back out, however, when Mary Lou spoke up. "You'd best take her on up to the store," she said to Cole. "Martha will be going home pretty soon to fix supper. I imagine she'd like to know her daughter-in-law's come home."

"Reckon you're right," Cole replied. "Let's get along then." He walked to the door and held it open for Carrie.

Carrie glanced furtively at Mary Lou and said, "Thank you. I'll return your dress as soon as I can buy something." Then she walked toward the door, much like a convicted felon walking to the gallows.

"You're welcome," Mary Lou said. "No hurry about the dress. Keep it as long as you need it." Then she said to Harley, who was following Carrie out the door, "Harley, you and Cole can come on back here for supper."

"Yes, ma'am," Harley replied obediently, for her raised eyebrow and unblinking gaze indicated it was a command and not merely an invitation. "We surely will." He grinned and gave her a wink.

Martha Green looked up from the counter when she heard the door open. "Cole Bonner," she announced, surprised to see him. "We were wondering if we'd ever see you back here again." She craned her neck in an effort to see the slender young woman almost hidden behind the tall rifleman. "And who's this you've got with you?" Without waiting for an answer, she called out, "Douglas, Cole Bonner is here, and he's brought some people with him."

"Howdy, Miz Green," Cole returned the greeting. "This is Harley Branch. I don't believe he's ever been in here before, have you, Harley?"

Harley said that he hadn't.

Martha was more interested in Carrie. "And who's this young lady?"

Purposely stalling until Douglas came in from the storeroom, Cole waited until the burly storekeeper entered the room, preferring to report the sorrowful news just one time.

Carrie, thinking Cole might have suddenly become reluctant to impart such tragic news decided she should not saddle him with that burden. "Mr. and Mrs. Green," Carrie spoke up, stepping in front of Cole. "I'm Carrie, Robert's wife."

"Carrie," Martha echoed and looked toward the door, expecting her son to walk in. She stepped forward to embrace her daughter-in-law, having known her only through her son's letters. "Well, this is a pleasant surprise," she gushed as she gave Carrie a welcoming hug. "We weren't sure when to expect you." She looked past Harley to the door again. "Where's Robert?"

"He's not coming," Carrie answered.

Confused, Martha stepped back and awaited an explanation.

Carrie continued. "I'm so sorry to tell you this, but Robert's dead." She paused when she saw the shock registered in Martha's eyes. "We were attacked by a couple of outlaws on our way here and they killed Robert."

Cole stepped up in time to catch Martha Green before she sank to the floor. Her husband quickly moved in to help Cole settle Martha into a chair by the stove.

Carrie, with tears streaming down her cheeks, blurted out, "I'm so sorry, and I wasn't sure if you'd want me to come here without Robert." She appeared too distraught to continue, so Cole told them how he and Harley had happened upon her abductors and managed to free her.

By the time he had finished, both father and mother were staring stone-faced at him, scarcely able to believe this tragedy had befallen them. After a long moment, Martha recovered her senses enough to realize that it was Carrie's tragedy as well as theirs. She rose from the chair and went to embrace the young stranger again. "I'm so sorry, my dear," she said, making an effort to sound sincere. "Of course, you're welcome in our home. We fixed up the front bedroom for you and Robert, so now it's yours, and welcome." She looked at Cole and Harley then and thanked them for bringing their daughter-in-law safely to them.

"Yes, ma'am," Cole said, anxious to leave now that Carrie seemed to have been received graciously. "I reckon we'll be goin', then."

Harley, as eager to go as Cole, was already at the door.

Carrie caught Cole's arm as he turned to leave. "Thank you for everything you did."

"I'm just sorry we didn't get there soon enough to help your husband," he said, and turned to leave. Remembering his promise to help her, he said to Douglas, "Carrie's got a couple of horses down at the stable, plus a mule and the sorrel she rode in on. I told Leon I'd talk to him about buyin' 'em from her."

Green nodded and Cole followed Harley out the door.

Carrie stood there, watching him go out the door, and once again felt abandoned. She turned to face her in-laws, discouraged by the awkward silence that suddenly dropped over the room. It was obvious that Douglas and Martha were trying hard to control their grief while confronted with a daughter-in-law they had never met before. She wished then that she had not come to Cheyenne. It was hard not to wonder why God had chosen once again to place her in a situation she desired not to be in. When she'd met Robert, she had thought that at last she could lead a normal life, married to a good man. Early in her life, she had made unfortunate choices that had caused her considerable grief. That was all behind her and forgotten when Robert asked her to marry him. And for the better part of a couple of years, it appeared that she had at last found peace and the comfort of a solid marriage. And now this. She wondered if Douglas and Martha would come to blame her for their son's death.

Further thoughts on the subject were interrupted when Martha spoke. "Come on, honey. I've got a few things to deliver to the postmaster's wife. She's been sick with a fever and I told her husband I'd stop by to see her before I went home. You can go with me if you want." She took Carrie's hand and led her to the back room of the store.

Outside, Cole found Harley waiting. "That wasn't a helluva lot of fun, was it?"

"Reckon not."

While Cole and Harley were delivering Carrie to the dry goods store, a couple of strangers pulled up short of the stables when something caught the eye of one of them. "You see what I see?" Troy Womack asked.

"Where?" Travis responded.

"Yonder," Troy said and pointed at some horses tied up in front of the stable. "I ain't ever seen another saddle like that Mexican rig Malcolm owned. But damned if that don't look like one on that little roan, tied up beside that big Morgan."

"Damned if it don't," Travis quickly agreed, and both men became immediately alert.

"We mighta just had us a big favor handed right to us," Troy said. "I'm thinkin' there just might be the initials, *MW*, cut into the left fender of that saddle. And if there is, we just mighta saved ourselves a long hunt."

There appeared to be no one around when they rode up to the hitching rail and dismounted.

"That's Malcolm's saddle," Travis said, certain of it before he even got to it. He lifted the saddle fender on the left side and peered at the bottom side of it. "By God," he swore and held the fender up for Troy to see their brother's initials, just as Leon walked out of the stable.

"Somethin' I can help you fellers with?" he asked, more than a little curious about their interest in Cole and Harley's horses.

"Yeah," Troy answered. "Who's the feller who owns this saddle?"

"Harley Branch," Leon answered before taking the time to decide if he should or not. Upon taking a closer look at the two men, he thought he might have made a mistake. So he quickly attempted to water his statement down. "Leastways, Harley was usin' it today. He ain't had it no time a'tall."

"Where is he?" Troy asked. "I need to talk to him."

"Why, I don't rightly know," Leon stuttered. "He

just said he was gonna leave his horses. Didn't say where he was goin' or when he'd be back."

"Is that so?" Troy said. "So if I take a look in them stalls, I ain't gonna find nobody back there, right?"

"No sir," Leon replied. "You're welcome to take a look. There ain't nobody back there but my son, Marvin. I ain't got no reason to lie to you."

Troy stared at the suddenly nervous man for a few long moments before deciding he was telling the truth. Finally he said, "Come on, Travis, let's go look in the saloons. Ain't nobody hidin' in them stalls. You'd recognize the son of a bitch if you saw him, wouldn't you?"

"I'm pretty sure I would," Travis said, recalling the fearsome image he had beheld as he'd raced away from the small stream where his brother was killed. Clad in buckskins like a wild Indian, standing tall as a tree with his rifle raised, waiting for Malcolm to look up over the bank, he was a man Travis would not likely forget.

They left the visibly shaken stable owner and started up the street, past the saddle shop, toward the first of three saloons. Having no reason to spend any time in that saloon because there were only a few customers in the small room, they left the Cowboy's Rest and headed for the Sundown Saloon.

"It's still pretty early," Travis said. "Maybe he's gone to take supper at that hotel down at the end of the street."

"Maybe," Troy allowed, "but we might as well look in those two saloons on the way."

CHAPTER 5

Unaware of the remote possibility that someone was even now searching every saloon between the stables and the hotel with the intention of killing them, Cole and Harley sat at a table in the hotel dining room. Maggie Whitehouse made an extra effort to make them feel welcome.

"Sure is good to see you back in town again," she said to Cole. Then as an afterthought, she added, "You, too, Harley." But her main interest was in Cole. Although Mary Lou had never admitted it, Maggie knew the real reason she had called off her wedding to Gordon Luck. And that reason was sitting at the table right now. "When you left here, we thought you and Harley were heading up in the mountains for good."

"I reckon that was more or less what we had in mind," Cole admitted. "But we hadn't figured on meetin' up with Carrie Green, so we had to make sure she got back here to Crow Creek Crossin' all right."

There were a couple of things that Maggie wanted to say before Mary Lou returned from the kitchen with a fresh pot of coffee, so she didn't hesitate. "If Mary Lou hadn't told me you were back, I mighta had to take a second look to make sure that was you." Puzzled by the remark, Cole merely shrugged, and Maggie continued. "You looked pretty much like an Indian when you walked in the door. I suppose that's natural when you're living up in the mountains with nobody but the squirrels and bears, and Harley, here, for company. I expect you'll be cutting your hair short again, now that you're back with the white folks. First thing you know, people will be worried about losing their scalps when you walk in the door." She forced a chuckle to make him think she was just teasing him.

Cole exchanged glances with Harley, puzzled by Maggie's seemingly meandering conversation. She acted as if she had never seen a man wearing buckskins before, and he didn't really care if people thought he was an Indian or not. He preferred to go clean-shaven, like the Crow men, instead of wearing hair all over his face, like Harley. The length of his hair didn't bother him as long as it was woven into two long braids, so as not to be in his way. Maggie always was a little strange, he figured, but then, again, most women were, and that included Mary Lou, who came from the kitchen at that moment.

"I'll try not to take any scalps while I'm in town this time," he declared, in answer to Maggie's comment, and winked at Harley.

Dumb as a stump, Maggie thought when it was obvious Cole was not aware she was hinting that he should do away with his wild-man look and return to the old civilized Cole Bonner. "Well, I'll get back to the kitchen," she announced to Mary Lou when she started to pour the coffee.

"Now, that surely hits the spot," Harley said after taking a sip of the steaming hot liquid. "You must have a special way of boilin' it."

"Well, I'm glad you find it satisfactory," Mary Lou responded. "We wouldn't want you going around telling folks our coffee wasn't good." Although trading playful comments with Harley, her eyes were cocked toward Cole, who sat silently studying her face.

Arthur Campbell had said that Mary Lou had called off her wedding with Gordon Luck. The news had caused Cole's brain to go numb at the time. He could have been truthful just now, when Maggie inquired about his plans to remain in the mountains for good. He could have admitted that he was prompted to retreat to the wilderness when Mary Lou had told him that she had accepted Luck's proposal of marriage. He could only speculate on the reason for her change of mind, and he was lacking the confidence to express his feelings for her. Further thoughts on the matter were suddenly interrupted when they were startled by a piercing scream from the street outside.

Jolted from thoughts of Mary Lou, Cole came out of his chair, along with all the other diners in the room, and went to the window to seek the cause for the scream. What he saw caused him to snatch up his rifle, yell to Harley, "It's Carrie!" and ran for the door.

In the moments before Carrie screamed, Troy and Travis Womack had walked out of The

Sidewinder Saloon and climbed onto their horses when suddenly Travis reined his horse back hard. "It's her!" he'd blurted. "It's her! That's the woman!" He'd pointed to a buckboard, pulling out from behind the dry goods store with two women in it.

"Who?" Troy demanded. "What woman?"

"The one me and Malcolm had! Carrie Green, the one that son of a bitch took from us."

Carrie had screamed when she'd recognized Travis.

He gloated, "Well, ain't that somethin'?" An evil grin spread across his face, pleased when he saw the horror reflected on the young woman's face. "Hello, Buttercup," he said, even though she was too far away to hear him.

"Well, shut her up before she gets the sheriff on us!" Troy ordered, and they both galloped to cut the buckboard off. But it was too late. John Henry Black was coming out of the hotel at that point, just in time to see them racing toward the two women.

Martha Green fought to control her horse when the animal reared back to avoid the charging riders amid screams of terror from Carrie.

Running, Sheriff Black yelled at the two riders, "Hold it right there! Rein those horses back!" He drew his weapon to show he meant business. Troy Womack was quick to respond. Two shots from the gunman's .44 caused the surprised sheriff to fall to his knees and collapse on the boardwalk.

Seeing the sheriff go down, Travis pulled up beside the buckboard and reached for Carrie.

"Leave her, damn it!" Troy yelled at him. "We've

got to get the hell outta here!" Without waiting to see if his brother followed, he wheeled his horse and galloped away.

"I want her," Travis replied, "and she ain't gettin' away this time."

Carrie tried to fight back, but his grip was too strong until he suddenly let go with the simultaneous thud of the first of two .44 rifle slugs that slammed into his body. He slid from his horse as it bolted away after Troy's.

Cole cranked another round into the chamber as he ran from the dining room door in an attempt to get a clear shot at the fleeing brother. But he was not in time to take it before Troy, leading a packhorse, galloped out of sight between the saddle shop and the post office. Concerned then for Carrie, Cole turned and ran back to the buckboard, pausing only a moment to make sure Travis was no longer a threat. He reached the buckboard a step or two behind Douglas Green, who had run from his store and was trying to calm the horse down.

Once the horse was under control, Douglas and Cole went to the aid of the two distraught women while Harley, only a few steps behind Cole, went to check on the sheriff.

"It was him!" Carrie cried when Cole asked if she was all right. "He came to get me!" she exclaimed, thinking that Travis had somehow followed her to Cheyenne.

Recovering from her fright more quickly than Carrie, Martha put her arm around the shaken girl's shoulders and held her close. "We're all right now. You're safe now."

"That's right," Cole said. "He ain't gonna bother

you no more. He's dead." He turned when he heard Harley yell.

"The sheriff's alive," Harley declared as he knelt beside the wounded lawman. "But we'd best get him to the doctor right away. He's bleedin' pretty bad, got two bullet holes in him."

"Put him on the buckboard," Douglas said. "We'll take him to Doc Marion's."

Cole went at once to help Harley carry the wounded man. They laid him as gently as they could in the back of the buckboard as Douglas climbed aboard and took the reins from his wife.

"Better hurry, Douglas," Arthur Campbell said, running up to join them after having witnessed the shooting from the door of his hotel. "We can't afford to lose him. First Jim Thompson, now John Henry. We'll have a helluva time replacing him."

Douglas turned the horse, and with the two women crowded in the seat beside him, headed toward the edge of town to the doctor's office. Wedged in between her in-laws, Carrie turned to gaze over her shoulder at Cole. It was a frightened look of distress like that of a child who was being taken from her parents, and Cole couldn't help feeling a little concerned for her. She was safe from the man who wanted to violate her, but she had yet to find what her life would be with parents she had never known. He guessed it was a natural emotion that she had come to feel safe with Harley and him. *She'll be all right, once she gets to know them*, he told himself.

A sizable crowd of spectators had gathered, now that the shooting appeared to be over. Most of them were gathering around the body of young Travis Womack.

In a minute or two, Horace Smith, a barber who also served as an undertaker, showed up to gawk at the dead gunman. "Reckon it's up to me to haul him off and bury him," he said and looked around at the gathering as if waiting for someone to offer payment for his services.

Since it was obvious that no one saw it as their responsibility to help out, he sighed and muttered, "I'll go get my wagon."

"He's wearin' a Colt .44 and a gun belt full of cartridges," Cole spoke up. "That oughta help cover your expenses."

"Why, yes sir, that would, indeed," Horace had assumed that Cole would strip the body of those things, as well as any other valuables, since he was the one who shot him. "I thank you very kindly." It was a fair assumption on his part, for Cole, being a practical man, was not above claiming the spoils resulting from his shooting.

He hoped to pick up the dead man's horse for his part. He turned when Arthur Campbell walked up to him.

"Reckon we've seen the last of that fellow?" Campbell asked. "You think he'll make another try to get that woman?"

"I don't know," Cole said. "I ain't so sure it was Carrie they came after. They mighta been lookin' for me, since I shot his brother and took Carrie away from them." The thing that baffled him was how they knew he would be in Cheyenne.

"I'm thinking there ain't no way we can be sure

we won't get another visit from that gunman," Campbell said, "and maybe lose another one of our citizens."

Harley cocked his head around to catch Cole's eye. Like Cole, Harley knew what Campbell was getting at.

Cole paused a long moment before responding. When he spoke, it was with a deadly sense of responsibility. "I know what you're gettin' at, and I don't reckon I blame you, but I ain't no lawman."

"You're the only man with the guts and the skill to track him down," Campbell insisted. "He shot our sheriff. There ain't nobody else to do it. We're trying to build a respectable town, and we're making good progress. We can't let drifters and gunmen think they can come here and have their way. As mayor, I can appoint you sheriff, if that's what bothers you."

"What if he gets me before I get him?" Cole asked. "You're makin' a risky bet."

"I've seen you in action," Campbell said.

"Ain't much else we can do here to help right now," Cole said to Harley. "I'm gonna go back to the stable and get my horse." He nodded toward Travis's body. "I wanna see if I can run his horse down before it wanders off somewhere. Maybe it didn't get too far before it quit runnin'." He turned back to Campbell. "I'll go after that fellow, because I reckon I'm the one that caused your sheriff to get shot. I won't be needin' a badge."

"I figured that," Harley said. "I'll be ready to ride, but I need to get a little drink to warm my insides first." He nodded toward the closest saloon,

the Cowboy's Rest. He was confident that Cole
didn't need him to go after one man, so he was
counting on Cole to say as much. As often happened of late, he was afraid he might slow him
down, and after the gunfight just ended in the
street, he felt the need for a drink.

Cole figured as much. "Why don't you stay here
and help Carrie sell her horses? She'd most likely
appreciate it. And I ain't got no idea how long I'm
gonna be gone."

Leon Bloodworth, who had come running to
join the spectators, fell in step beside Cole as he
walked back to get his horse. "Looked like that one
feller was after the lady," Leon said, "but they was
after you and Harley."

"How do you know that?" Cole asked. "How'd
they know I was in town?" Having recognized the
man he had just shot for the second time—this
time for good—he could believe that Travis was
hunting him. But surely they could not have followed him to Medicine Bear's village, waited him
out, then followed him to Cheyenne.

"Tell you the truth, I don't think they did know
you were here," Leon said. "They looked mighty
surprised when they spotted that fancy saddle of
Harley's. Asked me who rode in on that horse, and
where he was. I told 'em it belonged to Harley
before I thought about what I was sayin'. But I told
'em I didn't have no idea where he was. So that's
who they were lookin' for, the man who had that
saddle."

That sounded plausible to Cole. The Mexican
saddle was the spark that had set off the shoot-out.
And poor Carrie had just happened to ride into

the scene at the wrong time. He was well aware that neither Carrie nor Harley was the real target. According to what Carrie had told him, the men who'd killed her husband and carried her off were two of a three-brother clan. He had to give serious thought to the possibility that the one who had just escaped was the third brother and would make another attempt to avenge his brothers.

That possibility was the reason Cole had to find him before he found Cole and made good on an attempt. It was the reason he'd told Campbell he would accept the responsibility, and start out after him before his trail became stone-cold.

There was another reason as well. The man had shot, maybe killed, the sheriff. Like Arthur Campbell had said, that evil deed needed to be punished, and as far as Cole could determine, not one of the town's citizens was willing to step up to do the job. He couldn't honestly blame them. They all had families, so that left him as the only candidate for the job.

I'm the one he wants, he thought. *I'm the one who killed his brothers, so it's sort of up to me to settle this thing for good.* He was not content to leave Travis's horse to run loose, however. He needed the money the horse might bring in a sale, not to mention the saddle and no doubt a rifle riding in a saddle scabbard. "I'm wastin' time," he muttered.

At the stable, he took the essentials he thought he couldn't do without from the packhorse, telling Leon that Harley would pick it up. Then he backed Joe away from the rail and rode back to the Cowboy's Rest, where he found Harley engaged in conversation with the bartender.

Refusing the offer of a shot of whiskey, he told Harley what he planned to do. "I ain't comin' back until I run that bastard to ground."

"Damnation, Cole," Harley replied. "You don't even know who he is, or what he looks like. Don't let the mayor talk you into takin' no careless chances."

"I got a glimpse of him," Cole said. "I think I might recognize him if I was to see him again, and if my hunch is right, I figure his name is Womack 'cause Carrie said there were three brothers. I don't know how long it'll take, but if you ain't here when I get back, I'll see you back in Medicine Bear's camp." He turned and walked to the door before Harley could express more words of caution.

Just before going out the door, Cole turned and declared, "You better hope I run him down, 'cause he's lookin' for the man that straddles that Mexican saddle, and he knows his name is Harley Branch."

Guiding Joe between the saddle shop and the post office, he looked for the tracks of the three horses in the light snow. He spotted them at once, since no other tracks had been left there since the snow had fallen. With no other thoughts beyond overtaking the gunman, he pushed Joe a little harder in hopes of lessening the head start already taken. Tracks of the fleeing horses led across a creek, then cut back to the west, toward the Laramie Mountains.

After a couple of miles, the gunman cut back on a course that would intercept the Union Pacific Railroad tracks.

Upon approaching the railroad, Cole spotted the stray horse with the empty saddle. A bay gelding, the horse had evidently given up the chase when it decided to stop and drink at a small stream. Cole reined Joe back to a walk and approached the bay slowly. The horse watched him attentively, but made no move to flee, permitting Cole to ride up to him and secure him with a lead rope. The fact that the man he chased had made no attempt to catch his brother's horse told him that he had nothing in mind beyond running. Already leading a packhorse, he evidently figured an extra horse would slow him down too much. In fact, he might not have even known the horse was following him.

With the bay in tow, Cole resumed the chase, following the tracks of only two horses. They continued to the railroad, but instead of crossing, they turned to follow the road beside the tracks. It seemed that his man was heading for Laramie. Encouraged, Cole thought he had a better chance of catching him in town than he would searching the mountains for him. Forced to pull Joe back to a walk again to keep from tiring the horses too soon, Cole consoled himself by thinking that Womack would have to do the same. Otherwise, he would soon be walking.

Fortunately, there had been no other traffic on the narrow road since the snowfall, so tracking Womack was easy. Cole wondered why that thought hadn't occurred to Womack.

Only a short while after thinking it, the tracks stopped when the gunman had crossed a wide stream. So maybe he wasn't heading directly to Laramie.

Intent upon losing a tail or setting up an ambush? It

was an indication he at least suspected someone might be tracking him.

Upstream or downstream? Cole had to make a choice. He looked upstream, which would lead him into the foothills of the Laramie Mountains. Downstream might mean Womack was heading toward the Medicine Bow Mountains on the other side of the valley.

Cole paused to again consider whether or not Womack was intent only on escaping, or still of a mind to double back in an attempt to kill the man who'd killed his brothers. Cole shrugged, thinking it didn't make much difference, and decided to go upstream. Womack would likely think that was the best chance to lose anyone following or find a place to wait in ambush.

Cole gave Joe a light touch with his heels and the big Morgan entered the stream. Keeping him in the middle of the rapidly moving water to see the stream as Womack had seen it, Cole figured he could more readily see the best place to exit without leaving tracks.

Within a short time, he came to a flat rock jutting out from the bank. Thinking it a likely spot to leave the water without leaving tracks, he rode up on it and dismounted. He found no tracks on or around the rock as he'd expected, but upon finding open sand and gravel beyond the rock, also with no imprints from two horses, he knew Womack would have had to have wings. Back in the water, he continued upstream, watching the banks on both sides as the stream led him toward the top of a narrow ravine.

Halfway up the ravine the first shot was fired. It

struck Joe in the chest, causing the big Morgan to stagger sideways. Cole instinctively slid over to the side of the horse's neck in time to avoid two more shots that snapped over his head only inches away. A fourth shot caught the courageous horse in his withers, and he stumbled several more steps before going down heavily on his side. Cole managed to draw his rifle from the scabbard as the horse collapsed on the bank, but he didn't get his left foot out of the stirrup in time to avoid being pinned under the heavy weight of the big Morgan.

He was trapped! Try as he might, he couldn't pull his leg out from under Joe. The best he could do was to swing his right leg over and lie flat behind the big horse. No more shots came from above, which led him to believe Womack was waiting to see if he was going to come out from behind the fallen horse. Frantically straining to free himself, he pulled and pulled with no success.

He paused for a moment to evaluate his situation. His leg felt compressed under Joe's weight, but he felt no pain to indicate it was broken, as he had at first suspected. He could only speculate that the sandy bank of the stream permitted the leg to be driven into the ground instead of snapping on impact. That might have been good news, but he was trapped under the horse nevertheless, so he went back to pulling with all his might.

"He can't get out from under that horse," Troy muttered after several long minutes waiting for Cole to move out from behind the fallen horse. "He can't get up! The son of a bitch is pinned down!"

Suddenly the tables were turned and the advantage was his. "I killed your damn horse and now I'm gonna kill you," he shouted. First, however, he had to leave the rocks he had chosen as his firing position and move along the ridge until he could see enough of his target to get a clear shot.

He was almost gleeful as he worked his way from tree to rock to tree again, trying to find the angle that would give him a clear field of fire. *Shooting fish in a barrel,* he thought. He was to find, however, that the slope of the ridge did not seem to accommodate him, for the tree line where he needed to go stopped short of a grassy patch that would expose him if he moved to the edge.

He finally settled on a position where he could see Cole's hat and part of his shoulder. *I'll settle for that,* he thought. *I'm close enough with my rifle to hit anything I aim at. And there's no danger of hitting Travis's horse, still tied to a lead rope from the Morgan's saddle.*

As he rested the barrel of the Winchester on a small boulder and steadied his aim, Womack blew on his fingers, which were stiff from the cold. Then he concentrated his gaze on the hat and grinned when he saw it moving slightly. He knew that meant a head was in the hat. Confident he could hit the small target at that distance, he drew a deep breath to steady his aim, then slowly squeezed the trigger. With the crack of the rifle, the hat was immediately blown out of his sight.

Right on the money, he thought as the shoulder dropped behind the horse's body as well. Anxious to make sure of his kill, he jumped up and ran into the grassy patch, ejecting the spent shell as he ran.

He was right in thinking he could get a clear view of the man lying behind the horse, but he had not counted on seeing that man flat on his back, waiting for him with a Henry rifle aimed at the edge of the clearing.

There was no time for Womack to react, for the slug from Cole's rifle was already on its way. With the impact of the bullet, he staggered backward a couple of steps before falling on his backside, stunned by the sudden surprise. Unable to move for a long moment, he felt a burning pain in his side. His fingers fumbled as he unbuttoned his coat and looked at the patch of blood already spreading on his shirt. Panic set in, for the blood was flowing freely, and he was struck with fear that he had to get some help before he bled to death.

Frantic, he pushed himself backward until reaching the cover of the trees, afraid he might die if he didn't get to a doctor. The closest was in Laramie, about twenty miles away. With no thought other than to save his life, he pushed to his feet again, although unsteady, and concentrated on one thing only—get to his horses. The man pinned under the dead horse was of no concern any longer. He would probably stay pinned under the horse until he starved to death or the wolves ate him, he told himself. *But I ain't gonna die on this mountain with him.*

Feeling as if his life was draining out of him, the wounded outlaw made his way stumbling back up the slope to his horses. He rummaged through his saddlebag until he found his spare pair of socks, which he stuffed against the hole in his side in an effort to stop the bleeding. They soon became soaked with blood, which only added to his panic. With no other option, he grabbed the saddle horn, pulled himself up into the saddle, and started down the other side of the ravine, bound for Laramie as fast as his horses would permit.

All around him, the ravine had become silent. Still Cole listened, intent upon picking up any sound that might indicate Womack was working his way farther down the ravine for a better spot to shoot from. Trapped as he was, with his leg pinned under the heavy horse, he would be helpless if the outlaw circled around to come up behind him. He knew for certain he had hit Womack, but didn't know how badly he was wounded. When his shot had struck him, he had staggered backward out of sight.

Cole could do nothing but lie there and wait, hoping Womack was dead. It was not long, however, before he thought he heard the sound of loose gravel stirred up by horses' hooves coming from the other side of the ravine. As best he could guess, it sounded as if the gunman was leaving. Cole was not ready to assume that, knowing it could be a ruse. Listening intently, he wondered if Womack was hoping he would carelessly present a bigger target.

Cole continued struggling to free himself as best he could while lying flat on his back. What was stopping Womack from simply riding around behind him? Assuming he had managed to get to his horses, he should certainly have been able to circle back to a position where he would have a clear shot at Cole. who could do nothing to protect himself.

Finally, after waiting for what seemed an extremely long time, he decided that the sounds he had heard were, indeed, the departure of Womack. *I'll soon find out,* he thought and rose to a sitting position. When that didn't result in a wave of rifle fire, he knew the outlaw had fled.

I must have wounded him pretty badly, he thought. Although the immediate task was to free himself from his horse, thoughts he had had no time for leaped to the forefront of his mind as he placed a hand on the Morgan's neck and stroked the already cooling body. Joe was more to him than just a horse. He had been a partner, more like family, especially since the family he had known had been taken from him after such a short time. He had ridden the powerful Morgan all the way from Lancaster, Nebraska, when he first took his new wife to the land he had intended to farm on Chugwater Creek. It seemed like a hundred years had passed since then. *I wouldn't have made much of a farmer,* he thought. *But for her sake, I was willing to try like hell.* With the death of the faithful horse, the last living memory of his life before his family was destroyed was now gone.

Shaking away the memories, he turned to the task of freeing himself. The only tool he could reach was his skinning knife. Using it and his hands, he went to work on the cold sand under his leg. With no better plan, he concentrated on cutting a trench under the trapped limb in hopes that he could eventually clear out enough to let his leg settle a little deeper. He hoped the weight of the horse would still be supported by the ground on each side of the trench and he could slide his leg out.

As he labored away, he occasionally glanced up at the bay gelding, frustrated to think of that horsepower going to waste, and how it would have made his task simple. The bay patiently watched the strange efforts of the trapped man, possibly wondering why he didn't just order the Morgan to get up.

After a half hour that seemed more like an hour, he had succeeded in digging a trench down to his knee, but he could get no farther due to the weight concentrated on the lower part of his leg. So far, he had been successful in gaining some movement in his imprisoned leg, but he was still held fast from his knee down. And there was the matter of freeing his boot from the stirrup. Discouraged, he took a look at the long knife in his hand, wondering if the only chance he had was to try to cut his leg off. "To hell with that," he spat, knowing it to be impossible. Frustrated with his lack of success, he placed his free foot on the seat of his saddle and strained to move the horse off of his leg, no longer worried about the possibility of Womack's return.

"Damn it, Joe!" he exclaimed. "Why in hell did you have to fall at an angle like that?"

As if in response, the big Morgan's stomach seemed to heave slightly, and Cole heard what sounded like a large release of wind. For a split second, he felt a slight movement of his leg. He didn't hesitate. With his other foot still planted firmly on the saddle seat, he pushed with all the strength he could summon. Nothing happened at first, then he suddenly slid backward when his leg came free.

Scarcely able to believe he was no longer trapped, he rubbed his leg, cautiously testing it, lest it might be broken after all. He soon determined that there had been no real damage with only an aching knee from having been locked in a twisted position for so long. His boot was still in the stirrup under the horse and he stared at his stocking foot, wondering if Joe had responded to his frustration as one last service for his partner. He thought of Walking Owl, the medicine man in the Crow village. He would have no doubt said that Joe's spirit had seen to it that the leg was released. *I ain't gonna question it,* he thought, then said to the horse, "I wanna thank you for turnin' me loose. I appreciate it, and I'm sorry I cussed you before."

Finally free, Cole turned his attention to the job to be done next. He took hold of the bridle of the bay that had been watching him in curiosity. It was a sturdy-looking gelding. He had to admit that Travis Womack had ridden a fine horse. "I reckon it's you and me now," he said softly as he continued to calm the horse. "But I don't think much of that saddle. I'd rather have mine, so whaddaya say we get to it? Then we'll see if we can get after that son of a bitch that shot Joe."

Working quickly, with only one boot on, he took the coil of rope from Travis's saddle and tied it to the saddle horn on his saddle. He tied the other end to a tree on the bank. With his saddle secured in place, he undid the cinch, then looped one end of his lead rope around Joe's neck, and the other to Travis's saddle. All set to remove his horse from his saddle, he took the bay's bridle and led him till he took the slack out of the rope. "All right, let's go, boy," he encouraged the bay and pulled on the bridle.

The bay hesitated when he felt the resistance from the dead horse, then hunkered down and easily pulled the Morgan away from the bank and off his saddle. Once Joe was off the stirrup, Cole halted the bay and retrieved his boot.

When the saddles were swapped, Cole left Travis Womack's rig, along with his bridle, beside the creek. The only possessions he took were a Sharps rifle and a cartridge belt. With a sad farewell to Joe as well as a heartfelt thanks, he turned the bay toward Laramie.

"Gone?" Mary Lou exclaimed. "Gone where? When's he coming back?" She caught herself then, suddenly realizing she might be revealing emotions she preferred to remain hidden. In an attempt to toss it off as unimportant, she laughed and remarked, "He never could stay in one place very long, could he? What about you? Are you heading out right away, too?"

"No, ma'am," Harley said. "I'll stick around for a day or two." He was not fooled by her attempt to trivialize Cole's sudden departure without so much as a fare-thee-well. He was perturbed at his friend as well.

Cole Bonner was as smart as any man he had ever met, except when it came to women. There was not a doubt in Harley's mind that Mary Lou had called off her wedding to Gordon Luck because she couldn't bring herself to close the door on Cole. And Cole was too damn blind to see the two of them were tailor-made to couple up.

At the moment, Harley was tempted to tell her of the many times during the past year, when Cole thought he was alone with his thoughts, and he'd stood gazing absently at the snowcapped mountains. Harley was sure his friend had been thinking what might have been, but he hesitated to say, however, thinking maybe it wasn't his business.

"No, ma'am," he repeated. "I'll be here for a while. Cole figured he didn't have no choice. He done for two of that feller's brothers, so he was gonna have to settle up with him sooner or later, and sooner was better before anybody else got killed. That feller's already shot your sheriff, and maybe killed him. I don't know. And if Cole don't stop him, who will?"

"Why is it always Cole who has to right all the wrongs?" she blurted before she could stop herself from showing her irritation. "I mean, I know the sheriff got shot, and I surely hope he's gonna be all right, but there are other men in this town that could go after the man who shot him. It's the town's business, not Cole's."

Harley fully understood the woman's frustrations. And, in a way, he felt sorry for her for having feelings for a man like Cole Bonner. And he couldn't help it, either. It was just his lot in life to be caught in the path of mankind's violence. He had once tried to live the life of a simple farmer, but fate put a stop to that when his wife was murdered.

He didn't know squat about farming, anyway, Harley thought. "Like I said, it ain't just the matter of the sheriff gettin' shot. Sooner or later that feller is gonna come after Cole for killin' his brothers. It's better for Cole to be the one stalkin' the other." He gave her a grin then. "I can tell you this, when it's over and he's still standin', he's gonna wanna come back to find you."

Mary Lou exhaled a long sigh and nodded without replying. It was going to take a little more time. She smiled at Harley then and said, "I expect I'll see you in the dining room while you're in town."

"You can count on that," Harley replied with a wide grin. When she turned to go back to the dining room, he called after her and repeated. "Cole said he was comin' back here when he finished what he had to do."

CHAPTER 6

"Who the hell's bangin' on my door?" Doc Evans yelled when awakened from a sound sleep.

"Open up, Doc." The anxious reply came from the other side of his front door. "Open up! I'm bleedin' bad. I need doctorin'."

"Who is it?" Evans demanded. He lit a candle by his bed and looked at the clock. "It's three o'clock in the mornin'." He picked up a .44 Colt from his bedside table and walked out of the bedroom to the parlor, where he lit a lantern before going to the door.

"Troy Womack," the voice came back, "and I'm bad hurt."

"Womack," Evans grunted under his breath, not particularly happy to hear who was calling. "You got the law after you?" Doc Evans had treated a good many gunshot wounds since he'd settled in Laramie, because his practice was almost entirely made up of outlaws. With the recent purge of that wild element from Laramie, he feared he might come under the scrutiny of the vigilance committee. And he knew Womack was one of the more recent drifters who had evidently befriended Big Steve Long.

"No, Doc," Troy pleaded. "There ain't no law after me. Open up, else I'm liable to die on your doorstep."

"All right," Evans relented and unbolted the door. He needed the money and outlaws paid with cash money instead of trying to pay with cabbages or chickens. "Good God, man," he exclaimed when he held the door open and saw Troy's blood-soaked clothes.

Before closing the door, he stuck his head out and looked back toward town. Seeing the lathered horses standing, heads hung down, at his hitching rail, he asked, "You sure ain't nobody chasin' you? You ain't led none of that vigilance committee to my door, have you?"

"No, Doc," Troy pleaded. "I swear, I got shot by some jasper halfway between here and Cheyenne. He ain't no lawman and he ain't comin' after nobody no more. I left him under a dead horse." Even as he said it, he couldn't help cursing himself for not shooting Travis's horse as well to make sure the man was on foot, in the event he somehow managed to get himself out from under his horse.

At the time, however, Troy had been so afraid he was dying, he couldn't think of anything beyond getting to the doctor.

"All right. Get over here on the table and let's take a look at it." He led Troy to his examination table on one side of the parlor. "Get your coat and shirt off, so I can see the damn thing." While Womack did as instructed, Doc went to the small stove in the center of the room to revive the fire in the still-glowing ashes. Once it showed signs of life, he placed some wood on it, then placed a bucket filled with water on to heat up.

"It's cold as hell in here," Troy complained, sitting on the table with his shirt off.

"Is that so?" Doc replied. "If you'd made an advance reservation, I'd have a rip-roarin' fire goin' and maybe serve some refreshments."

"I wasn't sure I was gonna make it here before I ran out of blood," Troy said, ignoring Doc's sarcasm. "Can you fix me up? I need to get outta town. I can't stick around here waitin' for the good citizens of Laramie to decide they wanna stretch my neck just because I was a friend of Big Steve Long's."

"I don't know," Doc replied. "I'll know after I get a look at what you've got. Have you got any cash on ya, enough to pay my bill?" After Troy assured him that he would be paid, Doc set his lantern close on the table and examined the wound. "I'll need to clean it up first." He went to the stove and poured some of the water in the bucket into a basin, even though it had barely had time to take the chill off of it.

When the first rays of morning light crept across the Laramie River, the patient was sleeping off the lingering effects of the ether, a fresh bandage wrapped around his waist. In place of the bucket that had been on the stove, a coffeepot was bubbling away.

"Wake up," Doc ordered, "and get your ass outta

here before somebody sees those horses out there and thinks they oughta find out who owns 'em."

Reluctantly, Troy sat up on the table and remained there for a few minutes, fighting a wave of nausea that had swept over him. "How bad is it? It hurts like hell."

"It ain't that bad at all," Doc said. "The bullet went all the way through, and near as I can tell, didn't hit nothin' important. Most of the blood that soaked your shirt came out the hole in your back. You'll be all right, long as you don't get any dirt in it."

"I don't feel worth a damn," Troy complained. "Sick in my belly."

"That's most likely from the ether. I don't have no more chloroform, or I'da used that instead." Doc took him by the elbow and helped him off the table. "I'll pour you a cup of strong coffee. That'll fix you up, then you'd best get on your way."

"How much do I owe you?"

"We're all square," Doc replied. "I took my fee outta your coat pocket—didn't wanna disturb your sleep. Figured it'd save you a little time this mornin'."

"Is that a fact?" Troy responded, feeling more of his nasty disposition returning since he no longer feared he might be dying. He picked up his coat and pulled a roll of money from the inside pocket. A quick count showed him to be thirty dollars short. "That's a pretty stiff bill for bandagin' a wound, ain't it? You didn't even have to get a bullet out."

"There were some extra charges you wouldn't have gotten if you'd come in durin' my usual office hours," Doc said. "Gettin' me outta my bed in the middle of the night, the cost of that ether I had to use so you wouldn't feel too much pain, bandages, coffee—them things add up."

"You damned old crook," Troy said. "I'll let you get by with it this time. Hell, I might need some doctorin' again sometime. Otherwise, I'd consider shootin' you."

Not impressed by the idle threat, Doc went to the front door and looked out. It was still early, so nothing was stirring but Troy's weary horses, standing at the rail, still saddled. "Don't seem to be much goin' on. You'd best finish your coffee and get along before somebody comes by askin' questions."

"It'd be their bad luck if they did," Troy replied, feeling his confidence restored, in spite of the worrisome thought that Cole might somehow have freed himself after all.

"Go somewhere and get a steak or some beef liver. You need to build your blood back up." Doc walked him to the door and watched as he pulled himself up into the saddle, relieved when he rode away from his house. He took another look toward town to see if anyone had seen his patient ride away. He could still see only one or two people moving about on the street. *Damn Boswell,* he thought, cursing the sheriff. *If somebody doesn't kill him, I'm gonna have to try to run a respectable office practice.*

Feeling weak and wasted, Troy led his horses toward the Bucket of Blood Saloon. Like Doc

Evans had advised, he needed some solid food in his stomach and a little sleep. The short time he had spent under ether didn't seem to have helped him in his need for sleep. In fact, the only result was a slightly sick stomach, but he decided to get something to eat in spite of it.

Maybe my empty stomach is contributing to the queasy feeling, he thought.

He had gone no farther than a dozen yards when he realized the sign was down over the door of the Bucket of Blood and the doors were closed and padlocked.

Damn, he thought, *I reckon Fred Wiggins ran outta whiskey to sell.*

He was going to have to find something to eat somewhere else, and he wasn't that familiar with anyplace other than the Bucket of Blood. There was a small diner next to the train depot, run by a woman named Mabel Ryan. He had never patronized it, having always eaten at the saloon before.

Reckon I can try it this morning, he decided, although it was still pretty early and they might not be open. He turned around and walked his horse back up the street toward the train depot.

The lights were on in Mabel's Diner, so he tied his horse at the rail. But when he tried the door, he found it locked, only then noticing the CLOSED sign. Ignoring it, he tried the door again, rattling the knob noisily in the process. He kept at it until he heard the bolt slide and the door open wide to reveal a stubby gray-haired woman wearing a no-nonsense expression on her chubby cheeks, her face flushed red from standing over a hot stove.

"Mister, you must be powerful hungry," she

greeted him, and pointed to the CLOSED sign. "Either that or you can't read."

"I reckon I can read," Troy replied brusquely. "But it's gettin' past time for breakfast and I need somethin' to eat."

Mable gave him a more thorough looking over before continuing. "I don't believe I've ever served you before, else you'd know I open up for breakfast at six o'clock." She turned her head to look at a clock on the wall across the small dining room. "And according to my clock, it ain't but five thirty. I'm still cooking."

Troy realized right away that he wasn't going to get anywhere if he tried to bully the feisty little woman, so he decided to try her pity. "I'm sorry, ma'am. I just came from the doctor's office, and I ain't had nothin' to eat since yesterday mornin'." He unbuttoned his coat far enough to let her get a glimpse of his bloodstained shirt. "I kinda lost track of the time. I reckon I shoulda looked at my watch."

Mabel softened a little. "What happened? Somebody shoot you or something?" She peered inside the gap in his coat.

"Yessum," he replied. "They sure did. Jumped me on my way back from Cheyenne. I reckon the Good Lord was lookin' out for me, though, 'cause I made it back here to Doc Evans."

At the mention of Doc's name, Mabel jerked her head back and remarked. "Doc Evans? It's a wonder you're still alive. He ain't no real doctor, you know. Just calls himself one." Thinking that letting Doc work on him was a second time the stranger had suffered bad luck, she stepped back and said, "Come on in. I'll get you a cup of coffee and rustle up some breakfast for you. I've got biscuits about ready to come outta the oven." That served to remind her, so she turned her head and yelled, "Lou, look at my biscuits!" Back to Troy then, she asked, "Why did they shoot you? Robbery?"

"I reckon," he answered.

"Can you pay?" she thought to ask him then.

"Yessum," he replied. "I can pay. Like I said, I got away. The feller that shot me ain't likely to cause nobody no trouble no more. He messed with the wrong man that time." He couldn't resist crowing a little.

His boast failed to impress Mabel. In fact, she took another hard look at him, remembering then that maybe she had seen him before. "You were a friend of Big Steve Long's, weren't you? I believe I've seen you and a couple of your friends down in front of the old Bucket of Blood." He didn't answer, but she knew she was right. "You ain't the first customer I've picked up since that saloon closed. Ain't no place else to get breakfast since Sheriff Boswell shut that place down." She pointed to a table by the kitchen door. "Set yourself down," she said before continuing her commentary. "Like I said, I've picked up a few, but there's a lot of jaspers that left town when they saw what happened to Long and his half brothers."

"I reckon I'll likely move on, too, soon as I heal up a little." Troy said. "I wouldn'ta been hangin' around here before, if I'da known about Steve Long's unlawful dealin's, him and the Moyers. I thought him being the sheriff, he was honest as the day is long. You can't be too careful these days."

"I guess not," Mabel said, eyeing him even more closely. He had "liar" written all over his face, as far as she was concerned. "I'll get you something to eat," she said after a pause and went into the kitchen. When she returned, she had a cup of coffee and a plate holding three biscuits and a slab of bacon. She paused to watch him attack the bacon and biscuits for only a few seconds before commenting, "Well, I reckon you weren't lying when you said you ain't ate for a while." *But I don't know about that other part of the story*, she thought.

He took only a few minutes to finish his breakfast and stayed just long enough to get another cup of coffee. Still feeling weak and unstable, he had no desire to hang around town for any length of time. As soon as he finished, he paid Mabel the twenty-five cents she requested, but not without complaining that he should have gotten a full meal for that price.

"You did get a full meal," she replied. "Three biscuits and a slab of bacon, washed down with two cups of coffee. You feel full, don'tcha?"

"Ha!" he snorted. "You and Doc Evans oughta get together. You'd make a good pair."

By the time Cole had saddled up and was ready to ride the night before, it had already been too dark to follow a trail, but he was not content to wait for the next morning's light. He'd decided to head for Laramie, thinking that was the likely place that Womack would head. He was sure Womack was hit, and from the haste in which he departed, Cole guessed he was trying to get to a doctor as fast as he could. Hoping to shorten the distance between them while Womack was at the doctor, he started out for Laramie.

The first rays of morning light found him a good ten miles from Laramie, riding a tired horse. When he came to a healthy stream, he decided he had to give the bay a rest and catch a little sleep, himself, in spite of the urgency he felt for catching up with Womack. He was feeling the effects of not having slept the night before, and it wouldn't do to go after the outlaw with a woozy head.

Even though he had slept an hour longer than he had intended, it was still early in the morning when Cole walked the bay past the railroad depot. The aroma of fried bacon drifted across his path, causing his stomach to remind him of his neglect. The smell came from a small building close by with a sign identifying it as MABEL'S DINER. He was tempted to stop and buy himself some break- fast, but he wanted to find the town's doctor, if it had one.

He rode on until seeing a man come out the door of a general store. "Mornin'. I'm lookin' for the doctor's office.

The man looked him up and down as if decid- ing whether or not Cole was an Indian. Finally, he spoke. "You talkin' about Doc Evans?"

"If he's the doctor," Cole replied and waited for an answer. "Is he the only doctor in town?"

"Yep, least he's the only one in town that prac- tices medicine. He says he's a doctor."

"Well, where can I find him?" Cole asked, by this time losing patience.

"In his office, I reckon," the man replied. When Cole's impatience grew large enough to show on his rugged face, the man quickly blurted, "On down that way, next to the stables."

"Much obliged," Cole said and nudged the bay with his heels. *Ain't a very friendly town,* he thought, unaware of the town's recent troubles with outlaws and drifters.

He found the doctor's office next to the stables, just as the man had said, and tied the bay at the rail. He stepped up on the porch and knocked several times before the door opened and Doc Evans stood frowning at him, a coffee cup in his hand.

"Damned if people don't pick the damnedest time to knock on your door," he grumbled. "It's either when you're trying to sleep or trying to eat." Seeing the puzzled look on Cole's face, he blurted, "Well, what can I do for you?"

"I'm lookin' for somebody. Thought he mighta come here last night or this mornin'." A quickly raised eyebrow told him that his hunch might have been accurate. "A big fellow, ridin' a gray horse and trailin' a packhorse," Cole continued. "Think he mighta needed treatment for a gunshot wound."

"Nah, I ain't seen nobody like that," Evans declared. He figured this must be the man Womack said he had left under a horse. Doc didn't give a damn about Womack, but he still counted himself as part of the outlaw element that accounted for the biggest portion of his income. "Now, if that's all you want, I'll go back to my breakfast." He closed the door.

Cole walked off the porch and stood by the hitching rail for a few minutes while he thought about his next move. *Helluva friendly town*, he thought as he looked back toward the upper end of the street. He hadn't learned what he needed to know, but he felt sure the odds were good that Womack had been to see Doc Evans, judging by Doc's reactions to his questions. While he was pondering that, he saw a man walk out of the stable next door and stand judging the quality of the day just born.

Cole untied the reins and walked over to the stable, leading the bay. "Mornin'," he started again.

"Mornin'," Grover Taylor returned, and blatantly looked Cole up and down, a practice Cole was becoming accustomed to since entering Laramie. "Ain't seen you in town before. You lookin' for Big Steve Long?"

"Nope," Cole answered. "I'm lookin' for a fellow named Womack. Have you seen him this mornin'?"

"Womack," Grover echoed. "You a friend of his?"

"Nope," Cole said again. "I'm just lookin' for him."

"You the feller that shot him?"

The question surprised Cole. He figured Womack would be trying hard to keep people from knowing about his wound. "Maybe," he answered. "He shot the sheriff in Cheyenne yesterday and he was headed this way. Sounds like you've seen him."

"I saw him. He ain't been in here, but I saw him comin' outta Doc's house this mornin'. The way he was movin', kinda gingerlike, I figured somebody mighta shot him. His brother was in town, lookin' for him a few days ago, but I didn't see him with Troy today. Just saw Troy." He paused for a moment, then asked, "You a lawman?"

"Nope," Cole answered, "just somebody who wants to catch up with him. Which way did he go when he left the doctor's house?"

"When he left Doc's, he headed up the street toward the railroad depot." He watched Cole's reaction as he considered that for a long moment. "Mister, you're about three hours behind him. And if you're wonderin' if there's a gray like the one Troy was ridin' in my stable, you're welcome to take a look for yourself."

"Much obliged," Cole said. There was no point in looking in the stable. He was sure Grover was telling the truth. He stepped up into the saddle and turned the bay back toward the railroad depot. Possibly someone on that end of the street might have seen which way Womack went from there. *Three hours behind him,* he thought, not as far as he had suspected, after having slept longer than he had wanted to.

There was one man at the depot and he had just come to work an hour before, since there was no train scheduled to stop in Laramie before noon. That left Mabel's Diner the only other possibility. Cole tied the bay to the rail in front of the diner and went inside.

"You're a little late for breakfast," Mabel informed him. "We'll start again at noon."

Cole couldn't help feeling disappointed. The pleasant aroma of baked biscuits and fried bacon still filled the small dining room, causing him to realize he was hungry. It would probably not have put him that much farther behind in his search if he had taken a few minutes to eat. "I'm sorry I missed breakfast, ma'am, but I'm lookin' for a fellow that mighta passed by this way this mornin'. And I was wonderin' if you mighta noticed." He paused a moment, waiting for her reply. "Big fellow," he continued, "ridin' a gray horse. Mighta come from the doctor's office."

She knew then that her earlier suspicions about Womack were justified. "Whaddaya lookin' for him for? You a friend of his?"

"No, ma'am, I'm not. His name is Troy Womack. He shot the sheriff over in Cheyenne."

She shook her head slowly and thought about Troy's version of how he'd received the gunshot wound in his side. At the time, she wondered if she could believe his story. Now she wondered if she could believe this young man's claim. He looked for all the world like a wild Indian, even though he spoke softly and respectfully. "Are you a lawman?"

"No, ma'am," Cole replied.

"Well, then, how come you're tryin' to catch him? That sounds like the law's job."

"He shot my horse," Cole stated simply.

"Oh." Mabel responded, understanding. Then she made a decision. "Yeah, that fellow was in here at five-thirty this morning. I fed him some breakfast. He said some robbers had waylaid him and that was how he got shot."

"Do you know which way he went when he left here?"

"Sorry, I don't," Mabel said. "I didn't pay him no mind after he went out the door."

"He crossed the river and headed north on the other side," a voice came from the kitchen door. Cole turned to see a large, heavyset woman enter the room.

"How do you know that, Lou?" Mabel asked.

"I was out back, dumpin' some dishwater, when I saw him ride away," Lou said. "He crossed over and followed that trail that runs along the river."

"Much obliged," Cole said. He started to leave but hesitated long enough to say again that he was sorry he had been too late to get breakfast. "I'd like to have tried some of your biscuits."

Mabel turned to Lou and asked, "Did we have any of those biscuits left?"

When she said that they had two or three, Mabel turned back to Cole. "You want a couple of biscuits?"

"Yes, ma'am, I sure do," he replied at once.

Following the faint remains of an old game trail, Troy Womack grimaced with the sudden sharp pain that shot through his side when his horse hunkered down to climb the steep part of a slope. "Damn quack," he complained. "Ain't no tellin' what kinda mess he made of that wound. Good thing I'm almost there." Before he could complain further, a sight caught his eye that caused him to rein the gray back to a sudden stop. *Smoke!* Coming from the chimney of the little cabin he and his brothers had used. A dirty ribbon of smoke was trailing up into the frosty winter sky. Somebody was in his shack, and he had not been gone much longer than a week. He pushed the gray a little farther down the slope until able to get a better look, a spot that enabled him to see a corner of the corral. This caused some concern, for he could see at least three horses. There might be more. It was hard to tell. *I ain't in no shape to take on three or four,* he thought. The squatters could be anybody—outlaws, drifters, prospectors, settlers—anybody. He decided against settlers, because there was no wagon. Undecided as to what he should do, he contemplated his next move. Even though he felt the cabin was rightfully his, he wasn't ready to ride in and claim it until he had a better idea of the situation. He finally decided to move in closer to the trees lining the riverbank to get a better look.

After tying his two horses where he was sure they couldn't be seen from the cabin, he moved closer on foot until reaching a thicket of bushes clinging to the bank. He settled himself to wait, thinking that sooner or later someone was bound to have to come outside to answer nature's call, if nothing else. Then maybe he would be able to make a judgment on his best course of action. *If it's a bunch of sodbusters, I'll just shoot the place up till I either kill them or run them out,* he thought.

Flint Yarborough got up from the bedroll he had been using as a seat. "I reckon if I get any closer to the fire, I'll be in the middle of it," he complained. He and his two companions had crowded around the small fireplace as close as they could without singeing their clothes. "Whoever built this damn fireplace sure as hell didn't know how to build one. All the heat goes up the damn chimney."

"I swear, that's a fact," Red Swann said. "My belly's hot as hell and my back feels like a slab of ice. A shack this little, that fireplace oughta heat it up like an oven."

"I expect we'll get goin' again in the mornin'," Yarborough said. "See what's in that town." Red's comment was the first sign that he was getting back to normal after his adventure with the man dressed in buckskins at Murphy's Trading Post. His nose was considerably flatter than before and the deep bruises had not yet begun to recede. Yarborough was sure Red hadn't made peace with himself for the humiliation he suffered, but he seemed to be getting closer to his normal sour disposition.

"I'd just as soon we go on into town today," the third member of the gang said. "Find us a saloon and a couple of warm women."

His comment drew a snicker from Red. "What's the matter, Tiny? Ain't you satisfied with our company? Hell, me and Flint oughta be the ones bellyachin'. We're the ones tryin' to sleep in this little shack with you snorin' like a damn sawmill."

"I've had a lot better company, myself," Tiny Weaver replied. "Ain't nobody complained about me snorin' before. Besides, I'm about ready to spend a couple of nights on a bed, with a plump little woman to keep my back warm." He favored Red with a wide, foolish grin.

"Like that plump little gal in Bozeman?" Red asked, reminding the oversized simpleton of the circumstances that had instigated their early departure from that town. The childlike ox had broken a prostitute's jaw because she'd made fun of his clumsy attempts to make love. Ordinarily, that would not have caused much of a stir, except for the unfortunate fact that the whore in question was a favorite of the town marshal.

"Ah, Red," Tiny replied, "she didn't have no call to say what she did. You'da done the same thing."

"I wouldn'ta had to," Red crowed. "I don't get no complaints when I'm romancin' the ladies. That's the difference between me and you." He grinned and winked at Yarborough. "Ain't that right, Flint?"

"You two are makin' me tired," Yarborough replied. "I druther go outside and stand in the cold." He started for the door.

Knowing why he was really going out, Red called after him, "That's a pretty stout wind from the north. Best be sure you stand facin' south." He chortled heartily in appreciation for his wit.

Once outside, Yarborough didn't bother to walk very far from the cabin door to release most of the coffee he had consumed. He was not quite finished when he heard the voice behind him.

"You're under arrest for public indecency! Put your hands in the air!"

Startled, Yarborough whirled around, reaching for the handgun he forgot he wasn't wearing, stunned to find himself facing Troy Womack doubled over laughing. "Womack!" he cursed. "Damn you! Where'd you come from? You could get your sorry ass killed pullin' stunts like that."

Troy chuckled again. "Not when you ain't wearin' your gun. I noticed that right off." He gestured toward Yarborough's trousers. "Looks like you left a few tracks on your way back to the barn."

"I swear, you're lucky I ain't wearin' my gun," Yarborough grumbled while hurriedly buttoning his pants. "I'da shot you for sure."

Having heard a commotion outside, Red and Tiny were at the door by then, both with their weapons in hand.

"Well, I'll be . . ." Red started. "Troy! What the hell are you doin' here?"

"I oughta be askin' you that," Troy replied. "I've been usin' this shack for a little while and I didn't expect to find anybody in it when I came back. How the hell did you boys find it?"

"Hell, you're the one who told me where it was when I told you we might ride down this way," Yarborough answered. He glanced back toward the way Troy had come. "You by yourself? Where are your brothers?"

"It's just me now," Troy said. "We had a streak of bad luck and both of my brothers are dead. Malcolm first, then Travis, both killed by the same man, and I got a hole in me that I'm tryin' to heal up."

"I swear," Red responded. "Same man shot all three of ya? Who was he, a lawman?"

"No," Troy said. "I don't know who he is. A wild man, maybe a half-breed. He wears buckskins and braids his hair Injun style. Always carries a

Henry repeatin' rifle." He paused then to ask, "What in the world happened to you?"

"I reckon I ran into the same kinda wild man you're talkin' about," Red answered.

"Let me go back and get my horses," Troy said. "I'll take care of them, then let's go inside where it's warm and I'll tell you all about it."

"Ain't much warmer in there than it is out here," Yarborough said, still grumbling about the fireplace. He couldn't help being curious about the man Troy described—sounded an awful lot like the man who had rearranged Red's features.

After his horses were corralled with those belonging to his three friends, Troy returned to the cabin to tell his story. He was greatly encouraged when he found them at the cabin, thinking that the man whose name he thought was Harley Branch would now hesitate to attack four men. Consequently, he was disappointed to learn that the three of them were already planning to move into Laramie before dusk, having become tired of sitting in the small shack complaining about the cold.

"I need to lay low for a couple more days," Troy explained and opened his heavy coat. He pulled out his shirttail and showed them the bandage wrapped around his midsection. "Why don't you wait a couple of days before you go into town? We can get up a helluva card game. I've got a bottle in my saddlebag. Whaddaya say?"

"I don't know, Troy," Yarborough said, hesitating. "We've all got a pretty good dose of cabin fever already."

"I need me a woman," Tiny blurted.

"Yeah," Red added, "I reckon we're all ready to see what the hell Laramie's got to be proud of. You can rest up better in a hotel room, anyway. They got a hotel, don't they?"

"You boys are lucky you ran into me," Troy said. "You'd best take my advice and let Laramie be. This ain't no time to ride into that town. The folks there are puttin' a bounty on anybody that looks like an outlaw. That's why I came down here on the river." He went on to tell them the recent happenings in Laramie, about the demise of Big Steve Long and the Moyer brothers. "Hell, the Bucket of Blood ain't in business no more, and the vigilance committee is eyeballin' every drifter that rides through town."

His report caused a bit of hesitation from his three friends, but the dose of cabin fever was already severe.

Finally Yarborough expressed his opinion. "Well, damn it, I've had enough of this little shack. I need to go somewhere where's there's warm food and good whiskey. Maybe you're right, Troy. Maybe it ain't smart to hit Laramie right now with all that lynchin' fever goin' on. Why don't we just ride on down to Cheyenne? It ain't that far. Besides, I ain't never been to Cheyenne."

That was distressing news to Troy as well. "Hell, I can't go back to Cheyenne. I just ran from there. That's where that son of a bitch is that shot Travis and Malcolm and put a bullet through my side."

Yarborough favored him with an accusing leer.

"Ain't you plannin' to even things up with that jasper for killin' your kin?"

"Well, yeah," Troy replied, stumbling over his words. "I mean, hell yeah. 'Course I plan on evenin' the score. I just came back here to get fixed up by the doctor and get my strength back. Then I was gonna go look for that bastard."

"That ain't but one man you're talkin' about, right?" Red asked. "And you said you shot the sheriff, mighta killed him you said. That don't sound like you've got anything to worry about. If that feller's still around, we'll settle his bacon for him real quick. Sounds like that town oughta be wide open."

"It might be at that," Yarborough said. The more he thought about it, the more certain he became. "Hell, I'm ready to go. How far is it from here?"

"From the cabin here, it's a good day and a half," Troy said.

Yarborough cocked his head back to take a look at the sky. "We got a good chunk of daylight left. Whaddaya say we pack up and head on out right now? We oughta be able to eat up a lot of that distance before dark. Then we'd have all day to-morrow to get to Cheyenne. Whaddaya say, boys?"

"Whatever you wanna do," Tiny spoke up. As usually happened, he went along with anything Yarborough said to do.

Red agreed as well. "I don't think I've got any appointments on my calendar," he joked. "So let's ride." All three turned to gaze at Troy, waiting to hear his decision.

"I reckon I'm up to it," he said, rubbing his side

gingerly. "I 'preciate you boys helpin' me run this son of a bitch down." Truth be told, he had no intention of crossing paths with the sinister rifleman again. But with the added protection of three hardened gunmen, it put the odds of settling with his brothers' killer much more in his favor.

"All right, then. Let's get saddled up," Yarborough declared. "We're headin' to Cheyenne."

CHAPTER 7

Gnawing on the last of Mabel's biscuits, Cole crossed the river and found a narrow trail that followed along beside it. There were only a few tracks, most of them from days before, but he saw what he estimated to be fresher tracks from a couple of horses. They had to be left by Womack. *And as long as I've got tracks, I've got Womack*, he thought. He had ridden no more than a quarter of an hour, however, when he realized the fresh tracks he had been following were gone. "Damn," he scolded himself and turned the bay around, studying the trail more intently to see where Womack had left the common track.

Cole backtracked for less than a mile before discovering the place where the fresh tracks forked off and headed almost due west on what appeared to be an old game trail. Not having been in the country west of Laramie before, he had no idea where the trail might lead. For as far as he could see, there was nothing but wild, rolling prairie around him, with mountains in the distance. A thought crossed his mind then, reminding him that he had blundered into an ambush before while doggedly following Womack's trail. His carelessness had cost him the best horse he had ever owned. *If I make the same dumb mistake,* he thought, *I deserve to get shot.* Another thought occurred to him. He might not even be following Womack's tracks, but those of some trapper or settler on his way back from town.

"Damn," he cursed again. "I wonder if that ol' gal back there in the diner knows what she really saw." He'd gone too far to give up on it, however, so he decided to take it a while longer, just in case. At least the tracks were fresh and clear and they were the only trail he had.

Another couple of miles and he came to a low ridge running north and south. He rode up to the top, surprised to see what appeared to be a river, outlined clearly by the growth of trees and shrubs along its banks. Seeing a small cabin caused him to pause, however. Little more than a shack, it sat back among the cottonwoods. *So these damn tracks do lead somewhere,* he thought, and strained to see what appeared to be the corner of a corral behind the cabin.

He estimated a distance of almost a mile, so he couldn't quite tell if there were any horses in the corral or not, for he could only see that corner. He had to consider the possibility that he might be dealing with more than one person. He was suddenly struck with a feeling of caution, for he had to make sure he had not followed Womack to an outlaw hideout.

Cole looked long and hard at the cabin and the ground between him and the trees that guarded

the river. He decided it was too risky to follow the
trail that led straight to the shack and guided the
bay about halfway down the slope before turning
its head away from the trail to circle around to
the south and advance upon the cabin from downstream.

Making his way cautiously along the west bank
of the river, he stopped and tied his horse near the
water when he was within fifty yards of the cabin.
From there, he advanced on foot until he was close
enough to get a clear view of it and everything
around it. He could see no sign of any activity. The
corral was empty, and there was no smoke coming
from the short stone chimney. If he had been following Troy Womack's tracks from Laramie, and
not on a wild-goose chase as he had feared, then
he could conclude that Womack had already come
and gone. Maybe he would be back.

Cole took a few moments to decide what to
do—wait in ambush for him to return or figure he
was not going to.

Another possibility returned to caution him
once again. What if Womack knew he was being
followed, and was at that moment watching the
cabin from a spot upstream, with an ambush of his
own in mind?

Hell, Cole told himself, *I could spend the rest of the
day waiting for him to show up while he's making tracks
to someplace else.* That thought caused him to look
up at the sky. Not much daylight left. The thing
that worried him most, however, was the look of
the low-lying clouds moving in from the west. They
had the look of more snow coming. So far, he had
been fortunate in that there had been a mere

dusting of snow on the ground, making tracking easy. From the looks of the sky, that might not be the case come morning.

He took another long look at the cabin, sitting small and dark against the riverbank, seemingly deserted. "Hell," he muttered. "I'm goin' in, ambush be damned."

He walked back to get his horse, then rode cautiously up to the front of the cabin, holding his rifle in his arms, ready to respond if, in fact, he was riding into an ambush. There were no shots, however, and no ambush. *Wasted a lot of time,* he thought. One thing was confirmed before he even stepped down from the saddle. There were a multitude of tracks, both boots and hooves, so more than one person had been there. Many of the tracks were fresh. He was especially interested in the hoofprints leading out of the corral and heading directly down to the river. Whoever had been there had evidently left, and maybe not more than a few hours before.

A quick search inside the cabin told him that the recent occupants had left nothing behind, which led him to believe they had no intention to return. The fire had long ago gone out in the fireplace, but the ashes were still warm. He concluded that Womack had ridden to the dilapidated shack to meet someone, and then they had decided to leave together. Where they went was the problem.

Cole walked back outside. "Damn," he blurted as soon as he cleared the door, for he was met with the first flakes of snow falling to land softly on the doorstep. *If this keeps up,* he thought, *it won't be long before any tracks they left will be covered up.* Knowing he couldn't afford to waste any more time, he stepped up into the saddle and followed the tracks that led him down to the water.

Frustrated, for he was still not certain he was actually following Troy Womack, he decided to stick with it because it was the only option he had, other than giving up. With that discouraging thought in mind, he pushed on across the river to pick up the trail where it emerged on the east bank. All the while, he apologized to the bay gelding, for he had not rested the horse as he should have. He had to follow the trail for as long as he could before it disappeared under the snow, which was falling in earnest. Even when all traces were gone, he counted on at least knowing the party's general direction. And given that, maybe he could guess where they were heading.

As darkness settled in, he continued following the tracks of half a dozen or more horses until he finally lost them at the forks of two small streams. His horse was tired, and he could no longer see any tracks left by the men he followed. He had no choice but to call it a day.

Going about the business of making a camp. his first concern was for his horse. He pulled the saddle off, leaving the blanket on. Next, with his hand ax, he cut some of the smaller limbs from several of the cottonwoods beside the stream and peeled the bark from them to serve as horse feed. "Just as good as oats," he commented to the bay while it made short work of them. He gathered an armload of dead limbs from among the cottonwoods to start a good fire and carried them into a stand of pines on the opposite bank, where he made his camp for the night. Bending some young pines over and tying them together formed a scanty shelter. Soon he had the fire burning hot enough to burn even the peeled cottonwood limbs, one of which he used as a spit to roast some of the smoked venison he carried.

Once he'd eaten, he crawled under a flap of deer hide he carried and fell right to sleep.

During the night, he slept fairly well, waking in the early morning hours to discover that the snow had stopped. He shook off the inch or two that had found its way through his pine tent onto his deerskin cover. Placing more wood on his fire, he stayed until the first fingers of light filtered through his canopy of pines. Eager to see if there were any traces of a trail, he saddled the bay and was underway before any thoughts of breakfast or even coffee. He found out right away, however, that there was no need for haste, for the snowfall had done the work he had feared. He rode up from the forks of the stream to gaze out upon a wide snow-white prairie devoid of tracks.

All he had to go on was the general direction the party had started in. It was a guess at best. Based solely on his intuition, he decided the course suggested two different destinations. Even though he was not familiar with the country west of Laramie, he figured that if he continued in the direction he had been riding, he would end up somewhere near Iron Mountain on Chugwater Creek. The trading post there was well known as a hangout for outlaws and was one of the reasons he had chosen to take his hides to Fort Laramie to trade. On the other hand, the party could have turned back slightly south and gone to Cheyenne. He had to consider that possibility. Iron Mountain made more sense because Womack had just fled Cheyenne. And Raymond Potter, who owned the trading post at Iron Mountain, was more like the people Womack was inclined to deal with.

Cole nudged the bay with his heels and started for Iron Mountain.

Martha Green walked into the store from the storeroom in back carrying a bolt of calico. "I forgot I had this," she said to Carrie, who was dusting the shelves behind the front counter. "I think it would be just right for a dress you could wear when you're helping out in the store."

With her face lighting up in a big smile, Carrie exclaimed, "Oh, Mom, it's beautiful." Right from the beginning of their short relationship, the Greens had insisted that Carrie should call them Mom and Dad. She was still somewhat astounded by their generosity and acceptance of her as their daughter. After all the fears she had entertained before meeting them, she was eternally grateful for their warmth, and at last she felt that she was in a safe, comfortable place in her life. She turned to meet Douglas Green's smiling countenance. "What do you think, Dad?"

"You'll be pretty as a picture in a dress made outta that. Robert woulda liked that, too."

"But this is material you hope to sell," Carrie said. "I have that money Cole Bonner gave me. I should pay you for the material."

"No such thing," Martha insisted at once. "You've

got to stop trying to pay for everything. You're family, and family doesn't pay for things in the store. Isn't that right, Douglas?"

"That's a fact," he replied. "Family don't pay." He chuckled then. "Besides, that bolt of cloth has been settin' back there in the storeroom for over a year. Came in with the stock we hauled from Julesburg."

"You're both spoiling me," Carrie said.

"Ain't nothin' too good for our daughter," Douglas declared. It had been a hard thing to lose their only son, but the sweet girl he had left a widow was a genuine help in the healing. Now that Carrie was with them, it was a little bit like having their son still with them.

"When I get back," Martha said, "I'll dig in that drawer where I keep my patterns and see if I can find one that would be best for you." She went out the back door then to deliver a sack of flour to the hotel as a favor for Maggie Whitehouse. Outside, she was not aware of the dark cloud that an ill wind had just then gathered over the little settlement of Cheyenne.

Leon Bloodworth walked out the door just in time to see the four riders trot past his stable. He couldn't recall having seen three of them, but he immediately recognized the fourth. "Troy Womack," he muttered and stepped back against the door, astonished to see the outlaw back in Cheyenne. "Lord a-mercy, he's come back, and brung three more with him!" He was immediately struck by the thought that Harley's fancy Mexican saddle was sitting in his tack room and Harley's horse was in the corral.

Unable to move for a long moment, Leon didn't know what to do. He should tell somebody, but who? There wasn't really anyone in town who could stand up to the four obvious gunmen alone. It would take a gathering of the men who had answered to the vigilante call before and that wouldn't be easy. The altercation when Slade Corbett had been run out of town had taken the will to fight out of most of the men involved. Leon, himself, was one of the men who first answered the call to protect the town. He was the one who'd approached his fellow citizens to organize but was reluctant to risk his neck a second time. John Henry Black had been hired to protect the town and was laid up in his bed in the hotel, with still a long way to recover from his wounds.

Leon thought of Gordon Luck, the man who had led the vigilance committee before, and thought he should get word to Gordon down at the sawmill by the river. Leon had little doubt that every merchant in town would soon know Womack had returned. Before he saddled a horse and alerted Gordon to the danger, it occurred to the liveryman that it would be wise to warn Harley that Womack was back in town. Knowing Harley was usually found in his favorite saloon, the Cowboy's Rest, Leon headed there.

"Nice quiet little town," Flint Yarborough declared as he and his friends slowly walked their horses past the Cowboy's Rest, heading toward the hotel up the street. "I'm thinkin' this is just what we're lookin' for." He looked over at Troy riding beside him. "And you say the sheriff is dead?"

"I reckon he's dead," Troy replied. "I couldn't hang around for the funeral, but I put two bullets in him, and he didn't get up again."

"Yep." Yarborough repeated, "right nice little town. Just what we're lookin' for."

"I'm thinkin' we're passin' just what I'm lookin' for," Red Swann said. "Whaddaya say we pull over here and get a drink of whiskey?"

"Hold your horses," Yarborough said. "Hell, there's two more saloons up the street. I wanna get a look at the whole town first—see what we've got to work with here." He looked over at Troy again. "Besides, ol' Troy wants to see if that Harley Branch feller is still in town. Ain't that right, Troy?"

"That's a fact," Troy answered, secure in his resolve now that he had the backing of three hardened gunmen.

"Probably a good idea to take care of that son of a bitch first, so maybe we won't have to worry about gettin' shot in the back while we're settin' around in one of these saloons drinkin' whiskey," Yarborough said. Riding past the locked door of the sheriff's office, he joked, "I don't see no sign on the door that says HELP WANTED."

It brought a laugh from his companions. No one noticed the nervous figure walking hurriedly from the stable to disappear through the door to the Cowboy's Rest behind them.

They proceeded past the Sundown Saloon as the occasional person on the boardwalk stopped to gape before quickly stepping inside one of the stores.

One young lady caught Tiny Weaver's eye when she hurried into the general store next to the hotel. "Damn, did you see that?" he blurted, grinning, "Went in that store, there."

"Yeah, I saw her," Red answered him, getting only a glimpse of the woman's back.

Yarborough pulled up to the hitching post in front of the hotel. The others pulled up on either side of him.

"I'll be with you in a minute," Red told Yarborough. "I need to see if they've got some tobacco in that store."

"I'll go with you," Tiny said at once, eager to get another look at the woman.

"I'll see 'bout gettin' us a couple of rooms," Yarborough said.

"Might be a lot cheaper if we can take a couple of rooms in one of those saloons," Red said. "One of 'em has got two floors, so they most likely have rooms to let. I like livin' high on the hog, but the hotel will most likely cost us too much."

"Might at that," Yarborough replied. "But who said anything about payin'?"

Red laughed. "That's why you're callin' the shots. Come on, Tiny. I need some tobacco." He and Tiny looped their reins over the rail and headed for the store proclaiming itself as Green's Merchandise.

"Well, I'll be go to hell," Red muttered in disbelief when he walked into the store, his eyes focused on the young woman standing at the end of the counter. "Corina Burnett!" he declared emphatically. "I thought you mighta been dead. How the hell did you end up in a place like this? You workin' in one of the saloons here?"

Douglas Green, at first puzzled, was stunned when he realized the stranger's outburst was aimed at his daughter-in-law. He turned to stare at Carrie, his eyes wide with his confusion, when seeing the obvious alarm in the startled woman's face. Looking back at the leering faces of the two crude drifters, he sputtered thoughtlessly, "Can I help you?"

Carrie, whose very soul seemed to have frozen solid inside her, was speechless, the knuckles on her hand white from the desperate grip on the broom handle she had picked up moments before.

Equally puzzled by her reaction, Red went on. "What's the matter, Corina, don't you remember me? Last time I saw you, you was workin' in The Cattleman's in Ogallala. Flint Yarborough was with me. I know you remember him, big man with a handlebar mustache. I know I remember you."

She remembered him all right, but had made every effort to forget him and every man like him, especially the man he mentioned, Flint Yarborough. She had fled Ogallala to escape the brutish beast with the handlebar mustache who had become obsessed with possessing her. And now the nightmare had found her, seeking to destroy the opportunity to restart her life. Finally able to talk, she tried to speak in a calm voice, although her heart was racing. "You seem to have mistaken me for someone else. My name is Carrie Green, and I don't recall ever having been in Ogallala."

It caused Red to pause, unsure for a moment,

but for only a moment. "What the hell are you talkin' about? Your name's Corina Burnett. Carrie, huh? Is that what you're callin' yourself these days?" He didn't wait for her to answer. Turning to Tiny, he said, "Me and Yarborough was in Ogallala for a week, a couple of years back. We was in The Cattleman's every night just 'cause Corina worked there. She was the best-lookin' whore in town, no doubt about it. But the last night we was there, she was gone. Didn't nobody know what happened to her. I figured some damn cowboy, crazy out of his head with that rotgut they sold for whiskey, mighta killed her. But it got away with Yarborough somethin' awful. He liked to never got over it."

Totally unaware of the cannonball he had just dropped in their midst, he turned to the still paralyzed Douglas Green long enough to order. "Gimme some smokin' tobacco. You got it in them cans or them twists?" Turning back to Carrie, he said, "Me and my friends are gonna be in town for a few days. How about you and me gettin' together tonight—maybe before Yarborough knows you're here?" He turned to Tiny and grinned. "When Yarborough finds out she's here, he ain't gonna be sharin' her with nobody else."

Knowing her whole world was crashing down around her, a world that she had only recently discovered possible, Carrie had no choice but denial, even as she could see the shock registered in her father-in-law's eyes. "I'm sorry, sir," she replied, barely able to keep her voice from trembling. "I'm not this woman you knew. My name's Carrie Green, and I'm not the kind of woman you're talking about. So if you'll excuse me, I have work to do." With that she picked up the bolt of cloth and turned toward the storeroom door.

Again Red was stumped for a moment, looking back and forth between Carrie and the store-keeper. Then it hit him, *Carrie Green* and *Green's Merchandise*, and he threw his head back to guffaw loudly. "Well, damn me to hell," he bellowed. "I let the cat outta the bag, didn't I?" He gave Tiny a playful slap on the back. "Carrie *Green*. Now that sounds right respectable." He looked Douglas in the eye. "I gotta hand it to ya, you old hound dog."

When Douglas continued to stand there in shock, Red demanded, "How 'bout that tobacco? Leastways, I can get me somethin' to chew. I reckon we can find some female company in one of the sa-loons since ol' Corina has got herself respectable."

As if in a trance, Douglas went through the motions to fetch the tobacco for his offensive customer after Carrie disappeared through the storeroom door. He had no idea how he was sup-posed to respond to Red's horrifying accusations about his daughter-in-law. The only thing he could think to say was, "Carrie's not my wife. She's my son's wife."

"Is that a fact?" Red replied, still laughing at what he perceived as a really entertaining joke as he went out the door. "Wait till ol' Yarborough hears about this," he said to Tiny. "Carrie Green. Ha!"

Still dazed by the devastating encounter with the two men, Douglas stood motionless for a long moment, trying to make some sense out of what had just happened. Surely those two ruffians were mistaken, he tried to tell himself, but he could not rid his mind of the shock he had seen on Carrie's face. They seemed so certain that she was someone named Corina Burnett, a prostitute. *How can this be?* he asked himself. *She was Robert's wife, and he would not marry a whore. Maybe she had lied to them, and Robert and the real Carrie were still on their way here. But if that was the case, she would be foolish to attempt her charade. They would expose her as soon as they arrived in town.* Another, more serious thought entered his mind. *What if she was involved in Robert and Carrie's murder, and consequently knew Robert and the real Carrie would not show up?*

It was too much for his brain to handle. He had to know the real story and went into the storeroom, looking for Carrie, or Corina, whoever she was. He found her on the floor in the back corner of the room. Huddled against the wall, her face in her hands, she was weeping silently. He couldn't help feeling a tinge of pity for her, but he resolved himself to the task at hand—to find the truth, no matter how damning.

"You wanna tell me about this?" he asked. When she looked up at him with huge tears streaking her cheeks, she was so pitiful that he felt himself caving in.

At that moment, Martha walked in the back door.

"What's the matter?" she asked when she saw her daughter-in-law hovering in the corner, tears streaming down her face. Martha looked at once from Carrie to Douglas and demanded, "What did you say to her?" She hurried over to the nearby washstand to comfort the distressed girl.

Feeling a bit more authoritative with the prospect of his wife's support, Douglas answered her. "It ain't what I said to her. It's what she has to say for herself. She's got some explaining to do."

"What the hell are you talking about, Douglas?" Martha demanded as she tried to help Carrie to her feet.

"I'm talking about her name ain't really Carrie," he blurted. "It's Corina somethin', and according to one of those two fellows who was just in the store, she's a whore."

Taken aback, Martha released Carrie's arm and stood back to stare at the distraught young woman. "What is he talking about, Carrie? What happened here?" When there was no explanation from either of them, she demanded again, this time with angry impatience, "What happened here?"

Carrie seemed to pull herself together then, as if resigned to take what fate had in store for her. For it struck her that she was doomed to suffer the lot that destiny had written for her. And there would be no release from the hell she had known before Robert Green had stepped forward to save her. "I'm not the person I told you I was," she confessed. "I'm not who that man said I am, either, but I can't deny I once was the person he said I was."

As her husband had been, Martha was blind-sided by what Carrie's confession implied. At first looking helpless at Douglas, she turned back to face her daughter-in-law, hoping it was all a mis-understanding and Carrie would explain it away. When there was no such explanation forthcoming, she beseeched her husband to tell her what had caused his accusation. He told her of the two strangers who had just been in the store, one of whom had known Carrie before she'd married

Robert. Finding it impossible to believe, Martha turned to the shaken young woman, praying for a denial. Instead, she got a tearful confession.

"His name is Red," Carrie admitted soulfully. "I recognized him. He was one of a crowd of drifters and cowhands that came into the saloon. That was before I met Robert and changed my life."

Totally distraught, Martha could barely believe what she was hearing, first her only son's death, and now this shameful discovery. She felt she had been betrayed and deceived, and she immediately became angry. "You're a whore? Did my son know about your wicked past?" she demanded.

"Yes, ma'am," Carrie replied softly. "I told him everything. And he said nothing that happened before we met mattered."

"Well, it matters to me!" Martha snapped. "How could you take advantage of a gentle soul like Robert?" She glared at her husband, expecting him to join her in condemning this evil woman. When he did nothing beyond staring at Carrie with his mouth agape, she turned back to her daughter-in-law. "I'll expect you to gather your shabby belongings and get out of my house immediately."

"Yes, ma'am," Carrie replied, knowing there was no sense in trying to plead her case. It was obvious that Martha and Douglas were not interested in hearing about her impoverished childhood, drunken father, and the pitiful conditions that had forced her to do what she'd had to do to survive. "I'll go right now and get my things."

"I'll go with you to see you don't forget anything,"

Martha said, still fuming. She gave Douglas another scorching gaze to emphasize her disappointment in his lack of indignation.

Carrie turned at once and started for the door, well aware that Martha was going with her to make sure she didn't steal anything. If she was a whore and a liar, then she was probably a thief as well. *I guess that's only natural,* she thought.

Harley looked up when Leon Bloodworth walked into the saloon. He grinned when Leon looked over the half-empty room until he spotted him, then walked straight across the floor to his table. "Howdy, Leon, you come to join me in a little drink?"

"Hell, no," Leon replied. "I came to tell you there's four fellers lookin' for you, and I don't think you want 'em to find you. One of 'em is Troy Womack."

"Womack?" Harley responded. "What are you talkin' about? Troy Womack took off with Cole ridin' after him."

"I'm tryin' to tell you Womack is back in town. He's got three rough-lookin' fellers with him, and they are huntin' for Harley Branch."

Sufficiently alarmed, Harley asked, "What the hell are they lookin' for me for?" *If Womack's back in town, where the hell is Cole?*

Harley was at once anxious, afraid that his friend had come out on the short end in a confrontation with Womack. Knowing Cole was a pretty good tracker, Harley could only pray that Cole had lost

Womack's trail, but he feared that maybe the worst had happened.

"'Cause you've got that Mexican saddle that belonged to Troy's brother," Leon explained. "And they think you're Cole and you shot the other two Womack boys."

"How do they think that?" Harley asked.

"I don't know, but that's what they think for sure," Leon said, choosing not to admit that it was him who gave them Harley's name. "I'll tell them I don't know where you are, but I heard them talkin' 'bout checkin' all the saloons to see if you were in one of 'em. When they passed my place, though, they rode right on by this 'un, else you might be havin' a drink with 'em right now. You'd best make yourself scarce before they show up here."

"That might be the smartest thing you've ever said," Harley said, tossed down the rest of the whiskey in his glass, and got to his feet. He grabbed the bottle, went to the bar to settle up with the bartender, then followed Leon back to the stable to get his horse.

Harley considered hiding out in the stable, but Leon talked him out of it, saying he felt pretty sure that the four men would be back to the stable when they didn't find him in town.

"I didn't know who to tell about those gunmen," Leon said. "With Cole gone and John Henry laid up, I figured the only one who might do somethin' was Gordon Luck. I was fixin' to ride over to the sawmill to tell him after I told you to skedaddle. Why don't you ride out there instead and tell him about our visitors? Might be a good place for you to hide out."

Harley thought about the suggestion while he loaded the packhorse and threw his fancy Mexican saddle onto his horse. Luck had been active with the vigilantes before. He might want to face up to the four gunmen. If he did, Harley would help him, and maybe John Beecher at the blacksmith shop would join them. He had before when the vigilance committee went up against Slade Corbett. Harley was willing to help, but he had better sense than to go up against four gunmen by himself. He just wished Cole was there.

"I'll go tell Gordon what's goin' on." Harley tightened the girth strap and stepped up into the saddle. Then he waited until Leon took another look up toward the hotel to make sure the four visitors were still up at that end of the street. When Leon said their horses were still tied at the rail, Harley prepared to ride out the back door when he was confronted with Carrie coming in. She was carrying her few personal things bundled up in her arms. "Carrie!" he exclaimed. "What's goin' on?"

Startled to see Harley, she was initially at a loss for what to say. But she told herself there was no use in trying to hide the truth; he would know soon enough, anyway. "I guess it's just time for me to move on. I came to get my horse."

Fairly astonished, Harley dismounted. "Time to move on? What are you talkin' about? Where are you goin'?" Thinking about the trouble he and Cole had gone to just to get her to Cheyenne, he was confused by her talk of leaving town. He forgot for the moment about his own need to leave right away. "What's happened? Do Mr. and Mrs. Green know you're goin'?"

She took a moment to put her bundle down while she decided what to tell him. Again, thinking it useless to make up a story, she told Leon to fetch the sorrel she had ridden in on.

When he went to the tack room to get her bridle and saddle, she turned to Harley and said, "Harley, you and Cole are the only people who have ever bothered to help me without question, so I'll tell you the straight of it. Douglas and Martha kicked me out." She went on then to relate the unfortunate happenings that took place in the past half hour, pausing once when Leon left the tack room and went to the corral. "So now I'm leaving this place. I don't know where I'm going, but I know I can't stay here."

"My Lord in heaven." Harley exhaled, momentarily at a loss for words, but lost for a moment only, for he immediately responded. "You can't just go ridin' off by yourself. I'll go with you." He went on to explain his intention to leave town as well. "I'm glad I didn't ride out before you got here. I can't have you wanderin' all over the prairie by yourself. Cole would give me the devil for that. Tell you what. Lemme pack your things on my packhorse. There's four hardened gunmen in town lookin' for me, and from what you just told me, they'll likely be lookin' to find you, too. So we'll just make ourselves scarce, and find us a place that's better for our health. Whaddaya say?"

Desperate for help from any source, but especially relieved to be under his wing again, she gladly accepted his proposal. "I say yes," she replied at once. "But are you sure you want to help me? I mean, with all I just told you?"

"'Course I'm sure. Anybody's liable to make a mistake, especially when they're young and ain't got better choices. Besides, as long as I've known you, you're Carrie Green, and she's a mighty fine lady in my opinion."

She turned her head quickly to blink a tear from her eye as Leon led her sorrel back inside the stable.

"We'll stop by the sawmill and let Gordon Luck know what's goin' on," Harley said to Leon. He looked at Carrie again. "I was plannin' on headin' out by the river, anyway, so the sawmill will be right on our way." Ready to ride, they filed out the back door of the stable, heading for the river.

Behind them, Leon stood watching and puzzling over Carrie's decision to go with Harley. "I wonder what Douglas and Martha will think about this?"

CHAPTER 8

"I'm gonna need a couple of rooms," Flint Yarborough informed Arthur Campbell. "And I want two of them rooms up there facin' the street."

"Yes, sir," Arthur responded politely, not at all comfortable with the look of the man giving the orders, standing there with his rifle in hand. He tried not to make eye contact with Troy, who was obviously enjoying his return to town, as evidenced by the impish grin on his face. "How long will you be staying?" Arthur asked.

"Till I get ready to leave," Yarborough replied, causing Troy to laugh.

"Let me see what rooms I have available," Arthur said, stalling for a few moments while he tried to decide what to do.

The arrival of Troy Womack and his smirking friend placed the whole town in a particularly dire situation. Arthur had certainly never expected Womack to show up in Cheyenne ever again after he'd gunned down John Henry Black in front of the hotel. But Womack was back, big as life as if he had nothing to worry about—and with the sheriff still laid up in bed with the wounds that had almost killed him. Arthur was afraid to let the two outlaws know that Black was recovering in his room right there in the hotel.

To make matters worse, Red and Tiny walked in at that moment, having just left the general store.

My Lord, Arthur thought, *there are four of them!* He realized then that Yarborough's request for two rooms was not for a private room for himself and one for Womack. That shot down his initial hope of convincing Yarborough to take only one room, thinking to separate that room as far as possible from John Henry's room at the end of the hall. Arthur didn't know what to do. He was given a few more minutes to think of something when the two other men grabbed Yarborough's attention.

"I got somethin' to tell you that's gonna tickle you, I guarantee ya," Red declared as he swaggered up to join them at the desk.

Yarborough turned halfway around to respond with a dubious expression.

It caused Red to grin confidently. "You remember that little gal you took a shine to in that saloon, The Cattleman's, down in Ogallala?" He winked at Tiny, who was grinning as wide as he, for they knew that Yarborough had taken more than a casual interest in the young woman.

Yarborough paused to think a few moments before answering. "Yeah, I remember her. Can't call her name right off. What about her?"

"Corina Burnett," Red reminded him, knowing full well that Yarborough remembered her name.

"I just saw her, right next door in the general store. Calls herself Carrie Green now." He gave out a hearty chuckle when he saw the light of recall in Yarborough's eyes.

"Well, I'll be . . ." Yarborough muttered. Two years had dulled the flame of obsession he once had for the pretty young prostitute, but it had never gone out completely. "Corina Burnett. Are you sure? I'd sure like to see her again. Did she remember you?"

"She remembered me," Red stated emphatically. "She played like she didn't—tried to tell me she warn't the same gal—but she didn't fool me."

"When we get through here," Yarborough said, "we'll go back and see if she's the same gal. I got a thing or two I'd like to tell her."

Speechless to this point, but equally amazed, although for a different reason, Troy Womack could scarcely believe the woman Malcolm and Travis had abducted was, in fact, a common dancehall prostitute. His initial reaction was one of anger when he heard her name, thinking his brothers had been taken for suckers. The whole time she had been held by his brothers, Travis said she had cried and screeched like a Sunday school teacher over her dead husband. If she had owned up to it, she could have hooked up with them, and maybe caused a hell of a lot less trouble. He tried to remember the two women driving the buckboard that night when he and Travis charged it. He'd gotten a good look at her face when Travis tried to pull her out of the seat, but the memory had been dulled by the image of Travis falling dead a moment later. Finally he spoke. "That's the woman that caused Travis to get killed, only he didn't know her name was really Corina whatever you said."

"Well, I'll be . . ." Yarborough started, getting even more stirred up. "Is that a fact?"

Troy nodded slowly.

"Well, I know I gotta get a look at this woman now," Yarborough said. "See if she's the same one." He shook his head, amazed, still doubting the possibility. "Damned if she ain't a real sidewinder, ain't she?"

As aghast as any of them, Arthur Campbell found himself stunned by the new portrayal of the seemingly innocent young widow of Robert Green. So astonished was he that he had to remind himself of the problem he had yet to solve regarding the recuperating sheriff in the room upstairs at the end of the hall. It might be impossible to keep the four outlaws from finding out the sheriff was lying helpless only a few doors away from their rooms.

Although he preferred not to rent his two best rooms to the rowdy four facing him, Arthur could think of no other option. "Well, if you gentlemen are going to the store right now, I'll make sure your rooms are ready for you. I'll rent you my two best rooms upstairs, right up front where you can look out the windows and see everything that's going on in the street below. How's that?"

"You ain't got nothin' better?" Yarborough countered.

"No, sir," Arthur replied, thinking he had already answered that question.

"Then I'll take 'em," Yarborough came back.

"That's what I want. We'll go upstairs and look 'em over." He turned to Red and said, "Then we'll go see that gal you think is Corina. It's been about two years or more since we was in Ogallala. You mighta seen somebody that just looks like Corina."

Red just laughed, sure of what he had seen.

Already in a state of total dismay, Douglas Green was alarmed to see the two men return to his store with two others. And one of them was the gunman who had shot Sheriff Black. His first thought was that he was about to be robbed, and he knew there was nothing he could do to prevent it. They obviously knew there was no sheriff to stop them. With no option other than to give them whatever they demanded, he stood silently watching, hoping he would at least be alive after they left. He was somewhat surprised when one of them asked a question.

"Where's Corina?" Red asked, anxious for Yarborough to see her.

"C-Corina?" Green stuttered, still not used to the name. "Oh, Carrie . . . she's not here."

"She was here a few minutes ago," Red insisted, and looked at Tiny for confirmation.

The simple giant nodded vigorously.

Red turned back to Douglas. "Hell, man, we was just in here. Where the hell did she go?" Remembering then, he asked, "Is she in the back room yonder?" He pointed to the storeroom door, for that was where she'd gone when she'd left the store.

"No, sir," Douglas replied. "She ain't in the back room. She's gone, and I don't expect she'll be back."

Red was rapidly losing his patience with the bumbling storekeeper. He reached over the counter, grabbed the front of Green's shirt, and yanked the startled man halfway across the counter. "Well, where the hell did she go? And don't tell me you don't know, 'cause I'll shoot a liar quicker 'n I'd shoot a snake."

Douglas Green had never considered himself to be a coward, merely a peaceable man. At this moment, however, with the toes of his boots barely touching the floor, he could feel the bitter bile of cold fear creeping up into his throat, causing him to whimper pathetically. "Please," he begged, "I swear I don't know where she went. She's gone for good. When we found out who she really was, we told her to get out. She's gone, and that's the God's honest truth."

"You kicked her out, huh?" Red released the terrified man's shirt, letting him drop squarely onto his feet again. He drew his .44 and stuck the muzzle inches from Green's face, aiming right at his nose. "I reckon her kind ain't good enough for you. Is that right?"

"No, no," Green pleaded. "She's good enough. She just shouldn't have lied to us!"

Red cocked the hammer back on his pistol. "I'm fixin' to blow a hole through your head."

It was too much for Green's nervous system to handle. His knees failed him, causing him to drop to the floor, landing in a sitting position against the shelves behind the counter. His face frozen in terror, he stared up with wide-open eyes at the cocked handgun as Red leaned over the counter to keep it trained on him.

"Bam! Bam!" Red suddenly yelled, then roared with laughter when Green flinched in response. The outlaw released the hammer and holstered the weapon as Tiny and Yarborough joined in the laughter. Red turned to Tiny and said, "He thought he was a goner, didn't he?"

"He sure as hell did," Tiny replied, still chuckling at the frightened storekeeper. "That was a good one, Red. You had me fooled. I thought you was really gonna shoot him."

Red laughed again, pleased with the entertainment he had provided.

"I reckon he thought so, too," Yarborough said, "if them wet spots on his britches are what they look like." No longer amused by his partner's antics, he turned a serious eye toward the terrified storekeeper. "Now that the fun is over, suppose you tell me where Corina went. And don't make no mistake about it. If I pull this .44 ridin' on my hip, I aim to fire it."

"Yes, sir," Douglas pleaded pitifully. "I swear I won't lie to you. I don't know where Carrie, I mean, Corina was gonna go. She just went to the house with my wife to get her belongings. I don't know if she's still there, or where she would go after that."

"Where's your house?" Yarborough demanded. "That buildin' out back?"

"Yes, sir," Green replied. "Right across the yard. But please, don't harm my wife."

"Not if she behaves herself and don't give me no

trouble," Yarborough said. "She just better answer my questions and she'll be all right."

"Don't worry, old man," Womack piped up. "I've seen her and there ain't one of us that'll wanna lay a hand on her." He laughed, enjoying his attempt to make a joke.

Martha Green stood by the back door after she had watched her daughter-in-law disappear beyond the outhouse on her way to Leon Bloodworth's stable. At least, that was the direction she had taken, carrying her pitiful belongings in her arms. Standing now, staring at the empty snow-covered alleyway behind the post office, Martha could still see the image of the distraught young woman in her mind's eye. She wondered if she had been wrong in sending her away. It was a hard thing to do, but the woman was a prostitute, and had probably lied to trick Robert into marrying her. It made Martha angry to think that Robert had not told them about Carrie's background—if he, in fact, knew.

She shook her head violently in an effort to drive away thoughts of guilt. She had done what had to be done. She told herself that it was not Douglas and her responsibility to take a common whore into their home because of their son's foolish mistake. "She'll no doubt light somewhere else," Martha finally announced, trying to close the door on the issue, "and likely be better off than staying with Douglas and me." With that, she closed the back door and went to the front of the house, intending to return to the store.

Passing the front window, she happened to see four men walking down the tiny path between the store and her house. The sight stopped her cold before she reached the door. Two of them were probably the men just in the store, the two who had identified Carrie. All four looked capable of doing any amount of harm. *Why are they coming to my house,* she wondered, immediately alarmed. Why would Douglas permit them to come to the house? *Unless he couldn't stop them,* she thought. She went at once to the fireplace and took Douglas's shotgun from over the mantel. After checking to make sure it was loaded, she stood facing the door, awaiting a knock. It never came, and she was startled when the door was flung open and the four, led by Flint Yarborough, strode into the parlor.

Recovering her wits, she calmly informed them, "Most civilized folks knock before they come busting in somebody's house."

"Whoa!" Yarborough yelped when confronted with the shotgun pointed at his midsection. "Take it easy with that thing, lady. Don't go doin' somethin' that'll wind up with you gettin' yourself killed."

"What are you doing busting in here? You've got no business in my house, so you'd best turn yourself right around and get outta here. Where's my husband? Have you harmed him? 'Cause I'll shoot you down like the mad dog you are."

When Red and Tiny moved away from Yarborough to spread out a little, in case she pulled the trigger, she motioned them back. "You two just stand right where you are," she commanded, then directed a threat at Yarborough. "There aren't but two shots in this gun, but if one of them tries something, you'll get the first load of buckshot.

Her warning stopped Red and Tiny in their tracks, but Yarborough held up his hand to stop them as well. It was plain to see that the skinny little woman wasn't bluffing. "Hold on a minute, ma'am," he said politely. "We didn't come to do you no harm. You're right. I reckon we've been away from civilized folk too long. We just wanna talk to Corina for a minute."

"Is my husband all right?" Martha asked.

"Yes, ma'am," Yarborough answered. "We didn't have no reason to harm your husband. He's all right."

"Just wet his pants a little bit," Red couldn't resist commenting. It brought an amused grunt from Tiny, while Troy took a step back in an effort to get behind Yarborough in case the angry woman cut loose with her double-barreled shotgun.

Ignoring Red's attempt at humor, Yarborough continued. "Like I said, we didn't come to cause trouble. I'm just wantin' to see if she's the same woman I knew a couple of years back, so how about callin' her out here?"

"She's gone from here," Martha said, "and she ain't coming back."

Yarborough considered that for a moment. The feisty little woman was probably telling the truth, and he wasn't quite sure why he was determined to see Corina. But he had taken quite a shine to the young girl and been plenty aggravated with her when she ran off and hid from him when he went looking for her. She deserved a little payback for treating him like that, he concluded.

He was going to have to see for himself if she was in the house or not. "We'll just take a quick look to make sure she ain't slipped back in the house without you knowin' it." He nodded to Tiny and took a step to the side.

"No, you don't," she charged and brought her shotgun to bear on him, taking her eyes off the huge man beside him. Caught in the unfamiliar action of cocking the hammers back on her weapon, she was not ready for the sudden move from Tiny.

Grabbing the shotgun by the barrel, he turned it straight up as she pulled both triggers, resulting in landing her on her backside and creating a gaping hole in the ceiling. The simpleminded giant stood over her, grinning down at her.

"Now, I expect you'd best just get up from there and go set yourself down on that sofa and behave yourself till we get done looking through the house," Yarborough told her. "Troy, there, will keep you company while we look. Tiny, you stand by the door and set her husband down with her when he comes runnin' to the house." He looked back at Martha. "If he don't come a-runnin', I believe I'd run him off, if I was you."

There was little doubt that she was helpless to resist the invasion of her home, so she got up from the floor and went to the sofa.

Yarborough watched her until she was settled, then said, "Come on, Red, let's see if that little bird is hidin' someplace. And best be careful. There might be another gun in the house."

He and Red were looking in the kitchen when they heard Tiny welcoming Douglas at the front door.

"Well, I reckon maybe his missus might not run him off," Red said with a chuckle. "He showed up."

The search was thorough, but resulted in no sign of Corina. They checked a shed out back as well as the outhouse before concluding that Martha had spoken truthfully. Corina was gone.

"Who's watchin' the store?" Yarborough joked when he walked back into the parlor and saw Douglas seated beside his wife on the sofa. "Ain't you afraid some outlaws might clean you out while you're at home visitin' with your wife?"

His three companions laughed at his joke.

When Douglas sat there meekly with no desire to reply, Yarborough said, "It's a damn good thing you came a-runnin' when you heard that shotgun go off. She said if you didn't, you'd be sleepin' on the back porch tonight."

Tired of the entertainment enjoyed at their expense, Martha finally spoke. "All right. You've bullied us and had your fun. Your Corina ain't here, so get out of my house. We've got to get back to the store."

"Yes, ma'am," Yarborough mocked, "just as soon as you tell me which way she went."

"I told you I don't know which way she went," Martha retorted emphatically, even though she could have told them that Corina started out toward the stable. "And I don't care which way she went," she added.

"I believe you don't," Yarborough said. "Come on, boys. Let's go."

Douglas and Martha sat there for a few minutes after the four outlaws had filed out the front door.

"I guess I'd best get back to the store, in case they take a notion to go back and clean us out," he said.

She nodded in response.

Ashamed of the humiliation he had been forced to endure, he attempted to apologize for his lack of backbone.

"Don't be silly, Douglas," she responded. "You couldn't fight the four of them. They would have killed you, and then where would I be? With John Henry laid up in bed, the town is at the mercy of all the good-for-nothing outlaws that happen to drift through here. I just hope Arthur Campbell doesn't let them know the sheriff's laying helpless right there in the hotel. I'm afraid they might decide to finish him for good."

Mary Lou Cagle paused just before opening the door when she heard the heavy tread of boots and the boisterous conversation outside in the hallway. She automatically looked back at the bed, where John Henry Black lay weak and defenseless. She placed her forefinger to her lips, lest he might start to say something. It had to be the four outlaws outside the door on their way to the two rooms at the front of the hall. Holding a tray with the sheriff's supper dishes in one hand, she listened until she was sure there was no one else in the hall before slowly turning the knob and easing the door open. When she saw the empty hall, she took another quick look back at Black before stepping outside. Placing the tray on the floor at her feet, she quickly locked the door, picked up the tray again, and hurried down the back stairs.

"How's he looking?" a concerned Maggie White-house asked when Mary Lou came into the kitchen.

"Better," Mary Lou answered. "At least he's feeling a little more like eating now, a little more than yesterday, anyway. But he still ain't ready to sit up for no longer than it takes me to feed him."

"I hope that scum ain't planning to stay in the hotel very long," Maggie said. "I don't know how long you can keep being a nurse to John Henry before they get wise to something going on in that room."

Mary Lou could only respond with a shrug and a long sigh. She had been the one person Arthur Campbell thought of when a nurse was needed. It wasn't the first time she had been called upon to take that role. That time had been voluntarily on her part, however, when she had watched over Cole after he had been shot. The thought brought an image to mind of a wounded mountain lion, tame under her care. A slight smile parted her lips as she compared that picture with the image he presented when he'd returned recently, a year later. With his long sandy hair in braids and dressed in animal hides, he looked more like a wild Indian, but he still created that special feeling inside her. Her smile suddenly gave way to a frown when she reminded herself that he had yet to declare his interest in her. Although she would never admit it, she had turned Gordon Luck down because she had made up her mind to wed Cole Bonner.

Maggie suspected as much, but Mary Lou would deny it until the knot was tied. And if they never married, she would take it to the grave with her. Her thoughts were interrupted when Maggie broke into her reverie.

"What in the world are you thinking about?"

"Nothing," Mary Lou replied. "Wondering if we were going to have those four coyotes coming in here to eat, I guess."

"Is that so?" Maggie said. "Looked more to me like you were off someplace else in your mind. I asked you twice if you wanted me to clean up the dishes so you could take care of John Henry. And you ain't answered yet."

"No, I'll help with the cleanup. John Henry oughta be all right for the night. He's got his bedpan and water beside the bed. I'll check on him before I go to bed." Mary Lou paused, realizing Maggie had voiced concern about the four men. "Maybe, if we're lucky, they'll eat their meals at one of the saloons, like most of their kind."

In fact, the four outlaws were intent upon checking the saloons as soon as they parked their saddlebags and war bags in the two hotel rooms.

"I'm bunkin' with Flint," Red announced before any of them entered a room.

Still too new to the gang to be particular about a roommate, Troy shrugged and carried his belongings into the room with Tiny, unaware of the sly wink Red aimed at Yarborough. He would find the reason for Red's preference, however, when going to bed that night. Tiny, on the other hand, could not care less who bunked in with him, for he always fell fast asleep within minutes of closing his eyes. Consequently, he never suffered the problem of trying to sleep in a room resonating with the sound of a lovesick moose. As he had often explained, he had never stayed awake to hear how loud he snored.

With their gear stowed, they left the hotel to begin a search of the three saloons in town, looking for the man called Harley Branch. Starting with the Cowboy's Rest, they worked their way down the street, having a drink in each place and questioning the bartender about Harley. The results were the same in all three, no one had seen Harley, and from the response they received, it appeared that no one had ever heard of the man.

Tossing his shot of whiskey back, Yarborough smacked his lips in loud appreciation of the fiery liquid. They had drunk their way down to the last of the three saloons, the Sundown, so named because it was on the western end of the short street. Troy suggested that it might be a good idea to go back to the stable.

"I reckon we could do that," Yarborough said. "He'd likely know if Harley Branch was back in town." Like his friends, Tiny and Red, Yarborough was rapidly losing interest in finding the man who had killed Troy's brothers. He was fine with the idea of killing the man, but his main interest was in the possibility of looting the town of Cheyenne. It appeared to him that they had found themselves in the right place at the right time. And, so far, there appeared to be nobody to stop them, adding icing to the cake. *To hell with Harley Branch,* he thought, but as a last friendly gesture to Troy, he said, "All right. Let's go to the stable."

Faced again with the four dangerous-looking faces, Leon Bloodworth hoped his nervousness was not as apparent as he feared. "No, sir," he responded politely. "As far as I know, Harley Branch has left here for good, and he didn't say where he was headin'. He came in not long after you fellers rode by here, settled up with me, and left. I asked him where he was headin', but he just said away from here."

"Well, that about ties a knot in that piece of rope, I reckon," Yarborough said, turning to Troy. "There ain't any more we can do about him. Maybe we'll run into him somewhere down the line." He paused a moment, waiting to see if Troy had anything to say about that. When Troy simply shrugged as if accepting the missed opportunity for vengeance, Yarborough turned his attention back to Leon. "I don't reckon you've seen hide nor hair of Corina Burnett, have you?" Seeing Leon's startled look, he mistook it for confusion. "You might know her by Carrie. Does she keep a horse or maybe a buggy here?"

"Uh, no, sir," Leon stammered. "Carrie ain't got no horses here."

"She might be hid out with some of these other folks here," Red suggested. "She'll show up somewhere. This town ain't big enough to hide in."

"Reckon you're right," Yarborough said. "Anyway, what was your name?"

"Bloodworth, Leon Bloodworth."

"Right, Leon," Yarborough continued. "We're gonna put these horses up with you. Water 'em good and feed 'em some grain. They ain't had any in a while. We're gonna stay a few days in town, so you just start us up a bill and we'll settle up when we're ready to leave."

Leon hesitated, wondering if he should tell Yarborough that his usual policy was to collect his stable rent in advance when it came to new customers. He couldn't bring himself to do it when he met the penetrating stare of Flint Yarborough, seeming to dare him to demand money. "Yes, sir," Leon finally muttered. "I'll take good care of 'em for ya."

"Good," Yarborough said. "We'll just leave 'em with you and you can pull the saddles off and stow our gear in your tack room." Feeling in complete control now, he turned and started walking back to the saloon. "Come on, boys. Let's see what the town has to offer. We might wanna stay here permanent. They ain't got no sheriff now. Maybe I'm the man for that job." It was an idle comment, but the thought of taking over the town, like Big Steve Long had done in Laramie, had entered his mind. He could see that Cheyenne was already growing and could provide a lot of opportunity for a man like himself to get rich. If he did make a move like that, he'd have to be a little more careful about it than Long had, ending up with a rope around his neck.

The four unwelcome guests walked out of the stable. They left a shaken Leon Bloodworth watching them and wondering what they might do if they found out that John Henry Black was not dead.

Gordon Luck was not at the sawmill when Harley and Carrie got to the river. One of the young boys who worked for him told Harley that Gordon was repairing some benches in the church building. Harley thanked them and headed for the church, explaining to Carrie that Gordon was a preacher as well as a sawmill man. When they got to the church, they found evidence that Gordon had been working there—a couple of benches were upside down and braced underneath with new lumber—but he was not there.

Harley and Carrie walked back outside and stopped on the steps when they heard Gordon call from the house behind the church. Harley called back and in a few seconds they saw him walking to meet them.

"Harley," Gordon called out, "I thought that was you. Who's this you've brought with you?"

"This is Carrie Green," Harley answered.

"Oh, yes, I shoulda guessed that," Gordon replied. "I've been too busy at the sawmill to get into town for the past few days, but I heard you'd come to live with Douglas and Martha. I was powerful sorry to hear about your husband, and I was hopin' I'd see you in church this comin' Sunday." He nodded toward the door of the church. "I've been busy fixin' up some of the benches, so you won't take a chance on landing on the floor." He smiled broadly at Carrie, but was puzzled by the grim expressions on both their faces. He was somewhat surprised to find the young lady in Harley's company to begin with, so he guessed there might be an explanation coming. "What brings you out this way today?" he asked, becoming more serious.

Harley glanced at Carrie, not sure how much of the story she was willing to divulge. "Well, in the first place, we came to tell you 'bout some bad trouble in town. I know you heard about the shootout that landed John Henry Black on his back in the hotel."

Gordon nodded.

"Well," Harley continued, "the feller that done it has come back to town, and he's brung three gunmen with him."

"Oh, my Lord . . ." Gordon started. "That ain't good news. Have Arthur and the others got the vigilance committee together?"

"No, they ain't," Harley replied. "That's why we stopped by to let you know what's goin' on. Tell you the truth, I don't think anybody wants to tangle with these four fellers. They're a mean bunch."

"What about Cole Bonner?" Gordon asked. "From what I heard, he was the one that did most of the shootin' when that one feller was killed."

"Cole went after that Womack feller, but he ain't come back. And since Womack is back in town with his three friends, I'm afraid Cole mighta run into an ambush and got himself killed."

Gordon scratched his head while he considered the problem. Finally he asked, "So you're tellin' me that the town is in the hands of four outlaws and nobody's gonna go up against 'em?"

"That's what I'm tellin' you," Harley said. "I told Leon Bloodworth I'd tell you what's goin' on, in case you wanna see if you can get the vigilance committee together again. I thought about helpin' if you did, but I'm obliged to take Carrie somewhere safe." He turned to look Carrie in the eye. "And right now I'm thinkin' about goin' back to Medicine Bear's village. I'd go somewhere to look for Cole, but I ain't got any idea where to start."

The indecision was apparent in Gordon's eyes as he thought the situation over. He had responded to the call before to rid Cheyenne of outlaws. Like Arthur Campbell and Douglas Green, he was not eager to face up to four hardened killers again. He had done his part in helping to build a law-abiding town. Let someone else take a turn. "Are you plannin' to take Mrs. Green, here, to that Crow camp?" He directed his next question to Carrie. "Is this all right with Douglas and Martha?"

Harley shrugged, hesitant to answer.

Carrie smiled at him and said, "Everybody's gonna know soon enough, Harley." Then to Gordon, she said, "It's all right with Douglas and Martha. They asked me to leave, and not to come back, and I said I would."

"Why in the world would they ask you to do that?" Gordon exclaimed.

"They had their reasons," Carrie said and left it at that.

Gordon was astonished to think the Greens sent her away. "Maybe they're concerned for your safety," he suggested. There was an extended period of silence while he tried to determine what he should do. After he thought it over, he decided he'd let the town take care of itself. "I'll defend my sawmill and my church, but the citizens of Cheyenne are gonna have to take care of their own."

He looked at Carrie and shook his head as if apologizing. Then another idea struck him. "You don't have to go with Harley to live in a Crow village, if you don't want to. You can stay here at my house. I've got a spare room all fixed up to suit a lady. It was gonna be for me and my bride, but she changed her mind about marryin' me, so nobody's usin' it. I don't sleep in there, so it's just like brand new." In fact, he had closed the door to the room so as not to be reminded of it.

Harley looked at Carrie to judge her reaction to Gordon's invitation. He could see that it had caused her to give it some thought. "Well, that might be more to your likin' than goin' back to an Injun village." Thinking Gordon seemed sincere in the offer, Harley waited for a moment while Carrie considered the suggestion. "You would be far enough from town, so nobody would likely know you were here. 'Course, it's up to you. You know Moon Shadow and Yellow Calf would welcome you for as long as you wanted to stay." *At least*

for as long as that little camp of old folks can make it
before they're forced to go to the reservation, he couldn't
help thinking. He was afraid that time would not
be far off. The young men had gone and he didn't
know how much longer he would be able to supply
the camp with meat. He was getting long in the
tooth, himself.

Finally, Carrie spoke. "That's a mighty generous
offer and I thank you for it." Shifting her gaze to
Harley then, she went on. "It sounds like a wonder-
ful opportunity for me, but Gordon doesn't know
the whole story. And he should hear it before he
agrees to take me in." Turning back to Gordon,
she said, "I was a prostitute before I married
Robert Green and that's the reason I had to leave
Cheyenne. Douglas and Martha found out and
kicked me out of their home. I ain't a prostitute
anymore."

Her forthright admission had the effect on
Gordon that Harley expected. He was struck speechless for a long moment.

The sudden silence was interrupted by a comment from Harley. "That oughta give a preacher
somethin' to think about, I reckon."

It gave Gordon plenty to think about, all right,
but he tried to approach it with the forgiveness
that a Christian should embrace. He questioned
her on how she became a prostitute and she was
quite frank with her answers. After hearing of her
abandonment at a tender age, with no one to take
care of her and no place to go, he found he did
have some compassion for her plight. Since she
assured him that she had sought forgiveness for

her sins, and had traveled a sin-free path since meeting Robert, Gordon decided that the offer was still good.

"It ain't like I'm askin' you to marry me or anything else beyond just givin' you a place to live," he rationalized. "And since you ain't a whore no more, ain't nobody got any right to say anything about you rentin' a room in the parsonage."

"How much is the rent?" Carrie asked.

"Maybe you could help with the cookin' and washin'," Gordon said.

Both parties nodded their agreement and shook on it. Harley pulled the saddle off the sorrel and turned it out with Gordon's horses. After he had parked her saddle in the barn, he went inside the house where Gordon was showing Carrie around. When he walked in, he overheard Carrie comment that it was obvious the kitchen could use a woman's touch.

She'll be running this house in a week's time, he thought and smiled. "Well, I reckon I'd best decide what I'm gonna do," he announced.

"Why don't you stay here, too?" Gordon asked. His question brought a hopeful look to Carrie's eye.

Harley shrugged. "I reckon I could at that," he allowed. "I swear, I'd like to go look for Cole, but I'm blamed if I know where to start." The thought of his friend lying wounded or dead on the cold unforgiving prairie was not an image that rested easy in his mind. After he considered it for a few minutes, he decided. "What the hell? I reckon I'll stick around. I'll sleep in the barn with my horses."

Carrie nodded and smiled at him. She knew she

would be a lot more comfortable with Harley there, at least until she became used to the arrangement. It didn't strike her as a permanent solution to her problems, but for the time being, it sounded better to her than going back to live with the Indians.

CHAPTER 9

Never suspecting the possibility of what had taken place in Cheyenne while he had continued on to Iron Mountain, Cole reined the bay gelding to a stop on a low rise just short of Chugwater Creek. As best he could figure, he was about two miles south of Raymond Potter's trading post. If he had guessed right, he should reach the store while Womack and his partners were sitting around the fire, drinking Potter's whiskey and playing cards. He could have gotten there much earlier, but purposely had waited until later in the day. With odds of four to one, he needed to catch the outlaws when they were least on guard. He was counting on total surprise, since there was no reason for them to suspect that anyone was trailing them.

With a nudge of his heels, he signaled the bay forward.

Guiding his horse around a tight turn in the creek, he came in sight of the trading post, a group of three weathered board buildings that made up the general store and saloon. It had been some time since he had been to Potter's Place, as everybody called it. The combination general store and saloon being the closest trading post to old Medicine Bear's camp near the forks of the Laramie and North Laramie Rivers, Raymond Potter's tendency was to cheat his customers whenever he could, and Cole preferred to ride a little farther, to Fort Laramie, when he had hides to trade or a craving for a drink of whiskey that wasn't watered down. Aside from that, Potter seemed to cater to people on the wrong side of the law, and as a rule, you could expect to run into one or more men on the run from some lawman. It was the reasoning behind Cole's notion that Womack and his friends were most likely headed there.

As he approached the store, he held the bay to the western bank of the creek in order to come up on the blind side of anyone happening to be at the front door. Taking no chances, he held his rifle ready in case there was no time for introductions. While the bay plodded slowly across the side yard, Cole glanced at the horses in the corral beside the barn. Half a dozen horses were there, plus the four tied at the hitching rail in front of the store. That immediately captured his attention. Maybe he had not been as far behind the men he tailed as he had at first assumed.

It might have been a mistake to delay his arrival until suppertime. On the other hand, maybe the riders he trailed rode in on four of the horses in the corral. For there were no packhorses at the rail, and he was sure he had followed six horses from the shack on the Laramie.

He dismounted and looped his reins over the rail, his rifle still at the ready while he checked the horses tied there. None looked as if it had recently been ridden hard. So far, there was no indication that anyone had seen him ride up, so he paused for a moment to decide how best to proceed. He knew he could recognize Womack, but he had no idea what his three friends looked like. His immediate concern was what to do if he didn't see Womack inside. On the other hand, Womack's three friends didn't know him from Adam, either, so he figured he'd just trust his reactions to do the right thing.

Inside the saloon Raymond Potter was leaning on the end of the bar talking to a heavyset man with a full gray beard. Two of the three small tables in the room were occupied with two men at each table and all conversation in the room halted briefly when the door was swung open and Cole walked in. He shifted his gaze quickly, scanning the entire room, hoping to recognize Troy Womack at once, fully aware of the need to react instantly if he did.

After a second, the conversations resumed when everyone had determined the new arrival was no one they knew and, consequently, of no concern.

Cole immediately came to the conclusion that he had been wrong in guessing Womack and his friends had headed there. He didn't see Womack anywhere in the room, and Cole was struck with the thought that he might have made a serious mistake. *Womack and his friends might have gone anywhere, maybe even Cheyenne!* He had gambled on the idea that the wounded outlaw was interested only in clearing out of the territory. What if he and his companions had turned back toward Cheyenne?

Cole found himself thirty-five or more miles from Cheyenne with a horse already tired from the present day's ride. *Damn!* he thought, feeling he had been a damn fool for chasing snowflakes while his friends in Cheyenne might be suffering the vengeance of Womack and his three partners. With an urgency to get back to Cheyenne as quickly as possible, he started to turn about-face and delay not a second more, when Potter caused him to hesitate.

"Ain't seen you in a long spell," Potter greeted him. "You comin' in or goin' out?"

Thinking he might confirm what he had already decided, Cole answered. "I'm lookin' for somebody. I'm supposed to meet Troy Womack and three other fellows here today. Don't reckon they got here yet."

Potter looked genuinely at a loss. "Troy who?"

When Cole repeated the last name, Potter shook his head. "Don't know nobody by that name." He turned toward the patrons at the tables. "Anybody know a feller name of Troy Womack?" No one did, so Potter turned back to Cole. "Well, they ain't showed up yet. Matter of fact, there ain't been no four fellers ridin' together, showin' up around here. You sure you was supposed to meet 'em here?" Cole did not respond, so Potter asked, "Whatcha gonna have while you're waitin'? I've got some good corn likker that'll damn-sure cut a rut in your throat."

"Later maybe," Cole lied. "I've got something to do first." He turned around and headed straight for the door.

When the door closed behind him, Potter

commented to the man with the gray beard. "Well, ain't that somethin'? He's been in here before, but it was a while back. Looks like he's gone plum Injun."

Outside, Cole stepped up into the saddle, turned the bay's head back toward the way he had come, and started out along the creek bank at a lope. It was too much to ask of the horse to ride through the night, but he would push him pretty hard until stopping to make camp. Even with a stop to rest, he figured he could reach Cheyenne before noon the next day.

As he rode into the shadows of the cottonwoods along the creek, he could not help feeling that he should have stayed in Cheyenne instead of going after Womack. He was worried about Harley and the merchants in town, about the Greens and Carrie, but he was especially concerned for Mary Lou Cagle's safety. And it forced him to admit that he always had a feeling that it was a job he wanted— to take care of her. Headstrong and seemingly untamable, she nevertheless was who he wanted in his life, not just for now, but always. The problem was he had nothing to offer her, living more like a Crow warrior than a man capable of settling down and supporting a wife. He had tried to embrace the life of a farmer before his wife was killed, but he knew he was not suited for working the soil. With Ann gone, he had let the land he bought on the Chugwater go back, anyway.

That was when his existence as a hunter and avenger began. *It might be too late to change that,* he thought. Picturing Mary Lou in his mind, he had to admit he was not confident that she would be

inclined to cast her lot with him. She had turned
Gordon Luck down, and he was a strong represen-
tative of the new town's citizens. Frustrated as
always when he had these thoughts, Cole shook his
head and tried to free his mind of them.

The more Yarborough thought about it, the
more convinced he became that he had been
handed an opportunity that few men of his charac-
ter ever had. Finally deciding he would be a fool to
pass up the chance to take over the town, he informed his partners. "I'm fixin' to run for sheriff
of this town," he told them while eating breakfast
at the Cowboy's Rest. His comment caused barely
a ripple among his companions, none of whom
thought he was serious. "I'm runnin' fair and
square," Yarborough continued. "So we'll vote on
it right now. How many want me to be sheriff?
Raise your hands." He held up his arm and waited.

Red, his battered face barely inches from the
food on his plate, immediately held up his hand
without raising his head. Tiny and Troy, being in
doubt as to whether or not Yarborough was really
asking them to vote, hesitated, but under Yarborough's steady glare, raised their hands as well.

"There, then," Yarborough announced. "We've
had us an election and it was a unanimous decision.
I accept the job. The next thing is to let everybody
in town know. We'll tell everybody on both sides of
the street—soon as we finish eatin'."

When they finished and got up to leave, Yarborough said, "Might as well start with Abe." And he

called the bartender over to the table. "Just thought you'd like to know there's a new sheriff in town."

Abe looked genuinely surprised, startled in fact. "A new sheriff? I ain't heard nothin' about a new sheriff."

"You're hearin' about it now," Red informed him.

"That's right," Yarborough said. "There was an election and they voted me in as sheriff. I'll be settin' myself up in the sheriff's office right away and I'll need a key to the front door. Who do you reckon has it?"

"I don't know," Abe replied. "Arthur Campbell, I reckon. He's the mayor. Pete Little might have one. He used to work for John Henry, cleanin' the jail up and fetchin' meals for the prisoners."

"Where does he stay?" Yarborough asked.

"In the jail most of the time, but he's got a room in the back of the feedstore." Abe paused then and slowly shook his head. "So you're the new sheriff, huh?"

"That's a fact," Yarborough said, deadly serious. "And you'd best know that I aim to run a strict town. And I expect to get me and my deputies' meals free, too."

Abe cocked a suspicious eye toward him. "Hell, I can't do that. You'll have to talk to Mr. Knowles about that. He's the owner."

Yarborough paused to consider that. After a moment, during which he stared at Abe with menacing eyes squinting from underneath knotted eyebrows, he said, "I expect you'd wanna do it to keep any trouble from happenin' in here."

The intent of his message was not lost on Abe. "Maybe so."

"Good," Yarborough responded. "You wanna stay on the right side of the law."

They walked out without offering to pay for their food or the bottle Red picked up on his way out.

Outside, Red laughed and gave Yarborough a pat on the back. "Damned if you didn't buffalo ol' Abe in there. You had him so turned around on that sheriff story he didn't know what to think. Got us some free grub and a bottle, too."

"That warn't no story," Yarborough replied, causing Red to recoil slightly.

"You mean you meant what you were sayin'? Bein' the new sheriff and all?"

"Damn right I meant it," Yarborough came back. "I'm plannin' to milk this damn town for every penny I can get out of it. And the best way to do that is to be the law. That's what we're gonna do. The next one I wanna set straight is Arthur Campbell. Abe said he's the mayor, so he can let everybody else know that we'll be takin' care of the town."

"That's a helluva lot for these folks to swallow," Troy commented. He couldn't help wondering if Yarborough might be a little touched in the head. He was especially skeptical since everyone in town knew he was the one who shot the sheriff and high-tailed it. He had assumed that the sole reason they had come to town was to rob a couple of the businesses, and if they found him, kill Harley Branch. Then they would ride out of the territory to spend their money in Montana or Texas. "I ain't sure we can pull the wool over everybody's eyes."

"You just watch," Yarborough said. "They'll go

along without givin' us any trouble a'tall, 'cause they'll be scared not to. Now you and Red go on up to them other saloons and spread the word there's a new sheriff takin' over. I'm gonna go across the street to the sheriff's office and see if I can get in. I'll tell everybody I see 'bout the election. And Red, keep your eye out for Corina. She's gotta be hidin' somewhere."

They split up then to inform the town of the new deal.

Yarborough found the padlock missing from the door of the sheriff's office and smoke coming out of the stovepipe. He walked inside to find Pete Little sitting beside the small stove in the center of the room, drinking a cup of coffee. The meek little man was startled when the formidable figure of Flint Yarborough suddenly appeared in the open door, followed by the even more menacing hulk of Tiny Weaver.

Pete jumped to his feet, splashing some of his coffee onto the floor in the process. "The sheriff ain't here," he blurted.

"Yes, he is," Yarborough replied. "You're lookin' at him. Who the hell are you?"

"Pete Little. I help out around here—keep the place clean for Sheriff Black, bring the prisoners' food from the dinin' room—when we got prisoners—stuff like that. Right now, we ain't got nobody locked up, since the sheriff got shot." He looked back and forth between the smirking Yarborough and the grinning Tiny, not sure how he should react.

Yarborough took a minute to decide what to do with the little man. He seemed incapable of causing him any problems. "All right, I reckon you can keep your job, long as you keep a warm fire goin' and keep the place clean. I need a key to that padlock for the door. You got an extra one?"

"Yes, sir," Pete answered, "in the desk drawer." He watched while Yarborough opened the drawer and found the extra key. "You gonna be here permanent, or just till Sheriff Black gets back?"

Before Yarborough answered, the door opened again and Troy walked in. "Red said he'd meet you at the hotel. He's gone to the general store."

Ignoring him, Yarborough remained focused on Pete. "Whaddaya mean, till Sheriff Black gets back? He's dead, ain't he?" He glanced at Troy then, looking for confirmation.

Yarborough wasn't the only one staring at Womack, for Pete instantly recognized the man who had shot John Henry Black. It struck him then just who he was dealing with, and he feared that he had said too much if they had thought John Henry was dead. "I don't know," he blurted.

"You don't know?" Yarborough demanded. "You just said he was comin' back, and I don't know anybody that's come back from hell. Now, is he dead or not, and if he ain't, where is he?"

Pete was not the smartest man in town, but he was sharp enough to realize what was in the process of taking place. It looked like the same thing that had happened in Laramie when Big Steve Long took over the marshal's job. His eyes grew as large as saucers as he struggled to think how best to answer Yarborough without angering the fearsome gunman.

"He's stallin', Yarborough," Tiny decided and made as if to grab Pete by the shirtfront.

"No, sir! No, sir!" Pete fairly screamed, backing away. "I ain't stallin'. I just don't know for sure if John Henry's dead or not! All I know is that he was shot two times and he was pretty bad off, but I don't know what happened to him." He prayed they believed him, because the big simple-looking man seemed as if he would enjoy beating the truth out of him.

"You expect me to believe you don't know where they took him after he was shot?" Yarborough pressed.

"No, sir," Pete blurted. "I mean, yes, sir. I just stayed low in my room till everythin' got quiet again. I'd sure-enough tell you if I knew."

"Where'd he stay before he got shot?" Yarborough asked.

"Most of the time he stayed right here, sleepin' in the cell," Pete lied, knowing he would be sealing John Henry's death if he told them the sheriff had a room in the hotel. "They took him outta town somewhere is all they told me."

"Was there a funeral for the sheriff?" Yarborough asked.

"No, sir, I don't reckon."

"Then he ain't dead." Yarborough looked accusingly at Womack. "I thought you said you killed the son of a bitch."

"I said I *thought* I killed him," Womack said. "I put two bullets in him and he went down." He paused, then added, "And he didn't get up again. Hell, I didn't have time to wait around to see how bad he was wounded. There was a helluva lotta folks shootin' at me."

Yarborough hesitated while he thought the situation over to decide if it mattered to him if Black was alive or dead. If he was hurt as bad as Yarborough had been led to believe, it was doubtful he'd be any threat to him. On the other hand, it might be better to eliminate the former sheriff so there wouldn't be any question of the outlaw's authority. "I wanna find the son of a bitch and make sure he ain't gonna be no trouble," he finally said.

"Most likely took him to one of the farms or ranches close by," Womack suggested. "Anyway, he ain't likely to cause us any trouble. Hell, he'll probably die. I put two slugs in his chest, dead center."

"I reckon you're right. Let's go to the hotel and talk to His Honor, the mayor," Yarborough said, much to the relief of a severely shaken Pete Little.

"Where's your daddy?" Yarborough asked Campbell's young son, Sonny, when the three gunmen walked in the hotel lobby. "I need to talk to him."

"He ain't back from breakfast," Sonny said. "Is there something I can help you with?"

His father had cautioned him to be polite to the four outlaws so as not to provoke them. The merchants of the town were going to have to do something about them, but for the time being he told Sonny they were forced to tolerate them. And hopefully, maybe they would move on to some other town before that became necessary.

Yarborough was about to tell him to go get his

father, but paused when he heard someone on the stairs behind him. He turned to see a man coming down from the second floor, a small black bag in his hand. The man hesitated for a moment as if undecided whether to proceed down the steps or not. Since it was not Arthur Campbell, Yarborough returned his attention to Sonny, only to pause again when a thought occurred to him.

Turning quickly then to catch the man before he reached the door, he took another look at the bag the man was carrying. It looked like the kind of bag a doctor would have. "You're a doctor, right?" Yarborough blurted.

"I am," Doc Marion answered and continued toward the door until Tiny stepped in his way.

"What's your hurry, Doc?" Tiny asked, thinking that Yarborough wanted to inform him that he was the new sheriff.

"I've got patients to tend to," Doc answered brusquely.

Struck with a feeling that he was on to something, Yarborough asked, "Like one you just tended to upstairs, right, Doc?" He was encouraged by the immediate look of concern he saw in the doctor's eyes.

"A lot of folks get sore throats and runny noses this time of year," Doc answered, hoping to discourage any more questions.

"Bullet wounds, too, right, Doc?" Yarborough pressed, enjoying the game of words. "How 'bout it? Is ol' John Henry Black gonna make it?"

Red and Troy were on to the game. They turned to grin expectantly at Doc Marion. Tiny, a step slower to appreciate their luck in bumping into the doctor, just continued to grin.

"I'm not at liberty to discuss my patients with anyone," Doc replied. "But this patient might have pneumonia, so I'm advising everybody not to have contact with him." He paused briefly. "I mean her," he added, hoping to discourage their interest in his patient.

He could see that his attempts to throw them off were in vain, however, when Red asked, "Is it the kind of pneumonia you catch from a .44 slug?"

His question was followed by chortles from the amused outlaws.

Disappointed that he had blindly blundered into the ambush, Doc tried to end it. "Well, I haven't got time to waste here. I've got patients to see."

"Right, Doc," Yarborough said. "We don't wanna keep your patients waitin', so you can go see 'em just as soon as you tell us which room John Henry Black is in."

Doc blanched, realizing he might have inadvertently brought disaster down upon the sheriff. Still, he tried to think of something to keep them away from his patient, who was lying helpless in his room upstairs. "I told you, that patient upstairs is suffering from pneumonia. Sheriff Black is dead and that's all I can tell you." He stepped around Tiny and hurried to the door.

Tiny drew his pistol and prepared to go after him, but Yarborough stopped him. "Let him go. You never can tell, one of us might need a doctor. Besides, he's already told us what we need to know, and this young feller can tell us which room Black is in." He turned to lock eyes with Sonny.

Sonny immediately began to fidget and took a step back from the desk.

"There ain't but five rooms upstairs," Yarborough reminded him. "Me and my boys are in two of 'em, so that don't leave but three to look in. You can keep your mouth shut and we'll just kick them other three doors off the hinges. Your daddy most likely wouldn't like that, so you might as well save us the time and your daddy's doors. Which room is he in?"

"Last room at the end of the hall, by the back stairs," Sonny answered. It was plain to see there was nothing he could do to keep them out of the sheriff's room, so he handed Yarborough the key when he held out his hand. And since they immediately started for the stairs, there was no way he could alert Black of their coming. He stood helpless until they all climbed up the stairs, then he ran to the hotel dining room to tell his father.

John Henry heard the key in his door and looked at the big clock on the wall. It was too early for Mary Lou to be bringing his dinner. It hadn't been that long since she had brought him his breakfast. Doc had just left after giving him two teaspoons of laudanum. There had not been enough time to expect any relief from the pain in his chest, and he winced when he had to raise his head in order to see the clock. Consequently, he refrained from raising his head any more than necessary, and as a result, he didn't know who his visitors were until they were already in the room.

"Good mornin', Sheriff Black."

The words struck a chord of doom in the wounded man's soul, no less than had they been spoken by Satan, himself.

"I'm here to make sure you're nice and comfortable," Yarborough said. "You shoulda saved me the trouble and died when Troy, here, shot ya." Hearing a raspy response from the helpless man that he couldn't understand, Yarborough leaned close and asked, "What was that?"

"I'll wait for you in hell," Black said as clearly as he could manage.

"Ha!" Yarborough responded, delighted with the doomed man's defiance. "Well, you'll be waiting a long time, 'cause I ain't plannin' to get there for quite a spell yet." He jerked one of the pillows from under Black's head and slammed it down over his face. When John Henry tried to open his mouth to get air, Yarborough stuffed one end of the pillow down his throat. The desperate man refused to die, clawing weakly at his attacker until Yarborough had to ask for help. "Die, damn you," he cursed. "Here, Tiny, give me a hand," he ordered, whereupon the hulking giant cheerfully complied, grabbing Black by his throat and wringing the life from him.

Having waited no longer than it took the four men to reach the top of the steps, Sonny ran through the hallway to the dining room door. Startled when he looked up from his breakfast to see his son burst through the doorway, Arthur Campbell was at once alarmed. He was certain if there was trouble, it had to do with the town's unwelcome guests. Seated at the table with him, John Beecher, the town's blacksmith, almost knocked his coffee cup onto the floor when Sonny cried out, "Sheriff Black!

"They went up to his room!" He did not have to say who.

Mary Lou and Maggie were equally alarmed and rushed to the table to hear Sonny's report.

"I didn't tell 'em the sheriff was up there!" Sonny implored. "They saw Doc Marion come down and figured it out right away."

What to do? Campbell and Beecher looked at each other, each waiting for the other to say. They were the only two customers left in the dining room, purposely having a late breakfast. It was actually a meeting to decide what to do about reviving the vigilance committee to handle the new outlaw problem, and the lack of interest from most of the merchants. The problem had occurred once before, resulting in several lost lives.

Finally, reluctant to volunteer, Beecher asked, "What do you think, Mr. Mayor?"

"I don't know," Campbell replied, then asked his son, "How long have they been up there?"

"No longer than it took me to run in here!" Sonny answered.

"Somebody's got to do something," Mary Lou interrupted. "We can't leave John Henry up there by himself with those killers."

"There's not much we can do," Campbell said. "With just John and me against four hardened gunmen, we wouldn't stand a chance. We need to get more of our men involved—Gordon Luck,

Jim Low, Leon Bloodworth—we need more than just the two of us."

"Somebody's got to do something to help him," Mary Lou insisted. "I'll go up there."

"No," John Beecher said, forced to volunteer to save face. "It ain't your place to go up against those outlaws. I'll go. I ain't heard any gunshots, so they might not be plannin' to kill him. Maybe I can make 'em see he ain't in any shape to give 'em trouble and they'll just leave him be."

"You can't trust those men, John," Campbell cautioned. "You be careful you don't get shot."

"You can count on that," Beecher said. He drew his handgun and spun the cylinder to make sure it was fully loaded. He retrieved his hat from the back of the chair next to his, settled it squarely on his head, and rose to his feet. With a determined nod to Campbell, he turned and started for the door.

Outside the dining room, he walked down to the end of the hall to take the back stairs up to the second floor. When he reached the top step, he saw the door to the sheriff's room standing open. He hesitated for a moment, reluctant to enter the room, before forcing himself to go on. When he walked through the open doorway, he was confronted by the four intruders, standing in a semicircle around the foot of the bed. Three of the four automatically reached for their guns.

Knowing he was already outdrawn, Beecher held his hands up before him. "Hold on!" he cried out.

Yarborough grinned, sensing Beecher's reluctance to fight. He was the only one who had not gone for the .44 on his hip. "Howdy, neighbor," Yarborough greeted the shaken Beecher. "Come to pay your respects to the sheriff, there? We did, too, but it looks like ol' John Henry has done checked out on us." He told his men to put their guns away.

"Is he dead?" Arthur Campbell asked from the doorway behind Beecher, having been conscience stricken to follow the blacksmith upstairs.

"Yes, sir, he is," Yarborough answered. "We came up to see him just now and this is the way we found him. Near as I can figure, he musta had trouble breathin' or somethin' and he just cashed in."

"He wasn't having any trouble breathing when I brought him his breakfast this morning." Mary Lou, a step behind Campbell, was carrying the shotgun Maggie kept in the kitchen.

Astonished to see the woman brandishing the shotgun, all four outlaws stood still while she went to the head of the bed to take a closer look at the deceased lawman.

"What's all this bruising around his neck?" she questioned aloud.

Yarborough decided it would not serve his purpose to simply kill the three of them to stop their questions. He reasoned that he would have need for their services before he was through raping the town, so he displayed a friendly smile for Mary Lou's benefit. "That's what I was wonderin'," he replied. "Right, boys? We noticed them marks right off. We was just talkin' about 'em when this feller walked in." He nodded in Beecher's direction. "Near as I can figure, Sheriff Black couldn't get his breath and he was grabbin' at his throat to try to get some air. I've seen it happen before when a man's about to die."

He saw the skepticism in the eyes of all three of the town's citizens, but he knew there was little they could do about it. "I'm sorry I didn't get a chance to talk to Black before he died," he continued with his charade. "I came up here to tell him 'bout my plans to protect the town and how I was lookin' forward to workin' with him when he was on his feet again. I'm glad you came up here, Mr. Mayor. I was lookin' for you, anyway. Wanted to let you know you didn't have to worry 'bout your town bein' without protection from outlaws."

It was a little too much for Mary Lou to swallow. She couldn't help herself from commenting. "How are we going to believe you aim to help protect Cheyenne?" She pointed to Troy Womack. "That's the man who shot Sheriff Black, when he tried to stop him from attacking a defenseless widow. Are you going to arrest him?"

"That was a case of mistaken identity," Yarborough quickly replied when he could not think of any reasonable explanation.

"She wasn't nothin' but a damn whore," Troy blurted.

"Like I said," Yarborough went on, "he thought she was somebody else. And it was Black's fault that he got shot. He shouldn'ta pulled on Womack. If he was alive, he'd most likely admit that it was his fault. He pulled that gun and Troy didn't have no choice but to protect hisself." He glanced from face to face to see if he was getting away with his story.

From the expressions he read, he had to conclude that he wasn't. *They ain't as dumb as I thought,* he told himself. *But whether they believe it or not, there ain't nothing they can do to stop me.* "Sometimes things don't turn out like they oughta. But all you folks in this town need to know is that we're here to take care of you. I'm your new sheriff and I'll be keepin' an eye out for anything that don't look right." He looked at Campbell. "Now, I reckon you'd like to clear this body outta your hotel."

"Yeah, I reckon," Campbell said while trying to hide his emotions of disgust and fear for his town.

"Come on, boys," Yarborough said. "We need to let the rest of the town know that everythin's under control, and we'll be takin' care of the law from now on." With a smug grin for Campbell as he walked by, Yarborough led his men out of the room.

When they were back on the street outside, Yarborough split them up to inform the rest of the merchants that there was a new sheriff in town and it was going to cost them for their protection. "Troy, you and Tiny start out on this side of the street. Red'll come with me. I wanna pay a little visit to the telegraph office. We don't want nobody to get any ideas of wirin' the army about what's goin' on here."

CHAPTER 10

Not sure if his hunch was right or not, Cole pointed the big bay toward the stable at the edge of town. He figured that to be the best place to find out if Troy Womack and the men he had met at the cabin by the river had actually returned to Cheyenne. He was still berating himself for having gone on a wild-goose chase to Iron Mountain when he should have been more concerned about staying close to Mary Lou and the other folks in Cheyenne.

Those were the thoughts that troubled him as he pulled up to the corral beside the stable.

"Cole . . . Damn . . ." Leon started as he strode hurriedly from the stable to meet him. He looked back over his shoulder toward town as if afraid someone might have seen Cole ride in. "I'm damn glad to see you, but I ain't sure you'll be glad you came back when you find out what's happenin' here." Before Cole could respond, Leon went on, spewing words in panic. "We thought you mighta been dead. That Womack feller is back in town and he's brung three gunmen with him. He's took over as sheriff, at least some feller with him has—"

"Whoa," Cole interrupted him. "Slow down. Who took over as sheriff? What about John Henry Black?"

"They killed John Henry—said he died on his own—but everybody knows they murdered him. Mary Lou said he was gettin' better every day till her and Arthur Campbell found him dead with them four gunmen standin' around his bed."

"Is she all right?" Cole asked, and when Leon said she was, he asked, "Is Harley still here?"

"No," Leon answered. "Him and Carrie left here, headin' for Gordon Luck's place. I don't know if they stayed there or not."

"Him and Carrie?" Cole responded, confused. "Go back and tell me exactly what's happened.

Leon went back to the beginning when Douglas and Martha Green found out about Carrie's life before she'd married their son. Like most everyone else, Cole was amazed to learn of Carrie's past life and was genuinely sorry to hear of the Greens' reaction toward her. Leon told Cole the circumstances that enabled Yarborough and his men to take over the town and the dire straits the towns-people found themselves in.

"What about the vigilance committee?" Cole asked. "The last time this happened, you folks got together and rid the town of that wild bunch."

"I don't know, Cole," Leon replied. "This time it's different, I reckon. There's four of 'em, and they all look like they'd just as soon cut your liver out as say 'howdy-do.' Nobody I've talked to wants to go up against 'em—and I reckon that includes me."

"Nobody?" Cole asked. "Beecher, Low, Campbell, Green—they've all got families and businesses to protect. What about Gordon Luck? He led the vigilantes before."

"I ain't heard nothin' from Gordon," Leon said. "When Harley rode out with Carrie Green, he said he was gonna tell Gordon what was goin' on here in town, but I ain't seen him. Harley had to get outta town 'cause them four killers were lookin' for him 'cause they saw that fancy saddle he had on his horse, remember? They think he's the one who shot Womack's two brothers."

Cole paused to consider the situation. It was difficult to imagine that the town was in serious danger of being destroyed by a ruthless gang of outlaws. And he found it hard to believe the men of the town were not going to rise up to drive the unwelcome visitors out. He could understand the reluctance of an individual to stand up to four hardened gunmen alone. He didn't care for those odds, himself. With safety in numbers, there should be a dozen men who could take up their weapons and overpower the four. Maybe they just needed a leader.

He decided to go talk to Gordon Luck. Gordon had led the citizens before. Maybe he would lead them again. And if he would, Cole would be the first volunteer to go with him. He wasn't a resident of the town, but there was someone he was concerned for. "You say these four men are stayin' at the hotel?"

"That's right," Leon answered. "They took a couple of rooms there."

"What about the hotel dinin' room?" Cole asked. When Leon looked puzzled, Cole asked, "The women who work there, are they all right?" He was reluctant to let on that he was especially concerned for Mary Lou Cagle.

"As far as I know," Leon said. "Maggie shut it down, since there ain't nobody in the hotel but them four outlaws, and they eat at the saloon. Leastways, that's what she told Arthur Campbell, but the truth of the matter is she ain't fixin' no food for the likes of them four. Most of Maggie's business comes from folks here in town, not just the hotel, so there's more'n a few folks wishin' she hadn't closed up." Leon shook his head when he thought about it. "I know I wish she hadn't shut it down. It's gonna make it hard on me. I never did care much for my own cookin'."

"They ain't even cookin' for themselves?" Cole asked, still trying to gain information about Mary Lou.

"They ain't even there," Leon replied. "They decided it wasn't safe for three women to stay there as long as Womack and his gang were upstairs over 'em. Maggie and Mary Lou went to stay with Beulah in that little shack she and her husband built up on Crow Creek."

"Good," Cole replied at once, a great burden having been lifted from his mind. He had been reluctant to ride out to Gordon Luck's sawmill and leave the women unprotected in town. That problem solved, he could ride out to talk to Gordon about organizing a lynching party for Troy Womack and his three friends. "I'll get goin'. Maybe Gordon and I can get this thing started and clean your new guests outta here."

"Watch yourself, Cole," Leon warned. "You'd best ride out the back. That one called Yarborough has set himself up in the sheriff's office, and he might see you if you go out the way you came in."

"Rider comin'!" Sammy Hill sang out. He dropped the drawknife he had been working with and picked up his rifle. Cooter, his younger brother, ran to the back of the shed to fetch his twenty-gauge shotgun. With all the trouble in town, Gordon Luck had cautioned his two young employees to keep an eye out for strangers. The boys were joined a second later by Harley Branch.

"Where?" Harley asked, having not sighted the rider yet.

"Yonder," Sammy said and pointed to the willows down by the creek.

Harley squinted, silently cursing his failing eyesight until spotting the lone rider coming up from the creek. A grin spread slowly across his face as he recognized the familiar figure riding in easy rhythm with the bay horse's gait. He walked out of the shed and stood waiting by a stack of lumber, the grin still in place. "Well, I declare, if you ain't a sight for sore eyes," he said as Cole rode up. "How come you're on that bay? Where's Joe?"

Cole greeted his friend, then told him about the ambush that took Joe's life. "I wasn't sure I'd see you here. Thought you mighta gone back to Medicine Bear's camp."

"I was thinkin' about it," Harley said, "but I had to change my plans."

"Carrie?"

"Yeah. You heard?"

"Yeah, Leon Bloodworth told me about it."

"I decided to stay on here a little while, just in case you showed up," Harley said. "Tell you the truth, I wasn't sure you weren't dead when that other Womack feller rode back in town like he didn't have nothin' to worry about."

"I lost his trail after a little snow covered up his tracks," Cole said. "Then I made the wrong guess and wound up sayin' howdy to Raymond Potter up at Iron Mountain while Womack and his friends were headin' here to Cheyenne." He went on to tell Harley that he had ridden out there to see if Gordon Luck was ready to get his vigilantes together again and take back their town. "Where is Gordon?" He looked behind Harley to see the two young Hill brothers coming out of the shed to join them, but he didn't see Gordon.

"Say howdy to Sammy and Cooter," Harley said and waited until Cole exchanged greetings with the boys before answering his question. "Gordon's up at the church rebuilding all his pews. I reckon he's plannin' on doin' some high-powered preachin'. Carrie's helpin' him with some curtains and stuff." The grin returned and he winked at Cole. "Looks to me like they're gettin' along pretty good."

Cole nodded, aware of the implication.

Harley's face turned serious then. "Gordon ain't plannin' on ridin' with the vigilantes again. He said the merchants have to learn to take care of

their own business and not count on him to come
save 'em every time a drifter shoots somebody."

"Seems to me this is a little bigger than a drifter
shootin' another drifter in a saloon fight," Cole
said. "I never figured Gordon would try to stay
outta the trouble. His business depends on more
folks comin' in to build businesses—just like the
stores and the saloons and everybody else."

"He's up at the church," Harley said. "Looks to
me like he's thinkin' more like a preacher now
than he did before. Thinkin' he's against hangin's
and such. Too much religion will do that to a feller.
Go up and talk to him 'cause you'll need all the
men you can get to go up against that gang of
killers." He shrugged and added, "'Course you
know you can count on me."

Carrie held up a curtain for Gordon to see and
give his approval. "I can make no claim to be a
seamstress, but I think they'll do the job."

"They'll do just fine," a beaming Gordon Luck
responded. "That was what was missing—a woman's
touch. Fixin' up the benches helps, but I never
thought about hangin' curtains on the windows."

Her smile told him that she was pleased by his
approval.

He paused to watch her as she walked back to the
room behind the rough pulpit to prepare the other
curtains. In the short time Carrie had been there,
the two of them had become very comfortable together. He couldn't deny having had concerns
about her past, which she openly confessed to.

He had prayed on the subject last night, and he decided his God would have already forgiven her for her sins, so how could he not do the same? She had expressed an interest in being baptized to wash away her sordid past so it would be as if she was all new again. He had been hit hard after Mary Lou Cagle first accepted his proposal of marriage, then changed her mind.

For a while, he'd thought he would never consider marriage again, preferring to live without a woman. But the last couple of days had prompted him to think anew about someone to share his life with. Besides, Carrie was younger than Mary Lou. Further daydreaming was interrupted when he glanced toward the open door and saw Cole and Harley approaching the church. He didn't have to guess the reason for the visit.

"Howdy, Cole," Gordon called from the doorway. "I'm glad to see you're alive. Harley, there, was afraid harm had come to you."

"Gordon," Cole returned. "Looks like you've been workin' pretty hard on the church buildin'." He noticed Carrie then, at Gordon's elbow, having heard his greeting from the back of the church. "Carrie. Glad to see you."

Feeling that she owed him an explanation, since he had saved her from the fate Malcolm and Travis Womack had planned for her, she immediately came out with it. "I guess you know by now that I wasn't completely honest about who I was, and I owe you an explanation."

"I don't see how you owe me anything," Cole said. "I'm just glad to see that you're all right." He nodded toward Gordon. "Looks to me like you found a good place to light."

Gordon nodded in return. "That's what I've been tellin' her." He was relieved to see there was evidently nothing between Carrie and Cole beyond a casual friendship. He had harbored some concern about the possibility, especially since Cole had rescued her from the men who had killed her husband. He would not have given it any thought had he known what everyone close to Cole and Mary Lou Cagle had figured out long ago—that those two were somehow fated to end up together.

Getting to the purpose of the visit by Cole, Gordon asked, "Are things any better in town? I reckon that's the reason you rode out here to see me."

"I reckon," Cole replied. "To answer your question, no, things ain't any better in town. Matter of fact, they're worse to hear Leon Bloodworth tell it. I ain't talked to anybody else 'cause I'm not ready to let Womack and his friends know I'm back. I figured we'd need to get up a sizable posse, so the odds would be too much for those four to put up a fight. What do you think?"

"I think you're right," Gordon said. "You're gonna need a right sizable posse. Trouble is, where you gonna get it? Jim Low came out to talk to me about the same thing, wantin' to know if I would lead them. I asked him, lead who? And he said that so far he could count on John Beecher and maybe Leon, and himself. Arthur Campbell and Douglas Green are the main two that want those outlaws run outta town, and neither one is willin' to put on a gun to help do it. The few folks that attend my church every Sunday don't have a lot to do with Cheyenne. They're farmers and ranchers, and they ain't interested in risking their lives to save that sinful town. So I reckon I ain't, either. I think the town folk are just gonna have to ride it out and before long those four gunmen will decide to move on before the army or the U.S. marshals come after 'em."

Cole was disappointed to hear Gordon's position on an attempt to retake the town from the criminal element that had moved in. And he could see that talk about the murder of John Henry Black would not be enough to change his mind. "Sounds to me like you've pretty much made up your mind on the matter."

"Pretty much," Gordon said. He hesitated a moment, but decided to offer his advice. "I know the town's in a bad fix right now, but it looks to me like you and Harley decided to cast your lot with the Crow Indians, anyway," It was an obvious reference to Cole's long braids and his buckskins. "You've answered the call to help the town folk before and still the town's in trouble. It ain't really fair to ask you to fight their fight for them again, and if I was you, I wouldn't stick my neck out this time."

"Maybe you're right," Cole said. "I'll think about it." He understood Gordon's attitude, but he could not in good conscience abandon the people of Cheyenne to the evil whims of four lawless predators. There were good people in Cheyenne, set on building a respectable town, and some of them were bound to become victims of the vicious killers. "Well," he said in parting, "I just wanted to see where you stood on the matter. I guess I'll be gettin' along now."

"The least I can do is offer you some food. Or coffee at least," Gordon said.

"Yes," Carrie spoke up. "Let me fix you some coffee. If you're hungry, there's a couple of biscuits left from breakfast."

"Thanks just the same," Cole replied, "but I've got some things to do before dark. So I'd best be on my way." He nodded good-bye to Carrie and turned to leave. He had maintained a feeling of responsibility for Carrie even after Douglas and Martha Green had graciously welcomed her into their home. He now felt that he could willingly pass that responsibility to someone else. And Gordon Luck seemed to be eagerly stepping up to accept it. It was a good fit for both of them.

With Carrie finally off his conscience, Cole's thoughts automatically shifted to Harley. His little elf-like friend was wearing a target on his back because of his fancy for Travis Womack's Mexican saddle. And to make matters more dangerous, Troy Womack thought Harley was the one who killed both of his brothers. It was important to keep Harley out of range of any shooting wars in town. In spite of his bluster, Harley was getting old, and as a consequence, his eyesight was fading and his reactions were slowing down.

As Cole walked back to his horse, Harley fell in beside him. "Whatcha gonna do, partner?" he pressed. "You ain't still thinkin' 'bout roundin' up a posse, are you? 'Cause if you are, I'm afraid you're gonna find out that Gordon's right about that.

There ain't but a couple of men that'll volunteer, and they'll most likely back out when they find out nobody else is gonna join the party."

There was no response from Cole. He just continued walking toward his horse.

"Whaddaya think about what Gordon said?" Harley asked. "You think we might as well go on back to Medicine Bear's village and to hell with Cheyenne?" When there was still no answer from his silent friend, he asked, "You're goin' after them four fellers, ain'tcha?"

"I reckon," Cole finally spoke. "If somebody doesn't, Cheyenne's gonna be like Laramie with an outlaw for a sheriff and his gang of killers to back him up."

"Well, dad-blast-it, I reckon it'll just be the two of us, 'cause if Gordon Luck ain't willin' to lead a posse, ain't none of them town folk gonna step up."

"Reckon not, Harley. I've got another job for you. It's important and I need someone I can depend on." It had come to him that he could kill two birds with one stone. He could keep Harley away from potential gunplay while having someone watch over Mary Lou at the same time.

"You can depend on me," Harley said. "What is it you want me to do?"

"Leon said that Maggie and Mary Lou rode out to Beulah's house to stay till things quiet down in town. I don't know much about Beulah's husband, but from what little bit I do know, seems to me he's a little long in the tooth to protect three women. I need to know those women are gonna be safe, no matter what goes on in town. And if you're watchin' over 'em, I won't worry about 'em." He looked Harley in the eye. "What about it? Can I count on you to take care of 'em?"

Harley wasn't fooled. He knew the real reason Cole wanted him up on Crow Creek was to keep him out of harm's way. He also knew that he was getting too old to be going into a situation like the one in town, and might end up costing Cole if his young partner had to worry about him. He could also appreciate the way Cole had said it, in an effort not to hurt his sense of pride, so he responded enthusiastically. "You can depend on me. I'll make sure them ladies are safe."

"I knew I could," Cole replied. "I 'preciate it, Harley."

They walked to the barn. When he had fled with Carrie, Harley had brought with him Cole's pack-horse and all Cole's possibles that he had left in town. In addition to his cooking utensils, there were the various weapons Cole had acquired while disposing of Malcolm and Travis Womack, including his bow. Yellow Calf had helped him fashion the bow, and with the task ahead of him, he had a feeling it might come in handy.

When they returned to the front of the church where Cole had left his horse, he asked, "Do you know where Beulah's cabin is?"

"Not right off," Harley said. "I mean, I ain't ever been there, but I expect I'll find it easy enough if it's on Crow Creek like Leon said it was." He scratched his head while he tried to recall if he had ever been far beyond Gordon's sawmill. "Gordon most likely knows where it is. I'll ask him." He took a step back to give the big bay room to turn away from the rail. "Just what are you fixin' to do?"

"I don't know yet," Cole answered. "I'm gonna think about it." He nudged the bay with his heels and left Harley to stare after him until he disappeared among the willows on the creek bank.

"Lord, partner, I hope to hell you know what you're doin'," Harley muttered to himself.

He had not been lying when he told Harley he didn't know what he was going to do. He knew, however, that he had little chance of getting all four outlaws if he chose to seek them out in a saloon or hotel when they were all in one spot. In an out-and-out shoot-out, he might get two of them, and that was if he was lucky. He was going to have to take them on one by one and the first thing he needed to know was which saloon was their favorite. He needed to talk to Leon Bloodworth again. Leon seemed to have an eye on most of the activity going on in town.

It was past sundown when Cole got back to town. He thought it wise to come in behind the stable and enter through the back door, anyway. The odor of burned bacon told him that Leon was cooking his supper on the little stove behind the tack room. After dropping the bay's reins to the ground outside the door, he walked into the darkened stable to find Leon hovering over a small frying pan, tending his bacon. "Smells like you burnt it a little," Cole said as he approached.

"Whoa!" Leon exclaimed, startled. With the

frying pan still in his hand, he almost knocked his coffeepot off the flat surface of the stove. He looked around, spotting Cole then. "Cole!" he blurted, relieved when he saw who it was. "Damn, you scared the shit outta me! You've been livin' with those Injuns too long. Didn't nobody see you come in, did they? That bunch'll be down here in a minute if they did."

"Nobody saw me," Cole assured him. Then he couldn't help remarking, "I figured I oughta come by to help you cook some bacon that's fit to eat."

"I like it a little crisp," Leon claimed. "I wish to hell Maggie hadda kept the dinin' room open. I'm always cookin' everything too done or downright raw. You want some of this bacon?"

"No thanks. I'd enjoy a cup of coffee, though. You any better at makin' coffee than you are fryin' meat?"

"Well, it ain't hurt me none so far, so I reckon it won't kill you."

It just occurred to Cole that he had eaten nothing since breakfast that morning. He often forgot to eat when he had his mind on something important. Now that it was brought to mind, he decided that he was hungry. "I've got some dried deer meat in my packs. If I can borrow that fryin' pan, I'll cook some of it—enough for you if you want some."

Done with the small talk, Leon cut straight to the topic that mattered most to everyone in town. "Whaddaya gonna do, Cole? Is Gordon gonna round up a posse?"

"Reckon not," Cole replied between sips of hot

coffee. "He doesn't see that it's his problem. What about here in town? Is anybody willin' to fight yet?"

Leon shook his head. "I don't know. Right now everybody's kinda keepin' their head down." He stroked his beard thoughtfully, then commented. "I figured Gordon would be one of the first to help out. Hell, he was the main one when we had that deal with Slade Corbett."

"Well," Cole continued, "I really can't say as I blame him. From what you've told me, that's a pretty rough bunch to tangle with. Besides, I think he's got other things on his mind." He paused to turn the meat in the pan. "I need you to tell me where the four outlaws usually hang out."

"That's easy enough," Leon said. "This time of night they'll be at the Cowboy's Rest, eatin' and drinkin' and raisin' hell."

"All four of 'em?"

"Usually," Leon answered. "That big 'un, the one they call Tiny, will be upstairs with one of the women most of the time. Louella's the one he likes best. She said it was like 'rasslin' with a horse, said he ain't got a brain in his head. He claimed he was the one who killed John Henry, laughin' about how John Henry tried to fight, but he grabbed hold of his neck and wrung it like a chicken. Got big hands, Louella said. Said she could set her whole fanny in one of his hands." He shook his head when he recalled the conversation. "Louella told him to call on one of the other girls, 'cause she didn't like the way he was gettin' rough with her. She said he warn't too happy about that and left a good-sized lump on the side of her face."

"What about the Womack fellow?" Cole was especially interested in him for a couple of reasons. He was the one who put the two bullets into John Henry Black's chest and laid him up helpless in his room. And he was out to kill Harley, blaming him for the shootings that Cole had done. Losing Womack's trail had also caused him to ride a hell of a long way to a dead end at Iron Mountain. That hadn't set too well with Cole, either. Womack alone had been the only one Cole had a score to settle with. He knew nothing about the three Womack had hooked up with, other than what he had learned about them since they rode into Cheyenne.

"Womack's as bad as the other three rattlesnakes," Leon said. "But the king snake is the one they call Yarborough."

"Yarborough?" Cole reacted at once. "Did you say Yarborough?"

"Yeah, that's what they called him. He's the one callin' the shots. You can tell the others jump when he opens his mouth. And he's the one doin' all the talkin' about takin' the sheriff's job and protectin' the town.

It struck Cole then that Leon had mentioned one of the outlaws called Tiny. And he didn't even take notice. "What about the other one? Is his name Red?"

"Yeah," Leon replied, surprised. "How'd you know that?"

"I've had the pleasure of meetin' those three before," Cole said, not surprised that Yarborough would try to take over a whole town.

"That Yarborough feller's got a crazy streak in his head about Carrie Green, too, lookin' for her all the time, only he calls her Corina. He asks me if I've seen her every time he comes in here and I tell him every time that Carrie's gone from Cheyenne and ain't comin' back."

Leon started shifting from one foot to the other as he became more and more worked up about the siege the four villains had placed the town under. "And they ain't paid a dime for anything they buy. They order horse feed and hay like them horses belonged to the king of England and pay for it with promises. Douglas Green told me they've about stripped his shelves bare, and he ain't got paid a nickel."

By the time Leon had finished lamenting the certain demise of their town, Cole had gotten an accurate picture of the evil that had fallen upon them. He was more aware than ever that the town had to come together to stop the rape of the growing community.

"The killin's already started," Leon continued. "I ain't just talkin' 'bout John Henry Black. Day before yesterday, that one they call Red shot Harvey Settles down—said Harvey pulled a gun on him."

Cole pictured the meek telegraph operator at the train station.

Leon cocked an eyebrow at Cole. "Harvey Settles ain't never pulled a gun on nobody, especially a murderin' out-and-out gunman like Red Swann. Arthur Campbell said he figured Red went there to make sure nobody sent any telegrams asking for help from the U.S. Marshal Service or the army.

Harvey likely told him he couldn't hardly refuse to send a telegram if somebody wanted one. That was enough to cost Harvey his life. He shoulda just told that murderin' son of a bitch that he wouldn't send any. Arthur said he was fixin' to wire Fort Laramie for some help, but he didn't get to it before that feller got to Harvey."

There was little doubt what Yarborough and his friends had in mind. It was to clean the town out of everything they could with no hesitation to shoot anyone who protested or got in their way. And to Cole's way of thinking, they didn't plan to take long in doing it. Leon said they had killed the telegraph operator, but surely Yarborough had enough sense to know that the railroad would investigate the loss of contact with their operator. It was clear to Cole the looters had to be stopped right away before more innocent people were killed. *Hell*, he thought, *it's not my responsibility. If the folks in this town don't care enough to fight to save all they've built, it's not up to me to do it for them.*

He shook his head. There was no sense in thinking such thoughts. He knew he couldn't turn his back and walk away. Too many good people called Cheyenne home—Mary Lou and Maggie were foremost in his mind. But also the many people who had invested in the future of the town and built businesses to accommodate the growing population.

As if reading his thoughts, Leon asked, "Do you know where Jim Low's cabin is?" Low owned the saddle shop next to John Beecher's forge.

Cole said that he did not.

"It's about a mile down the creek just past the spot where it forks to go around a big rock. If you're wantin' to help, Jim's holdin' a meetin' there tonight with a few of the others to talk about gettin' rid of Yarborough and his gang."

It came as a surprise to Cole, since he had been told repeatedly that there was no longer anyone in town willing to risk going up against the outlaws. Maybe Low and the others were just smart enough to keep it quiet. They were going to need all the help they could get, so he decided to ride down there and see what they had in mind. "I'll leave my packhorse with you for a little while," he said to Leon. "I've got what I'll need for the time being and I'll come back if I need anything else."

"I figured with the way things are goin' around here, you and Harley might be thinkin' about goin' back to that Crow village. I don't know what you've got in mind, but you'd best be careful if you're gonna stay in town."

"All I've got in mind right now is to see how many men show up at Low's place tonight, and hear what they're plannin' to do. What about you? You goin'?"

It was fairly obvious the question made Leon uncomfortable, since he had taken a bigger role in organizing the vigilantes before. "Ah, no, I reckon not," he stammered. "One or two of them fellers usually show up here after supper to make sure I'm takin' care of their horses. I expect they wouldn't like it if I weren't here. Might cause some trouble."

Cole nodded, but made no reply. It was his

guess that a lot of the other men in town had their excuses as well.

Low's cabin was not hard to find, even after the sun went down. East of the town of Cheyenne, Cole remembered having seen the cabin before, but he had never had the opportunity to find out who it belonged to. The cabin was a simple affair with just two rooms, a main room with a stone fireplace that served as a parlor as well as a kitchen and bedroom. Being a bachelor, Jim had no need for anything of a fancier nature. Seeing several horses tied at the corral beside the cabin, Cole guided his up beside them.

"Evenin', Mr. Bonner." A soft voice belonging to young Sonny Campbell greeted him from the shadow of the cabin. He stepped out of the shadows as Cole dismounted.

"Evenin', Sonny," Cole returned. "I see you got the job as lookout."

"Yes, sir. I volunteered. Daddy's inside with the others, so I told 'em I'd keep a watch out to make sure none of those gunmen surprised the meeting."

"Good idea," Cole said. "And you're doin' a good job, too. I didn't know you were there till you said something." His comment pleased the young boy, as evidenced by his wide smile. Without thinking about it, Cole pulled his rifle from the saddle sling and went in to join the meeting.

There was a pause in the discussion when the door opened and Cole walked inside. It resumed immediately with greetings of welcome from some of the men gathered before the fireplace.

"Evenin'," Cole responded and settled himself on the floor on one side of the fire, the three chairs having been claimed by the early arrivals.

"I'd offer you some coffee, Cole," Jim said, "but you'll have to wait till somebody finishes with their cup."

"No, thanks," Cole replied. "I helped Leon Bloodworth empty his pot just before I rode out here." He looked around the half circle of men. There were only five—Harold Chestnut, Arthur Campbell, John Beecher, Douglas Green, and Jim Low. Of the five, Cole knew Chestnut, Campbell, and Green could not be counted on to participate in any gunplay. That left three possible guns, counting himself, and that was not enough for the job at hand.

"Glad you showed up, Cole," Jim said. "I wasn't sure you were comin' back." Guessing what Cole was thinking, Jim went on. "I was hopin' there'd be a few more showin' up. Maybe they'll show up yet. It's still early."

"Suppose they don't," Cole said. "You plannin' to go against those four outlaws with the six of us here? . . . seven if you're countin' Sonny outside."

The question brought a quick response. "No," Arthur Campbell replied at once. "You can't count Sonny in on this. He's too young. I promised his mother that he would not be involved in any kind of gun violence."

No one objected, since Campbell's son Claude

had been killed by a cold-blooded murderer named Sanchez only a little over a year earlier.

"We have to be realistic," Harold Chestnut, the postmaster, said. "I'm here to support you in any way I can, but I'm no good with a gun. Arthur and Douglas are in the same boat. We're not gunmen, and frankly, we're too old to try to act like we are. I doubt we'd scare any of those animals."

"I understand what you're sayin', Harold," John Beecher said. "But if we don't stop those bastards, they're gonna wipe us all out. Now, with Cole here, we've got a helluva lot better chance to overpower 'em and lock 'em up in the jail—maybe hold 'em till the marshal in Omaha sends a deputy to haul the lot of 'em to prison, or a cavalry patrol from Fort Laramie comes after 'em."

"Why bother with putting them in jail?" Douglas Green asked. "Why not just hang them? Hell, they've already killed the sheriff and a telegraph operator."

"Well, you're right," Beecher allowed. "We'd be justified in hangin' the four." He looked around the gathering, nodding enthusiastically. "But we need to be strong in numbers. If there ain't but three of us that goes after 'em, they ain't likely to back down, and somebody's gonna get hurt."

Cole said nothing as he listened to the discussion while it went back and forth. After an hour or more, it was easy to see that Beecher and Low were not going to be successful in persuading the other men to participate in an armed confrontation with the four hardened criminals. Finally, he decided he had heard enough, so he got to his feet. "Gentlemen, I reckon I've heard all I need to hear, so I'll be sayin' good night to you." With no further explanation, he walked out, leaving them to wonder.

He was already stepping up into his saddle when John Beecher came outside after him. "Cole," Beecher implored, "Are you sayin' just let the bastards gut the town and do nothing to stop them?"

"I didn't say that at all," Cole replied, turned the bay's head away from the corral, and rode back toward town.

CHAPTER 11

Louella Sykes prepared to go downstairs after a visit with one of the cowhands from the Lazy-C ranch. A young man, little more than a boy actually, the cowboy came to the saloon to see her every chance he could. Oftentimes, he didn't have the money to go upstairs with her, but even on those occasions, she took the time to have a social visit downstairs. Louella had practiced her profession long enough to have lost any belief in fairy tales and love's innocence. But she had to admit she was touched by the young cowboy's infatuation with her. He never called upon Lil or Junie, always Louella. At times, she had allowed her mind to fantasize about the possibility of escaping the world she had chosen for herself those many years ago— most recently, after she heard about the plight of Carrie Green—or Corina Burnett, as Flint Yarborough called her. She didn't know Carrie, but she knew about her. Prostitutes learned about everything that happened in a town the size of Cheyenne sooner or later. Men talk. She found that she felt happy and sad for Carrie Green, for she had climbed out of her sordid past to gain respectability, if only for a brief two years. It might have lasted longer were it not for the arrival of Yarborough and his scum. That thought brought to mind the simpleminded brute Tiny Weaver, and Louella unconsciously reached up to feel the bruise on the side of her face.

Finished with the straightening of the room, she lectured herself to put away foolish thoughts that only served to make her melancholy.

On her way back downstairs to join the evening crowd, she stopped at the head of the steps. There he was, that sneering oversized lout with a child's brain, a selfishly evil man-child who revolted violently when denied his wishes. He was looking for her, she knew that, and she told herself that she was not up to fighting off his barbaric advances, so she stepped back away from the stairs. If she was lucky, he might not have glanced up and seen her.

She hurried down to the end of the hall and went down the back stairs to the porch behind the kitchen. A cautious look in both directions told her there was no one to see her leave the saloon in the darkness of the alley, and she made her way quickly to the crude building that housed the rooms of the prostitutes as well as those of the kitchen help.

Once inside her room with the door bolted, she resigned herself to a quiet evening alone. She regretted retiring from the saloon while the evening was still fairly young, but her potential for earning much money was slight, anyway, and had been ever since Yarborough and his friends came to town. Lil and Junie should appreciate the lack of competition with her gone. Maybe Tiny Weaver would turn his attention to one of them. As soon as she thought it, she knew she wouldn't wish that on anyone. Further thoughts were interrupted by the sudden crashing of her door as it was kicked nearly off its hinges and slammed against the inside wall, making a sound like a gunshot. Louella's terrified scream drifted no longer than a few seconds on the night wind before the giant hand that clamped over her mouth silenced her forever.

With the smug expression of a petulant child, Tiny walked past the shattered door and stood outside for a moment to think about the woman lying on the bed behind him. A slow grin began to form on his rough features when he told himself, *she ain't gonna be nobody's woman but mine now.* An instant later, he felt the solid impact against his chest, causing him to step backward against the doorjamb. Thinking he had been hit with a heavy rock, he struggled to stand solid on his feet again until he felt the intense pain shoot through his chest like that of a white-hot poker searing his lungs. He looked down to discover the shaft of an arrow protruding from his body. Confused, he stared in disbelief at the cruel missile for a moment before he attempted to run toward the saloon for help, only to be staggered by a second arrow in his lower back. The massive outlaw took two more steps before crashing to his knees like a wounded buffalo. Poised there for only a moment, he slowly keeled over to land on his side.

Cole climbed out of the wagon bed he had used for cover and walked over to confirm his kill. He had found the wagon parked behind

John Beecher's blacksmith shop to be a convenient platform from which to fire his arrows, and he thought about the blacksmith at the meeting earlier that evening. *You've got one less to worry about,* he thought as he stood for a few moments looking down at the dying man.

It was his first look at one of the three outlaws that Womack had joined up with since he had encountered them at Murphy's Store, but it was easy to tell this was the one called Tiny. Although it was obvious Tiny was not likely to move, Cole took the precaution to relieve him of his weapon before he went to see if he could help the woman.

Inside the broken door, he found Louella lying sideways across the small cot she slept on. He shifted her limp body around on the cot and covered her with a blanket. Then he stood over her for a moment while he silently apologized for not getting there in time to prevent her brutal murder. *I could have done for him before he came to you, but I didn't think he would want to kill you.* He could have shot Tiny in the street when the hulking bully attacked a young cowboy in front of the saloon, sending the young man to find a doctor to treat a broken jaw. But had he shot him then, Tiny's three companions would have been alerted to the fact that he had tracked them down. By taking one of them quietly, the other three could not be sure it was not a random killing.

"I'm sorry, miss," Cole whispered, turned, and left.

Outside, he paused to check on the body lying in the alley behind the saloon. Tiny was still alive, but barely breathing. Cole was not sure if the brute was past suffering or not, but he did not want to use his handgun to make certain. He was not ready to call spectators out of the saloon with the report of a pistol. *We'll wait a while,* he decided. *Maybe your friends will come looking for you.* He looked around then for the best place to lie in wait and decided the wagon he had used before was his choice. He went back to it and crawled up in the wagon bed to wait out the cold night.

The wait was not as long as he had expected, for after an hour or so, one of the other women came out of the saloon and discovered the body lying in the alley. Her screams were enough to alert the town, even had she not run back inside to report the killing. In less than a minute, a small crowd poured out the back door of the Cowboy's Rest and gathered around the body. Cole's plan to eliminate one or more of the remaining outlaws was not to be, for about nine men and two women circled around the body.

The distance was not that great, but in the darkness of the alley he found that he could not make out the faces. He concentrated on one man who could possibly be Troy Womack, but he could not be absolutely certain and could not risk killing an innocent man. He was reasonably sure he recognized Yarborough and maybe Red Swann as well. Due to the darkness of the alley, however, he could not be positive, so he slowly drew his rifle back from the side of the wagon where he had steadied his aim. There was nothing he could do but watch.

Someone discovered the shattered door on Louella's room and shouted to the others around Tiny's body. Most of the men went inside the room to find Louella while four remained by Tiny's body along with the two women. Cole had an idea that Yarborough and Swann would surely come to view the body.

Before long, more people heard about the killing and came to see. Soon there was a sizable crowd of spectators and with it, less chance of getting a clear shot. They were too occupied with gawking at the huge body to notice the man slide out the back of the wagon behind the smithy's forge and casually walk out of the alley.

Behind him, one of the four men standing over Tiny's body suddenly realized he had been left with the three ruthless outlaws, so he decided to follow the gawkers in to see the dead prostitute. Thinking that any protection was better than none, Lil Jones moved a little closer to the imposing figure of Flint Yarborough, no longer seeking to avoid him. "Why would Indians attack a town for no reason at all?" Lil wondered aloud.

"Why would they kill poor Louella?" Junie asked. "Don't the Indians usually capture women and carry them off?"

The three men ignored the questions of the women, more concerned with the targeting of Tiny.

"One of these local bastards caught Tiny when he couldn't see where it was comin' from," Red commented. "It sure as hell weren't no Injun attack."

Troy Womack stared down at the lifeless hulk, his mind focused on the two arrow shafts. He vividly remembered the man who had shot him, even while still pinned beneath his dead horse, and he silently cursed himself for not killing him then. He had panicked, thinking he was dying if he didn't get to a doctor right away, telling himself the man was as good as dead. He feared the devil had somehow freed himself and had found him again. "You're right," he finally spoke. "It weren't no Injun, but it was a devil that looks like a damn Injun, wears buckskins, braids his hair like an Injun, 'cause he lives with the Crows."

"How you know that?" Red asked.

"That's what that feller down at the stables told us. Remember what he said? Harley Branch, he's the one killed my brothers and came after me. He's the one who rode the horse with Malcolm's fancy saddle on it." Troy was certain of it, although it did occur to him that he wasn't sure if Malcolm's saddle was on the horse he killed on that night in the ravine. In that critical moment, the Mexican saddle had been of no importance.

"Harley Branch, huh?" Yarborough replied. "I thought he took off for good when he found out we were lookin' for him."

"Well, I reckon he decided to come back," Troy said.

"Maybe," Red said. "But hell, maybe it was somebody else using a bow. Coulda been whoever shot Tiny just didn't want nobody to hear the shots. And it coulda been anybody in this damn town."

"You might be right about that," Yarborough said. "Coulda been anybody, but we'd best keep our eyes peeled for that son of a bitch Troy's talkin' about. Somebody lookin' like an Injun. And just to be sure, if you do see somebody like that, shoot the son of a bitch and ask questions later."

"Makes sense to me," Red agreed. "Too bad about ol' Tiny, though." He squatted beside the body and started searching Tiny's pockets for anything of value. "Whoever took his gun, got any money he was totin', too."

"I reckon we're gonna have to show the folks in this town that we mean business," Yarborough said. "They mighta started thinkin' about some vigilante stuff. We'll clamp down on 'em so's they'll think twice about pickin' us off one by one like they did with Tiny." He stood there a few minutes longer, still fuming over what he saw as possibly a secret resistance move by some of the town's merchants. "We'll see about that," he expressed aloud.

"Well, it ain't helping none to stand around here in the cold jawin' about it," he decided. "Ain't that right, ladies? Let's go back where the fire and the whiskey is." With that, he turned about and headed back inside.

Troy and Red followed close on his heels, but the two women remained.

"We've got to take care of poor Louella," Lil called after them. "We can't just leave her be."

"We'd best get Horace Smith to come get her and fix her up for burial," Junie suggested.

"Yeah," Red called back, "tell him he can pick ol' Tiny up, too, if he wants to." He took a few steps more, then added, "Or leave him where he is. Tiny won't give a damn, and I sure as hell don't."

Troy Womack wasn't the only one who recalled that the man who had chased him up that ravine could have passed for a Crow warrior, even in spite of his sandy hair. Now that he had struck the first blow in the town's war with the outlaws, Cole was aware that he could not move freely in the town unless he changed his physical appearance drastically. The one advantage he had was the mistaken notion the outlaws had that the man who had killed the Womack brothers was named Harley Branch. Red and Yarborough knew him as Cole Bonner. Changing his appearance might keep them from recognizing him at a glance. The same might apply to Troy Womack, who had also seen him as he was now, looking more Indian than white.

It was not unusual for Horace Smith to be called out at night to pick up a body, although it was normally the result of a bar fight that went too far. As the town's barber, as well as the undertaker, he knew that it was all part of the job. It was a little sad on this night, however, for Louella Sykes had been a fixture at the Cowboy's Rest saloon almost since the day it opened. Horace would do the best he could to make her look pretty before they put her in the ground. As for the body of the man who'd killed her, Horace moved it out of the alley only as a service to the town, for no one stepped forward to pay for a burial. He intended to merely dig a hole in the ground and dump the body into it. He had no intention of building a box to put it in. *It'd be a waste of good lumber,* he thought. *And from the size of the son of a bitch, it'd take about twice as much as usual.* In fact, he wished that he could personally thank the person who was responsible for Tiny Weaver's death. He didn't bother to remove the huge body from his wagon, thinking it might as well stay there since he planned to haul it off in the morning to bury it. It would be good if the other three outlaws could be taken care of in the same way.

With Louella still laid out on his table, he covered her with a heavy sheet, picked up his lantern, and started to leave his shop and return to the house. He was stopped by a knock on the door. "Who is it?" he asked without opening the door, wondering who could possibly be calling on him at this time of night.

"Cole Bonner," came the reply.

Surprised, but more curious than concerned, Horace slid the bolt and opened the door. As his lantern cast its light upon his visitor, he was at once struck by the image before him, and the picture of Tiny's body with the embedded arrows came immediately to mind. He knew without doubt that the two were connected. "Cole Bonner," he pronounced solemnly and stepped back to bid him come in. "You did it."

"Did what?" Cole asked, not happy that Horace assumed it without asking. He was convinced more than ever that his appearance had to be altered.

"Accounted for that load of shit in my wagon out back," Horace answered.

"This ain't got nothin' to do with that killin'," Cole said. "I've been gone from here a long time and I'm in need of your barberin' services so folks will think I'm civilized. I know it ain't your normal business hours, but I saw your light on, so I decided to stop in." When Horace didn't respond beyond looking confused, Cole explained. "I need a haircut."

"A haircut?" Horace repeated, astonished.

"I woulda just hacked it off myself with my knife," Cole explained. "But I didn't want it to look like that's what I'd done." He paused before saying, "If it's too late, maybe I can come back in the mornin'."

"I ain't surprised," Horace said, still working on the question of who killed Tiny Weaver. "It was you that stepped up when Slade Corbett tried to take the town apart." He nodded, satisfied with his deductions. "No, indeed, it's not too late. It'll be my pleasure to cut your hair for you." With growing enthusiasm for the project, he suggested, "You'll be needing a shirt and trousers, too, to replace those buckskins." He turned and pointed toward the back of the shop. "I've got a passel of clothes in that closet back there, all kinds. I betcha we can find something just like you need."

Cole was amazed by Horace's reaction, but he knew he might have been unrealistic in thinking no one would add two and two together and come up with him as the answer. He might have considered it a serious setback, but he was confident that Horace would keep tonight's conspiracy to himself.

Cole decided to take him up on his offer. It would help him a great deal if, in fact, there were some clothes in Horace's closet that would fit the bill. "I'll take you up on that. I knew it would be best to get rid of the buckskins, but I thought I was gonna have to wait till mornin' when Douglas Green's store was open."

"No, sir-ree," Horace insisted. "No need to spend your money on something I've probably got right here. Besides, if you go walking around town wearing brand-new clothes, you're gonna stand out even more. Come on, we'll go up front to the barbershop and I'll cut your hair for you." He paused to cast a critical eye on the project. "Probably wouldn't hurt to wash it while we're at it."

Cole couldn't disagree and realized his good fortune to have found Horace in his shop so late.

After his haircut, Cole was escorted back to the mortuary part of the building to shop the closet. They found a shirt and some trousers that fit fairly well and a heavy wool coat that was made distinctive by a bullet hole over the left side pocket. Footwear presented the only problem. The boots Horace had were all too small for Cole to wear comfortably, so the single concession they made to the Crow Nation was for Cole to continue wearing his moccasins. It was not an unusual habit, for many white men preferred the comfort of deerskin footwear.

When the shopping was done and Cole was outfitted in typical ranch-style clothes, Horace asked a question. "Where's your hat?"

"I don't have a hat," Cole answered. He had discarded his hat when Womack put a hole in it while he was pinned under his horse.

"What do you do when it rains?"

"I pull a deer-hide blanket over my head," Cole said.

"You need a hat, like everybody else," Horace insisted. "On the shelf." He pointed back to the closet.

Cole found one that wasn't too bad, even though it had seen more than a couple of hard seasons. He pulled it down squarely on his head and turned to get Horace's approval.

"It suits you," Horace said.

Cole was ready to go, all decked out in dead men's clothes. He really thought nothing could be more fitting, considering the task he had undertaken. "How much I owe you?" he asked when Horace walked him to the door.

"Not a red cent," Horace replied. "I'm just proud to give a hand to somebody who's not afraid to do something about the lawless gang of murderers that came to take our town. I'm not handy with a gun, so I wouldn't be much use in an attempt to arrest that bunch. I'm glad I was able to help you a little bit." He reached out to shake Cole's hand. "And don't worry none about this," he nodded toward the body lying in the back of his wagon. "I know how to keep my mouth shut." He held the door open for Cole. "If I can do anything else to help you, just let me know."

"You've already made my job a helluva lot easier," Cole said. He couldn't help being impressed by Horace's enthusiasm for helping him out. It reinforced his notion that there were other people in this town who had everything they owned invested here. And they were at grave risk of losing it all.

He thought at once of Maggie and Mary Lou. What would become of them if someone wasn't there to maintain law and order? And not in this one incident. What about after Yarborough, Womack, and the other one were finished? Cole decided then and there that if Yarborough could declare himself sheriff, then so could he. He reached up and settled his new hat firmly on his head.

"I'll be seein' you, Horace," he said and disappeared into the darkness.

"You want the rest of this coffee?" Maggie Whitehouse asked. "There might be a full cup left in the pot."

"No," Mary Lou replied. "You drink it. I don't think I could swallow another gulp of that coffee. Maybe Beulah will drink it, if she ever gets back from the outhouse. I'm surprised we haven't already used up all we brought out here with us."

Both women were sick of sitting around Beulah's tiny cabin doing nothing but drinking coffee and going to the outhouse. The first day they were there, they scoured the entire cabin, walls, floors, even ceilings. They cleaned all the dishes, pots, pans, and every surface they could get a scrub brush or a rag on. The cabin was not unusually dirty, for Beulah was not a lazy housekeeper. They did it as payment for Ralph and Beulah inviting them into their home.

As they finished up yet another pot of coffee, they could find nothing else to occupy their time. Mary Lou and Maggie were accustomed to being busy most of the time.

"I'm losin' money settin' around here on my behind," Maggie complained. "I hope there ain't none of that crowd messin' around in my dinin' room. The more I think about it, the more I wish I hadn't let those bastards run me outta town."

"I've been thinking the same thing," Mary Lou

confessed. "We've never let anybody else make us run."

"I don't know. It wouldn't take much to make me say to hell with 'em—go on back and open my dinin' room tomorrow."

"Maybe one more cup of this coffee?"

"That'd do it," Maggie responded with a giggle. "Whaddaya say? Are you up to it?"

"Hell, yes!"

Harley and Ralph came in the kitchen door after feeding Ralph's stock to find Maggie and Mary Lou on their feet, looking as if they were going somewhere.

In a few seconds, Beulah came in behind them. She, too, noticed the look of urgency on the faces of the two women. "I told you I was gonna be there for a spell," she said, thinking they were waiting to use the outhouse.

"We're goin' back to town," Maggie said. "We ain't lettin' that Yarborough trash run us outta our own town."

"Hot damn!" Beulah squealed. "I was wonderin' how long it would take. When are we goin'?"

"Now, wait a minute," Harley responded at once. "Cole sent me out here to make sure nothin' happened to you ladies. I can't let you go back into town without me bein' sure them outlaws are gone." He had never said as much before.

That caught Mary Lou's attention. "Cole sent you out here? I thought you were just laying low because those gunmen thought you were the one that shot the Womack brothers."

"No such a thing," Harley replied, offended. "I

wanted to stand with Cole, but he made me promise I'd take care of you." He hesitated before thinking to add, "And Maggie and Beulah."

Maggie and Mary Lou exchanged smug smiles.

"Anyway, if you're goin' back, I'm goin' with you."

"When are we goin'?" Beulah asked again.

"In the mornin'," Maggie answered. "But I don't know if you wanna go with us. I ain't sure if we'll even have any customers when we get back. I figure Mary Lou and I can handle it. Me and her ain't got a man to take care of. You'd best stay here and take care of Ralph till those gunmen decide they've got all they're gonna get and leave town."

"I expect you're right," Ralph quickly agreed.

Harley shook his head, troubled. "I don't know if Cole's gonna be all right with this or not," he mumbled. "I promised him."

"Don't worry about it," Mary Lou teased. "I'll tell him we sneaked away while you weren't looking." It had never occurred to her that Cole sent Harley to protect them.

CHAPTER 12

Harley looked right and left as he led the buckboard driven by Maggie Whitehouse through the back alley behind the hotel. Sitting uncomfortably in a beat-up old saddle that belonged to Sammy Hill, he was nevertheless considerably more at ease with his fancy Mexican saddle resting in Gordon's barn. *No sense in riding into town with a target painted on my back,* he'd told himself. He had spent some time the night before trying to talk Maggie and Mary Lou out of returning to town while Yarborough and his friends were still there, but to no avail. He should have known he was wasting his time, especially when two women as strong-minded as those two made up their minds to revolt. *Cole's going to skin me alive when he sees these two back in town.*

It was with a great deal of relief that he passed behind the Cowboy's Rest without anyone's notice and pulled up behind the hotel. "I'll help you tote your possibles inside first. Then I'll put the horses away."

Both women had rooms behind the kitchen,

making it easy to carry the few pieces of luggage they had left with when fleeing town. After they had checked on their rooms and found they had not been entered, they put away their belongings and hurried to the kitchen to be sure nothing had been disturbed there.

Harley insisted on checking the kitchen and dining room. Satisfied there were no serious threats to the safety of his two charges, he then went back outside to unhitch Maggie's horse and unsaddle his own, all the while keeping a cautious eye out. The hotel kept a small stable, strictly for the convenience of Arthur Campbell, his employees, and on rare occasions, some guests. Harley figured it was one of those rare occasions and corralled his horse with Maggie's after taking advantage of a sack of oats he discovered in the stable. With the horses taken care of, he went back inside to assume his position as kitchen guard.

By the time Harley got back to the kitchen, Arthur Campbell and his son, Sonny, had discovered that the women had returned. Campbell interrupted his conversation with them long enough to greet Harley before continuing his update of all that had happened since they left.

Mary Lou turned to Harley and said, "There's not but three of them now. Somebody killed one of them, the great big one."

"Cole?" Harley asked at once.

"Don't know," Campbell said. "At first we thought it was an Indian. They found the brute in the alley with two arrows in him."

"Cole," Harley stated with a confident grin.

"Maybe," Campbell allowed. "Nobody saw it.

Anyway, the other three are still here and they don't look like they're plannin' to leave anytime soon."

"Where's Cole?" Harley asked. "Have you seen him?"

"Nope," Campbell answered.

"Don't surprise me none," Harley said. "But he's here, all right."

"Well, we didn't come back to stand around and visit," Maggie finally announced. "Me and Mary Lou have got to get to work and fix some breakfast. It might be a little bit late, but maybe some folks will come in, anyway. Looks like my pantry ain't been raided, but I ain't looked in the smokehouse yet. We'll come up with something, won't we, Mary Lou?"

"We always do," Mary Lou replied.

"I'm damn glad to see you back," Campbell said. "My wife will be tickled, too. She had to go back to cooking three meals a day."

Arthur Campbell was not the only person who was pleased to see the dining room open again. Maggie's regular customers were unhappy with the fare offered at the saloons, as were the town's three unwelcome guests. When word got out that Maggie was back, and she and Mary Lou were preparing to reopen the dining room, the news was met with great anticipation. While still in the process of firing up Maggie's big iron cookstove, the women were already turning hungry customers away to give them time to prepare something to serve.

"My oven ain't near hot enough to put biscuits

in the pan," she told Harold Chestnut when he said he would like to sit down and wait for her to get breakfast ready.

"I ain't had a decent meal since you left town," the postmaster complained. "If you'll just let me have a cup of coffee, I'll wait for the food."

"If you don't let me get on with my work, there ain't gonna be no breakfast," Maggie complained. "We ain't got Beulah here today to help out. Mary Lou, is that stove hot enough to make the coffee yet?"

"Won't be long now," Mary Lou answered. Since the stove had been idle for the past couple of days, there had been no warm ashes banked in the belly of it, as would usually be the case.

Several other men drifted into the dining room and promptly began filling the benches on either side of the long table in the center. At Maggie's suggestion, Harley laid kindling in the dining room stove and soon had a fire started. It would take a while for that one stove at the end of the room to warm the place up to approach anything close to comfort. That didn't seem to dampen the spirits of the mostly single men who regularly started their day with a substantial breakfast at the hotel dining room.

The air was light and cordial among the eager patrons at last warmed by the contents of the first pot of coffee. The big metal pot was charged up again with backup from a smaller pot that was sometimes called in to keep the pitch-black liquid flowing. A lot of good-natured banter floated back and forth between eager customers, most of it at the community table in the center.

That is, until the door opened and Red Swann and Troy Womack walked in.

Conversation ceased at the end of the table nearest the door, and the wave of silence rolled along the long table as the two outlaws proceeded to make their way to one of the smaller tables on the side of the room. Walking with a swagger, both men sneered at the suddenly silenced customers as they passed by.

"Looks like ol' Abe was right," Red remarked. "Think I'll have a look in the kitchen and tell 'em to get us some grub out here right away." He left Troy to pick out a table and went through the kitchen door, almost colliding with Mary Lou on her way to the dining room with a stack of plates.

"Whoa! Hold up there, Honey-britches, before you drop all them dishes."

Taking a couple of steps backward, Mary Lou steadied her stack before responding to the crude outlaw. "Customers stay in the dining room, and my name's not Honey-britches. What do you want?"

"I want my breakfast, Honey-britches, and I don't wanna wait all day to get it."

"Breakfast isn't ready yet," Mary Lou replied. "And as you can see, there are quite a few folks ahead of you. Go sit down somewhere and we'll get to you in time. Or if you don't wanna wait, most of the saloons serve breakfast. You can go there." Dangerous men or not, she was not of a nature to keep her thoughts to herself.

Her remarks were met with a wide sneer. "I remember you. You were the one that came up to Sheriff Black's room carryin' a shotgun. Well, I think I'd best set you straight on how things are gonna go around here. I reckon you ain't heard, since you run off after ol' John Henry Black kicked off."

When Mary Lou tried to go around him, he stepped in front of her.

"If you don't get outta my way, I'm not gonna get the food ready," she said. "Then you might have to explain to that roomful of men waiting to eat why you're holding me up."

"You're a right sassy little bitch, ain't you?" He stepped up close, hovering over her, almost stifling her with the heavy stench of alcohol mixed with to-bacco. "Those yellow-bellied jaspers settin' around that table already know who's runnin' this town now. And the first one that forgets it is gonna find himself layin' in the street out there. So you best learn to mind your manners pretty damn quick, or I'll gut you like a fish." A wicked grin replaced the sneer as he added, "After I'm through with you." He took two cups from the tray of dishes she carried, walked over and helped himself to coffee from the backup pot on the stove.

Harley came in from outside, carrying an arm-load of wood for the stove, just in time to see him walk out of the kitchen. At once concerned, he dumped his wood by the stove and hurried to her to ask, "Is that one of them bastards?"

"No harm's been done," she quickly assured him, lest he thought to confront the belligerent bully. "He was just mouthing off, trying to get served before everybody else. He's the one called Red and he ain't nothing for you to get worried about. He knows better than to mess with me." She only wished that was true, but she was afraid Harley was going to try to stand up for her honor and get himself killed. "There ain't anything else you can do right now. Why don't you sit yourself down at this table by the kitchen door and I'll have you something to eat pretty quick." Late in coming, the thought occurred that it would be disastrous if one of the other men happened to call Harley by name. It would be better to have him sit at the small table by the kitchen door, away from the long table.

When he took her advice and sat down, Mary Lou hurried on out to distribute the plates on the tables, still trying to rid her nostrils of the foul odor of Red Swann when he had hovered over her.

He had obviously started his morning with a generous portion of whiskey. The man was half drunk at that early hour, which served to fuel her disgust for the lack of courage among the men of the town. Speaking softly so as not to be heard by the intimidating bullies at their table, she scolded her fellow citizens for sitting on their hands in the presence of the two gunmen. Her admonishment was met with heads down and eyes staring at the table in front of them.

When she got to Jim Low, she whispered, "Are you and the others going to do something? The big one is half drunk." She was aware of the meeting he had held at his cabin supposedly to unite the men against the town's occupation by the evil force. She paused, waiting for his answer.

He quickly shook her off with a rapid movement of his head, never daring to look up, lest he lock eyes with one of the two.

Mary Lou shook her head in disgust and moved

on down the table, aware that Red's eyes were following her every move. In spite of her fearless disposition, she could not repress the sudden chill that made her shiver under his gaze. Determined not to let him see it, she marched over to his table and placed two plates down in front of him and Womack. Avoiding direct eye contact with either of the outlaws, she promptly spun on her heel and went back to the kitchen.

"By God, that's a mighty fine-lookin' woman," Troy was inspired to remark as he studied Mary Lou's backside until she disappeared through the door.

"You just now noticin' that?" Red asked. "I took a shine to her first time I saw her, up in the room with John Henry Black. She's got a fair amount of mustang in her, and I'm plannin' to saddle break her before we're done here."

"You ain't the only one thinkin' about that," Troy said. "Been thinkin' 'bout that, myself."

"Is that so? Well, I've already got my brand on her. You'd best find you another 'un, 'cause I don't aim to share this 'un with nobody."

"That's a helluva note," Troy responded. "I thought we was partners. What about Yarborough? What if he says he wants a go-round with her, too?"

Red snuffled a grunt. "I ain't worried 'bout Yarborough. He's so tied up in knots over that gal that's hidin' from him, he ain't thinkin' 'bout nothin' else." He gave Troy a smug grin and teased, "You're the one that has to find your own filly. Might have to settle for one of those old mares at the saloon, though."

"What's the matter?" Maggie asked when she

saw the look in Mary Lou's eyes as she returned to the kitchen. "Have they already started trouble?"

"No, it's just the way that big one looks at me. I feel like I've been violated with him looking at me like I'm something on the menu."

"We ain't got no menus," Maggie replied without thinking.

"Well, if we did," Mary Lou said impatiently. "I wonder where the other one is, our brave new sheriff. Don't rats usually travel in packs?"

"Maybe," Maggie replied. "Rats I think we could handle, but we're dealin' more with wolves. I just hope to hell they clear outta here pretty soon without causing trouble. We'll just feed 'em as fast as we can get something cooked and maybe they'll be anxious to get back to the Cowboy's Rest."

"Maybe we can get them outta here before their partner comes looking for them and decides he wants to sit down and eat, too," Mary Lou suggested, unaware of the events taking place at the jail.

When the women had returned to town that morning, prepared to reopen the hotel dining room, Cole was already making his next move against the remaining three outlaws. Having learned from Leon that the three slept in their hotel rooms and usually ate breakfast at the saloon, he approached the door of the sheriff's office early. He found the door locked, but Leon had said that Pete Little was there most of the time during the day. He peered in the window and, sure enough, he saw the gray-haired little man sitting at the desk, drinking coffee. *Good*, Cole thought, *I could use some coffee.* He went back to the door and rapped firmly. He heard Pete hustling out of the chair, and in a few moments the door opened.

"Cole Bonner!" Pete exclaimed and stuck his head outside to look up and down the deserted street. "Whaddaya doin' here? That feller you was chasin' is back in town, and he brought plenty of help with him! He don't come here to the sheriff's office very much, but one of them with him does. He's took over as sheriff."

"That's what I heard," Cole said and stepped past Pete. "Any coffee left in that pot?"

Baffled by Cole's seemingly unconcern with what he had just told him, Pete impressed upon him. "Yarborough's the name of the feller callin' hisself the sheriff. He's the leader of the four." He paused then, remembering. "Least there was four. One of 'em got killed last night." He paused to think again. "Did you have somethin' to do with that?"

"Might have," Cole replied while examining the coffee cups sitting on a small table next to the wall. Selecting the least offensive one as far as dust and stain were concerned, he poured some coffee from the pot. His unhurried response only served to increase Pete's anxiety.

"Yarborough's liable to come walkin' in here any time now," Pete insisted.

"Good. Give me a chance to see him up close," Cole said between sips. "Damn, this coffee's rank. How old is this stuff?"

"Made it outta some fresh grounds yesterday

afternoon. There was still more 'n half a pot left. Didn't make sense to waste it."

Cole walked over to the door, opened it, and threw the contents of the cup outside. Pete stood by the desk, his eyes opened wide, obviously amazed by Cole's casual manner.

Thinking it best to enlighten him, Cole explained. "I heard how easy it is to win an election around here, so I had another one and I won this time. I reckon I'm the new sheriff." Astonished, Pete looked as if about to blurt something, but he remained silent and Cole continued. "How many keys are there to that lock on the door?"

"Ain't but two now. The one that John Henry carried never showed up—mighta been buried with him—but I got one, and Sheriff—" He paused. "I mean, Yarborough's got the other one."

"You just keep your key, and I'll get that one from Yarborough when he shows up."

"Yessir, whatever you say," Pete replied, still wide-eyed with disbelief. He couldn't hold his curiosity any longer, however. "You just gonna tell him he ain't the sheriff no more? Just like that? And you're the new sheriff?"

"Well, pretty much," Cole said. "'Course I'll tell him he just lost another election, fair and square, just like the one that got him the job. Then I'll arrest him and lock him up till I can arrest his friends."

Pete nodded as if he understood. In reality, he wondered if Cole had been chewing on locoweed, or maybe had gotten his brain frozen during all the time he and Harley were stomping around in the high mountains. Thinking of Harley, Pete wouldn't have been surprised if that was the case for the brash-talking little man, but Cole had always impressed him as a sensible man.

In any case, Pete was eager to see what was going to happen when Flint Yarborough showed up. At the same time, he was not sure it would be safe to be there when the bullets started flying. He was still undecided whether to stay or clear out when Yarborough showed up to check on things at "his office."

"Ohhh . . . shiiiit!" Pete dragged the words out slowly when he glanced out the window and saw Yarborough approaching from the saloon across the street. He turned to face Cole, but it was unnecessary to say anything.

"Yarborough?" Cole asked.

Pete nodded solemnly.

"By himself?"

Pete nodded again.

"All right, you just stand over there next to the cell door and don't get between us." Cole sat down at the desk facing the door and laid his rifle on top of the desk.

Yarborough opened the door and stood there for a moment, puzzled by the sight of Pete standing against the cell wall, his eyes as big as saucers. "What the hell's ailin' you?" he asked and closed the door behind him. It was only then that he discovered the man seated at the desk. "Who the hell are you?" he demanded.

"I reckon you'd be Flint Yarborough," Cole said.

"I know who I am," Yarborough came back. "Who the hell are you?" He made a gesture as if about to reach for the .44 he wore.

"That would be a mistake"—a soft smile parted Cole's lips as he raised the Henry rifle off the desk—"especially with that heavy coat in the way." He shrugged. "But hell, if you wanna make a try for it, it's up to you. You never know. Maybe I forgot to crank a cartridge in the chamber. Right now I can't recall, myself."

"Mister, you're makin' one helluva mistake," Yarborough growled. "I own this town, and you'll be dead by nightfall." He had a strong feeling he had seen Cole before. He looked familiar, but he was having trouble remembering where it might have been.

"Oh, there ain't no mistake. You see, while you and your friends were havin' your breakfast, we had another election here in town and damned if I didn't win. Too bad you didn't come in to vote.

"Well, enough of that small talk, you're probably wantin' to get into your cell, so you can relax." He gave a nod toward Pete. "Pete, open that cell door for Mr. Yarborough." Then back to Yarborough, he said, "Now I'll have you unbutton that coat and drop it on the floor."

Yarborough did as he was told.

"Now, unbuckle your gun belt. Not too fast!" Cole warned when Yarborough moved a little too rapidly. "Just let it drop on the floor and step over it."

Yarborough hesitated, not willing to surrender any chance he had to fight.

"I know what you're thinkin'," Cole said. "Will he pull that trigger? Let me answer that for you.

Yes, he will. And he'll be beholden to you for making the job easier than keepin' you alive."

Yarborough was convinced. When he did as he was told, Cole asked for the key to the lock on the front door. Yarborough, of course, claimed that he had lost it.

"I hope you ain't gonna make me strip you down naked. I bet it gets pretty chilly in that cell when the fire dies down in the stove. But it won't matter that much if we don't find that key. I'll get another lock at the store. It only opens the front door, anyway, doesn't open your cell. Now, step inside."

"You're a dead man, you smart-mouthed son of a bitch," Yarborough threatened. "There ain't nobody in this whole town man enough to face up to my boys. When they find out what you're tryin' to pull off here, they'll tear this jail down and go through you to do it."

"Don't sound too good for me, does it?" Cole replied. "Pete, take a look through those coat pockets, 'specially those on the inside, and see what you find."

"You're the sneaky son of a bitch that dry-gulched Tiny Weaver, ain't you?" Yarborough growled. "I'd like to see how you'da come out in a fair fight with Tiny."

"I don't do fair fights," Cole said. "Odds are better the other way." He paused then when Pete held up a double-barreled derringer. "Uh-oh, you musta forgot you had that."

A few moments later Pete produced the key.

Cole took the key and the pocket pistol and told Pete to give Yarborough's coat back to him.

Growing more and more enraged over finding himself in such an unexpected situation, Yarborough scowled as he snatched his coat through the bars when Pete offered it. The slight grin on the old man's face didn't help. To Yarborough, it seemed impossible for him to have been captured so ridiculously easily—one man, sitting behind the desk. He didn't even get up from his chair. The infuriating part of it was the fact that there was nothing he could have done to resist without getting himself shot. He had no doubt that Cole would have pulled the trigger, just as he immediately surmised that Cole was the one who put two arrows in Tiny. It had been a huge mistake to think the town had no backbone enough to resist him and his friends. Already, they had been cut in half, as far as the numbers were concerned, without their even knowing they were in a fight.

"Damn!" he suddenly blurted, unable to contain his frustration. When both Cole and Pete reacted with puzzled expressions, Yarborough demanded, "You're Harley Branch, right?"

His question served to deepen Pete's puzzled expression, but Cole was not surprised. Evidently no one had told Pete about the mistaken identity.

"Nope," Cole answered, "I ain't Harley Branch."

"The hell you ain't," Yarborough replied, choosing not to believe him. "You went after Troy Womack."

"That's a fact. I went after Womack, but I ain't Harley Branch." Cole couldn't resist japing Yarborough. "You'd best thank your lucky stars that

Harley wasn't on your tail, and you just had to deal with me." He turned his attention to Pete then. "Anybody ever break outta this jail, Pete?"

"Nary a soul," Pete said.

"That's what I figured. Those bars looked pretty stout to me, and that window's too small for even a man your size to squeeze through. What about the roof?"

"Four-by-six rafters with a double deck of two-by-fours, layin' crossways each other, come special from Gordon Luck's mill," Pete answered.

"Damn," Cole exclaimed and shook his head, impressed. "No wonder nobody ain't ever broke outta here. It'd take a man six months to go through that roof if he had a good axe to work with." Figuring that Yarborough had received the message, he said to him, "Now you'd best sit down and make yourself comfortable, 'cause you ain't goin' anywhere."

Like an angry bear chained to a tree, Yarborough sat down on one of the two bunks in his cell, scowling fiercely but unable to strike out at his captor. In a few seconds time, he jumped to his feet again when he suddenly remembered. "You son of a bitch! I shoulda gone after you with Red when you left Murphy's."

"Woulda saved all of us a lot of trouble," Cole replied. He motioned for Pete to follow him outside, and waited for him on the short boardwalk by the hitching rail. "The easy part of this thing is done. Now comes the hard part, tryin' to catch the other two. Does one or both of them usually come here?"

Pete said that it was not the usual case. So far, they had preferred to plant themselves in the saloons.

It was only Yarborough who liked to come by the jail, and he didn't stay very long when he did show up. Pete was of the opinion it was because Yarborough enjoyed feeling he had an official position of power. "I stay here most of the day by myself. I wouldn't hang around if he was gonna be here."

Cole paused to think about the situation he had created with Yarborough's capture. "Here's what we better do right now. We'll put the padlock back on the door and leave Mr. Yarborough by himself for a while. I've got to see if I can round up those other two and I ain't sure that's gonna be so easy. I don't want you here in case one of his boys come to get him out. I don't wanna worry about you with a gun held to your head." He knew that Pete would have to open up if threatened with his life. "Tell you what. You can do me one more favor if you let me buy you a drink at the Cowboy's Rest. If Womack is there, you can give me a little warning. I haven't seen him up close. Whaddaya say?"

Pete readily accepted the invitation. "Well, it's a little too early in the day for me, but if it'll help you out, I'll have a little shooter with you."

Cole closed the shutters on the one window in the front of the office before locking the padlock in place on the front door. Then he and a slightly nervous Pete Little walked the short distance to the Cowboy's Rest saloon. He stopped at the door while Pete took a step inside to look the room over. After a couple of minutes, Pete stepped back and said he didn't see Swann or Womack in the saloon.

"I reckon we took too long visitin' with Yarborough," Cole said. "We'll go on in and maybe they'll show up pretty soon." He had no real plan, just trusting his instincts to react to whatever happened when he finally came face-to-face with the two gunmen. But he needed Pete in case Troy Womack came in alone, and he hoped that would be the case. He'd much prefer to deal with them one at a time.

"Well, I'll be . . ." Abe started, surprised to see Cole in the saloon. He looked around nervously, even though he knew none of the three gunmen were there. "Howdy, Cole. I reckon you're still lookin' for Troy Womack. Tell you the truth, we thought he mighta turned the table on you, but I reckon he'da been braggin' about it if he did. You followed him right back where you started, all right, but he's got company with him. I reckon Pete's already told you that. Womack ain't here right now. He was here, but him and Red Swann, one of the fellers he hooked up with, walked up to the hotel dinin' room to get some breakfast. I don't know where Yarborough went."

Cole was not expecting to hear that. "The hotel? I thought the hotel dinin' room was closed."

"It was," Abe replied. "One of my customers in here a few minutes ago said Maggie came back to town and opened for business again."

"Just Maggie?" Cole pressed. "Was she by herself?"

"No, he said Mary Lou was with her. Beulah wasn't, though."

That was not good news to Cole. He had started his one-man track-down of the four ruthless killers, feeling safe in the knowledge that Mary Lou—and Maggie, too—were out of harm's way. He didn't say anything for a few moments while he tried to think of the best way to approach his problem. His first thought was to simply lie in wait for the two to leave the dining room and finish business with two quick shots from his Henry rifle. That was by far the quickest solution for the town's problem and the safest solution for him. But he soon discarded the notion, reminding himself that he preferred not to create a reputation as an assassin if there was a chance to capture them. That way a jury of the town's citizens or a judge could order a hanging.

His mind made up, he figured he shouldn't have any trouble picking out the two outlaws in the dining room. Since he didn't need Pete any longer, there was no reason to expose the little man to danger. "I reckon I owe you that drink I promised," he said to Pete, tossing a coin on the counter. "Give Pete, here, a drink of that whiskey you sell to your good customers."

"Where you goin'?" Pete asked. "Ain't you gonna have one?"

"No, I reckon not," Cole said, turning to leave. "I'll see you back at the jail in a little while."

Abe poured Pete's drink and set the bottle down. "Did he say he'd see you back at the jail?"

"Yep," Pete replied, smacking his lips. "He's the new sheriff."

When the food finally arrived on the tables in the dining room, it was devoured in rather hasty fashion by those plucky souls who had stayed to receive it. Over half of those who had come to eat breakfast had already gone, deeming it not worth the risk to sit around waiting for the two malevolent bullies to decide to amuse themselves at the expense of some unfortunate cowhand or store clerk. The uneasy exodus of many of the diners did not go unnoticed by Swann and Womack and, in fact, provided amusement for them while they ate the fried potatoes and beans with the sliced ham Maggie and Mary Lou served up.

"What the hell are you lookin' at?" Red demanded when Harold Chestnut glanced in his direction as he climbed off the bench, preparing to leave. Red reached as if going for his six-gun, then roared with laughter when Chestnut nearly fell over the bench in his haste to retreat. Troy joined in, enjoying the feeling of power derived from the obvious fear everyone suffered in their presence.

"Damn," Red declared, "I'm gonna need a drink of whiskey pretty soon. All this coffee I've been downin' has damn-near sobered me up." He got up from his chair and paused to watch Mary Lou carry a tray full of dirty dishes to the kitchen. "I'll tell you somethin' else I'm needin', too. And I aim to have it. But first, I've gotta go get rid of about a gallon of coffee." He headed for the door that opened to the back hallway and led to the outside door on his way to the outhouse.

As he walked down the hallway, he passed a couple of doors, and it occurred to him that the two women lived there at the hotel. *In one of these rooms, I'll bet,* he thought. Out of curiosity, he tried one of the knobs. Finding it locked only sharpened his curiosity, so he pressed a massive shoulder to the door and forced it open, splitting the jamb in the process. "Uh-huh," he murmured when he discovered it to be a bedroom. "I thought so."

He went inside the empty room to look around and it took no more than a few moments to confirm it to be a lady's bedroom. *I knew she lived in this damn hotel somewhere,* he thought, still not certain that he had found Mary Lou's room and not Maggie's. *I'm going to be visiting you pretty soon, Honey-britches,* he promised himself. Then he went back to the hall and continued on his way to the outside door to find the outhouse.

CHAPTER 13

Troy Womack tilted his chair back against the wall, his coffee cup in hand, as he surveyed the dining room, enjoying the almost visible cloud of fear hanging over the long table. It gave him a sense of power to witness the obvious signs of intimidation displayed by the men of Cheyenne. First one, and then another diner rapidly finished breakfast and hurried out the front door. He stared after them, but none would meet his eye. It was especially gratifying when he was called to remember the circumstances under which he had been forced to leave town before. Chased out of town by what appeared to be a half-breed Indian after Travis was shot down, he thought he would never return. But return he did, and no one dared stand against him. The thought twisted his lips into a smug, satisfied smile.

Another diner got up and hurried toward the door, leaving only two customers remaining at the long table. Troy looked at Mary Lou as she continued to pick up the dishes from the table. Red was right in thinking her a fetching young woman, and although he had staked his claim on her, he had no rights to her. *Might be, I'd best corral her before Red gets back from the outhouse,* he decided. *He ain't got no more claim on her than I have.*

His thoughts were distracted when the front door opened and another customer came inside. Tall, broad-shouldered, with sandy-colored hair, he was a stranger to Troy, even though he had a familiar look about him. *Must have seen him in the saloon,* he thought, then shifted his gaze back to Mary Lou, who had stopped abruptly when she spotted the man. She looked about to speak, but hesitated and glanced at Troy. The little man seated at the table next to the kitchen seemed to be startled as well. The stranger nodded briefly toward them and continued on toward the long table, but he didn't stop there. He continued on to Troy's table.

His curiosity aroused, Troy lowered his chair back down on four legs. Puzzled by the man's lack of intimidation, he began to wonder if he had reason to be concerned. The man carried a Henry rifle, but it was held in one hand, hanging at his side. No sign in his facial expression or in the casual way he carried the rifle indicated that Troy should be alarmed.

Thinking it better to be cautious, he set his cup on the table and reached down to draw his .44 as Cole walked right up before him.

"What the hell do you want?" Troy demanded.

The front sight of his pistol had not cleared his holster when he was knocked sideways out of his chair to land hard on the floor, the impact causing him to squeeze the trigger to send a shot into the ceiling. At the sound of the gunshot, Harley didn't hesitate, knowing Red would hear it as well. He jumped up and ran out through the kitchen to the back hallway door. He wanted to be in position to surprise Red when he rushed in to see the cause of the gunfire.

The butt of the rifle that had rendered Troy senseless for a few moments had been reversed and the barrel was pointing at his face.

"Drop it," Cole commanded. Troy did not respond at once, his ears still ringing from the blow to the side of his head. He stared at the blurred image of the muzzle of the Henry rifle staring back at him. Gradually, as his head began to clear, the image of the rifle barrel became sharp.

Troy released the weapon and Cole kicked it away. The sight of Cole's moccasin flashed like a sudden bolt of lightning in Troy's brain, instantly bringing the realization that the man before him was the devil that had pursued him.

"Who the hell are you?" he demanded, but didn't wait for an answer as he felt the side of his face where the skin was broken and blood was already trickling down across his cheek. "You're that son of a bitch that shot my brothers. You're Harley Branch." He looked frantically toward the back door, expecting Red to walk in at any moment.

"That's right," Cole said. "I'm the son of a bitch that shot your murderin' brothers and I say good riddance. But my name ain't Harley Branch. You've been lookin' for the wrong man all along."

"Whaddaya aimin' to do with me? Maybe you caught up with me, but I ain't by myself no more. You'd best turn me loose. My partners will be all over you in just a few minutes. Then it's gonna be a different story. You'd better run while you still can."

Cole glanced at Mary Lou, who had not moved since first seeing him come in the door. She nodded, then motioned toward the hallway door with her head. He understood then why Harley had run out the back.

"Your partner's outside," Cole said to Troy. "We'll just wait for him to come back."

"You've got more to worry about than just one." Troy moaned, his broken cheekbone throbbing from the blow that felled him.

Mary Lou warned Cole. "I think the other one went to the outhouse, but I haven't seen the third one, the one called Yarborough. He's liable to show up any minute."

"That's all right," Cole said. "I know where Yarborough is. I'm not worried about him, but I need to know where Harley is." Knowing he had clearly run out to intercept Swann, Cole thought for a moment, then said, "I need some rope. I need to tie this one up till I can go find his partner." He looked at the two men still sitting wide-eyed at the long table. "Either of you got any rope?"

He was answered by a shake of the head from both men.

"I've got some clothesline in the pantry," Maggie volunteered, having rushed to stand beside Mary Lou when she had heard the shot fired by Troy and Harley had rushed by her.

"That'll do," Cole said. "Get it."

In a matter of minutes, Maggie returned with a coil of clothesline cord. Cole took it from her and handed her his rifle. "Shoot him if he makes a move." He rolled Womack over on his belly and quickly tied his wrists behind his back and his ankles together with a short length of clothesline binding ankles to wrists.

"I've gotta go find the other one before Harley gets into trouble." Cole took his rifle from Maggie and offered his handgun instead.

She refused, saying she felt more confident with her twelve-gauge shotgun, which she kept behind the kitchen door.

"Shoot him if he tries to get outta those ropes— in the legs, if you can. I'd like to lock him up and let a judge decide what to do with him." He flashed a wry grin in Womack's direction and added, "Or maybe a jury of the good citizens of Cheyenne."

"Don't you worry about him," Maggie assured him as she broke her double-barreled shotgun to make sure it held two shells. "I'll be happy to see he doesn't go anywhere."

"We'll help out," one of the two men still seated at the table said, now that the monster had been rendered harmless.

Hearing three shots coming from the alley, Cole started toward the kitchen.

As he passed Mary Lou, she said, "Cole, be careful." That was all she could think to say, still surprised by his sudden appearance.

He gave her a worried smile, his mind occupied with thoughts of what trouble Harley might have gotten himself into.

With full confidence that Cole had the situation under control in the dining room, Harley had knelt beside the back porch steps, watching the door of the outhouse. He was concerned that Swann might go back inside before Cole had Womack under control. Never letting his eyes stray from the closed door of the privy, he began to wonder just how long Red could linger after surely hearing the shot fired from inside the building. The minutes began to pile up until finally Harley decided he'd better make sure Red was still in the outhouse.

Glancing from right to left, from the smokehouse to his left, back to the small stable on his right, Harley eased out from behind the porch steps. Seeing no one, he began a slow, cautious approach toward the closed outhouse door. With his .44 Colt aimed at the door, he advanced to within fifteen feet before he heard the sobering metallic sound of a hammer cocking behind him. He froze, instantly aware that he had been outfoxed, and was struck with a sick feeling of helplessness as a result.

With no chance other than pure luck, he had no choice but to try, so he spun around in time to face the .44 slug that tore into his side before he could even complete his turn. Staggered, he still tried to get off a shot, only to be stopped cold by a second shot from Red's pistol that knocked the wind from his chest. With his arm hanging limply, he fired a shot into the ground before he collapsed into a heap before a leering Red Swann.

Red could not be sure, but he had a feeling something had to have gone terribly wrong inside for this little bowlegged old man to have come looking for him. Consequently, he didn't waste much time over his kill. With a contemptuous sneer at the fallen man, he hurried to the cover of the hotel stable where he paused to decide what to do. Something had happened to Troy in the dining room. Or maybe he had just decided to shoot someone.

That didn't figure, Red decided. Maybe a group of the town's citizens had decided to act to defend their town. If that was the case, he'd best not take a chance on being surprised as Troy might have been. Best to find Yarborough and they could decide how to handle the problem. Hearing the sound of someone running on the long porch behind the kitchen, he was sure then that Troy must have been overpowered.

Red slipped out the back of the stable and headed for the Cowboy's Rest. Behind him, Cole paused at the back door. As a precaution to running headlong into an ambush, he eased the door open only far enough to permit him to see what awaited him. He felt his heart stop when he surveyed the alley behind the hotel. The yard was empty except for the body lying in front of the outhouse.

In a fit of panic, he burst through the door and was halfway across the yard before he thought to exercise any caution. He dropped to one knee, his rifle to his shoulder, and looked quickly around him. There was no sign of any threat and he had to remind himself that, had there been, he would most likely be lying in the alley beside Harley. Further thoughts of any danger to himself were quickly forgotten, however, as he hurried to Harley's side. He was overcome with a feeling of guilt when he gazed at the pitiful little body of his friend, for he felt that he was the cause of the tragedy.

As gently as he could, he turned Harley over to get his face out of the dirt and was startled to witness a slight fluttering of Harley's eyelids. He was alive, or maybe just going through the final moments before death. There was no way Cole could be sure, but he prayed it was the former. "Harley," he pleaded. "Can you hear me? It's Cole."

There was no response, but he could feel a weak heartbeat in the veins in Harley's neck.

"I'm gonna take you to the doctor, partner. You hold on. Don't run out on me. Just hold on." He laid his rifle on the ground and lifted Harley up on his feet so he could let him fall across his shoulder. When he felt his load was secure, Cole knelt down and picked up his rifle. Rising to his feet again, he hurried back to the hotel as quickly as he could. He had no thoughts of Red Swann nor concern for his getting away. Thoughts of making the man pay for shooting his friend would come later. All that mattered was to get help for Harley.

"Oh, my God," was all Mary Lou could utter when she opened the kitchen door.

"Send somebody to get Doc Marion," Cole directed as he carried his wounded partner into the dining room half filled with spectators who had heard the gunshots and were gaping at the trussed-up outlaw lying on the floor.

A young man who worked in the harness shop volunteered, and Cole said, "Tell him to hurry. Harley's hurt bad."

"Is he still alive?" Maggie asked, not certain from the lack of response from Harley.

"Just barely, I think," Cole answered.

"I'll get a blanket," Mary Lou said and ran to her room in the back hall, never noticing the split doorjamb on Maggie's door when she hurried past. When she returned, she spread the blanket on the floor next to Harley, then she and Cole lifted him over on top of it.

Both were startled when Harley whispered, "Did you get him?" The words were weak and halting, his lips barely moving.

It was the first time Cole had thought about Red Swann since he saw Harley lying motionless in the alley. "No," he answered, "but I damn sure will. You can count on that."

"Give me a little room here," Mary Lou said, "and I'll see if I can slow that bleeding down."

Cole backed away obediently while she stuffed a couple of towels over the two bullet holes. Knowing there was nothing he could do for Harley, he reminded himself that he had a prisoner he had left tied up in the other corner of the room.

Stepping between two of the spectators, Cole faced Jim Low, who was standing over Womack now, having taken responsibility for that job from Maggie. Cole could not help thinking that if Jim and his fellow citizens had stepped up sooner, maybe Harley wouldn't be lying on the floor with two bullet holes in him.

"Whaddaya aimin' to do with him?" Jim asked.

"Take him down to the jail and throw him in with his partner," Cole answered, his mind already working on the one gunman who had escaped.

"Jail?" Low responded in surprise. "Are you sayin' Yarborough's in jail?"

"Unless he broke out since I came in here," Cole said.

"Well, I'll be . . ." Low started. "So that's why he didn't show up to eat with his partners. You put him in jail?" He still found it hard to believe and thought that over for a few moments before commenting again. "So we've got two of the three captured then."

Cole nodded, even though thinking the term *we* was hardly the case. But maybe the pioneer spirit that had inspired men like Jim Low to brave the frontier had returned. He hoped so for the future of the town.

"What are we gonna keep 'em in jail for?" Low thought to ask then, thinking that the natural course of action would be to simply hang them.

"I reckon that'll be up to you and the mayor and the rest of your citizens," Cole said. "Try 'em, hang 'em, or wire the U.S. Marshal Service to send a deputy to pick 'em up." Satisfied that his prisoner was well taken care of, he went back across the room to see if Harley was still hanging on. He was kneeling beside him when Doc Marion came in.

A quick examination prompted the doctor to comment. "It's a damn wonder he isn't dead." He glanced up at Mary Lou. "It's a good thing you got some of the bleeding stopped. Maybe he won't lose too much more before we can get him over to my office. I can't do what I have to here, and I'm not certain I can do much, anyway. I'll have to find out how much damage those bullets have done."

One of the spectators said he had his wagon beside the hotel and volunteered it as a transport for Harley. Cole found himself in a storm of indecision between seeing Harley carried safely to the doctor's surgery or taking control of his prisoner. Foremost in his mind was his need to find Red Swann before he escaped, but he knew he had to make sure Womack was locked up before he could seek out Swann. He looked anxiously back and forth between the wounded man and Jim Low standing guard over Womack.

Feeling a hand on his elbow, he turned to find Mary Lou beside him.

"Don't worry about Harley," she said. "I'll go to Doc Marion's with him. You have to worry about that murderer over there. You need to make sure he doesn't get away."

He nodded, understanding his priorities when she reminded him.

"And, Cole, you be real careful. That monster, Swann, might still be in town."

He nodded again and started to turn away, but stopped after a couple of steps, looked back at her and said, "Thanks."

"Where's Yarborough?" Red Swann demanded when he rushed into the Cowboy's Rest.

"Up at the jail," Abe replied, surprised to see Red after news of the altercation at the dining room.

I should have checked there first, Red thought, considering the fact that Yarborough went there every morning to "play sheriff." "How long ago was that? Did he say when he was comin' back?"

"No, he didn't say," Abe said, feeling a bit more cocky in light of developments that had taken place that morning. "I don't think he'll be comin' back here a'tall." Although he had not left the bar, he was well aware of the arrest of Flint Yarborough. Word traveled very rapidly in a settlement the size of Cheyenne and since Red had left with Troy to go to the hotel dining room, how could he not know about Yarborough? Seeing Red's obvious anxiety in his efforts to find his partner, Abe could not help but be amused by the irony of the situation. It was especially satisfying, considering how the sinister foursome had ridden into town, killed the sheriff, and defied anyone to oppose them.

Red appeared to be thinking about what to do before turning to go back out the door, but he paused. "What did you mean when you said you don't think he'll come back here? You know somethin' you ain't tellin' me?"

Abe could only shrug in response, afraid he had already said too much, but Red's suspicions were aroused. Not sure exactly what had happened back at the hotel, he did not discount the possibility that the men of the town might have decided to fight back. He spun around and returned to the bar. He grabbed a handful of Abe's shirt and jerked him halfway across the bar while he whipped out his .44 with his other hand. "You'd better start talkin' quick, you son of a bitch, before I splatter your brains on that mirror behind you!"

Sufficiently motivated at that point, Abe blurted out. "Yarborough's locked up in jail!"

"What the hell are you talkin' about?" Red demanded, the barrel of his pistol barely inches from Abe's nose. "Who locked him in the jail?" He couldn't conceive of the possibility of anyone getting the best of Flint Yarborough. It had to be a vigilante action. "How many of 'em are there?"

"It weren't but one man," Abe choked out, "the new sheriff, Cole Bonner!"

Hearing the name of the man who busted his nose, Red was stunned for a moment, not sure he had heard Abe correctly. "Who'd you say it was?"

"Cole Bonner, he's the man that killed Womack's brothers. He's the one that killed your friend, Tiny," Abe sang out, holding nothing back in hopes of coming out of this alive.

His confession caused Red to become confused. "What about Harley Branch?" he sputtered while still holding Abe stretched halfway across the bar. "I thought he was the one chasin' Troy."

"Cole Bonner," Abe repeated.

The name finally sank in Red's confused mind, and he was not sure it could be the same man that had knocked him senseless at Murphy's Store. The realization that they were crossing paths again was difficult for him to believe. "This time, things are gonna be a little different," he vowed and shoved Abe backward, causing the frightened bartender to land on his backside. Red holstered his weapon and headed for the door, striding with confident determination to find Cole Bonner.

Outside, he got no farther than the corner of the building when he was stopped by a scene that was unusual since he and his friends had taken over the town. A mob of people were coming down the middle of the street from the hotel. At the head of the parade, he saw Troy Womack, his hands tied behind his back, being herded along by a tall, rangy fellow holding a rifle in his back.

At once cautious, Red stepped back into the shadow of the building. It looked for all the world like a lynch mob and the worst thing that could have happened to him and his partners—the vigilante committee had gotten the backbone to reorganize their hanging party.

"Damn," he cursed under his breath, his hand automatically falling to rest on the handle of his pistol. There was no question as to what he should do at that moment. He couldn't take on the whole mob of vigilantes.

He hesitated to run for a moment longer when the mob stopped at the jail and waited there while the rangy fellow herded Womack through the door. So it wasn't a lynching, at least not right away. It appeared they were going to lock Troy up with Yarborough, if Abe was telling the truth and Yarborough was in jail.

Red's choices were still few, only one that made sense actually. With nothing he could do against that many men, he had to become scarce and damn quickly at that. He needed to think about what he should do about Yarborough and Womack, if anything, or should he just head for parts unknown while he still had the chance?

Suddenly, Red became angry when he realized how this stranger Abe had called Cole Bonner had managed to pick the three of them off one by one. He was the only one left. Cole Bonner was the name of the man he had first seen at Murphy's Store, but that man looked like an Indian or a half-breed. The man he was seeing now wore no buckskins and had short hair.

If they had stayed together, the four of them

could have stood up to any number of do-gooder town folk. Maybe they could still do it. Tiny was dead, but Red thought if he could spring Yarborough and Womack from jail, the three of them would still be too much for the good citizens of Cheyenne to take down. And they could go ahead with their original plan to rape the town, a town that seemed so ripe for the picking. *Hell, I ain't ready to give up yet,* he declared to himself, his decision more than a little influenced by the desire to retaliate against the town.

The first thing he thought to do was to get out of sight while he studied the situation over. Reversing his path, he hurried back down the muddy street toward Leon Bloodworth's stable, glad now that they had not decided to keep their horses in the hotel's tiny stable. He was more determined than before to settle with the man called Cole Bonner. But he decided he had to be smart about it and wait for an opportunity when he would have the best chance of not being caught.

There was no one at the stable but Leon's son, Marvin, when Red hurried inside after pausing to make sure no one had spotted him. The young boy froze when he turned around to see the menacing gunman confronting him. His father had run to join the gang of citizens escorting Troy Womack to jail.

"What the hell are you gapin' at?" Red demanded. "Get your ass out there and get my horse outta that corral." When Marvin frantically replied that he didn't know which horse was his, Red hesitated just for a second before declaring, "The gray, bring me the damn gray."

The gray was Troy's horse, but it was a better horse than the roan Red had been riding. It might prove impossible to get Troy and Yarborough out of jail, so he decided he might as well take the best horse in case he had to hightail it. Thinking that a smart decision, he followed Marvin into the tack room and showed him which bridle was his. Then while the boy went to the corral, Red picked up his saddle and walked out between the stalls to wait for Marvin to fetch the gray.

While he saddled Troy's horse, he tried to decide what to do next. It was still fairly early in the day, and daylight was not his friend if he thought to hole up somewhere in town where he could see what was going on. He desperately needed to get back in his room in the hotel to pick up his extra ammunition and his saddlebags, but there was little chance of that without being seen by someone and getting trapped inside. Whether he ran or stayed to help his friends, he was reluctant to leave all his possibles in the hotel room. He was still of the opinion that, if he could free Yarborough and Womack, the three of them would be more than a match for the vigilantes. And if they could knock off this Cole Bonner fellow, it would be easier still. He decided it worthwhile to give it a shot, but he had to hole up somewhere and wait for darkness, so he could move about town without being seen.

Even though it appeared the menacing outlaw was leaving for good, Marvin could not find the courage to ask for payment of his stable fees. Relieved to see his departure, he stepped back well out of the way when Red stepped up into the saddle and wheeled the gray around to leave through the back door of the stable. Taking the same path that Harley had taken when he was thinking to escape the four outlaws, Red headed out back of the town toward Crow Creek. His only plan was to find a good spot to wait out the day, then, under the cover of darkness, return to look the jail over. If possible, he might try to somehow find a way to break Yarborough and Troy out of there.

While the day dragged by for Red Swann, it moved at a more rapid pace for the folks back in town. Motivated to help now that the odds were much more in their favor, Jim Low and John Beecher volunteered their time to stand guard at the jail, while Cole searched the town, looking for the one remaining gunman. His first stop, after checking with Abe at the Cowboy's Rest, was the stables, where young Marvin Bloodworth told him of Red's departure. It appeared that Swann had opted to skip town before risking the fate of his two cohorts in crime. Cole combed every shop and saloon in town, anyway, and had to conclude that Red had, indeed, decided to run for it. That might be good news for the town, but Cole was not ready to permit the ruthless outlaw to get away with shooting Harley, even if it meant another long chase.

After satisfying himself that Red was not hiding in town at the present time, Cole went to Dr. Marion's office on the edge of town to see how Harley was doing. He found Mary Lou in the parlor when he walked in. "How's he doin'?" Cole asked.

"He's still alive is all Doc will say right now," Mary Lou answered. "I just brought some food from the hotel for him and Doc. Doc was glad to get it. He's in the kitchen eating now, but Harley ain't in any shape to eat. How about you? Are you hungry?"

Cole hadn't thought about it before she asked. "No, I don't reckon. I could use some coffee, though. Got any of that?"

"We've got plenty of that," she replied. "Doc doesn't have a thimbleful of food in the whole house, but he does have coffee. Come on. I'll get you a cup, and you can ask Doc about Harley."

Cole wasn't surprised to hear about the lack of food in the house. Doc Marion was a bachelor and usually ate all his meals at the hotel.

"I'm surprised you aren't at the meeting," Doc greeted Cole when he followed Mary Lou into the kitchen. When Cole replied that he wasn't aware of any meeting, Doc went on to inform him. "The one at the hotel. His Honor, the mayor, called for a meeting to decide what to do with your prisoners. Seems he and Douglas Green have decided to crawl out of their holes since you took the outlaws off the street—holding a trial for them, I imagine. Douglas told me that Gordon Luck had showed up to go to the meeting. He said Gordon told him that he owed the town an apology for not jumping in to help before this."

That was especially surprising to Cole. Gordon had evidently had a confrontation with his conscience. Maybe it might have been a move toward getting Carrie involved with the community. He was surprised that Gordon would have left her alone at his house up on Crow Creek.

"No, I didn't know a meetin' was called," Cole repeated and took the cup of coffee Mary Lou handed him. "I reckon it's up to the town, what they do with those two." He shifted the conversation to a matter he was more concerned about. "What about Harley? Is he gonna make it?" He wasn't overly interested in what the men of the town decided to do with Yarborough and Womack. The only one of the three who held his burning interest was Red Swann, and he was sworn to make him pay for his attack on Harley.

Doc paused to pull a tough piece of bacon rind out of his mouth, examining it for a moment before scraping it off his finger on the edge of his plate. "I don't know for certain. I had to go pretty deep for that one in his chest. That man musta been standing right in front of Harley when he shot him. I got the bullet out of him, but it made such a mess, I'm not sure if it tore his lung up or not. We'll just have to wait and see how he does today and tonight and see if he's still with us tomorrow. I don't think we'll have to wait much longer than that to know for sure."

"That don't sound too good," Cole said.

Doc shook his head. "It's all up to Harley now, him and his Maker. I've done all I can do."

"I'm sure you have, Doc. Can I see him now?"

"He might not be awake," Doc said. He got up from his chair then and led Cole and Mary Lou into his surgery where Harley was still lying on the table. "Now that you can help me, I think it'd be a good idea to move him off my table and put him on that cot." He nodded toward a cot in a corner of the room. "It'll be a lot more comfortable for him."

As carefully as they could manage, the three of them transferred Harley to the cot. His eyes remained closed until he was settled onto the cotton mattress. Cole wasn't sure if he was dead or alive until his eyelids fluttered briefly and he asked the same question as before.

"Did you get him?"

Cole said no but promised that he would before it was over.

"Hurts like hell," Harley muttered painfully. "I believe he kilt me, but if he didn't, Doc's tryin' to finish the job for him." That seemed to be all the talking he could manage for the moment. He closed his eyes again.

Cole couldn't help but smile, looking down at the little man. *Thunder Mouse*, he thought. *He's gonna make it.* "You just do what Doc tells you and rest up, and I'll be back to see you."

Mary Lou walked out with him as far as the front porch. "Doc didn't say anything about Carrie when he was telling you about Gordon coming in. But I know you're interested in what happens to her, and in case you're wondering, Carrie came in with Gordon. She's staying at the dining room with Maggie and me till Gordon comes back for her."

Cole nodded slowly in reply and Mary Lou switched to another subject, one she was more interested in. "I guess you're going looking for that other killer now."

Again, he nodded in reply.

"Don't suppose he's already left this part of the country," she went on. "And you'll go after him even if he has."

"If he left a trail," he said.

"I hope to hell he didn't," she replied.

"I promised Harley," he protested.

"I know," she sighed impatiently. "Just don't get yourself killed." She turned about and went back inside.

CHAPTER 14

"How are the prisoners doin'?" Cole asked Jim Low when he got back to the sheriff's office. He looked at the cell room where the two were sitting, sulking silently at that moment.

"They ain't exactly enjoyin' it," Jim said with a grin. "And they're bellyachin' about bein' hungry. What are we gonna do about feedin' 'em? Pete Little said the hotel dinin' room always fed prisoners when John Henry was sheriff. Reckon Maggie will feed these two?"

"I reckon," Cole said, realizing there was more to being sheriff than simply arresting people. "I'll talk to Maggie about it."

Seeing Cole walk in, Yarborough got up from his cot and stepped up to the bars. "You might be thinkin' you've pulled a smart one on us, Bonner, but you mighta just signed your own death certificate. If you had a lick of sense, you'd know that I'm the only one who can save your life."

Cole did not reply, choosing to pause and look at him, waiting for him to continue.

"You didn't catch our partner, did you?" When

Cole still did not answer, Yarborough went on. "You ain't gonna catch him, neither. You ain't even gonna see him till he's ready for you to, and it'll be too late for you to stop the bullet with your name on it."

Ignoring Yarborough's ranting, Cole turned to Pete Little, who had returned to claim his prior duties at the jail. "Looks like you fellows are in good shape here. I'm goin' to the hotel now and talk to Maggie about feedin' these two birds." He turned to Jim Low. "You all right, Jim?"

"Everything's under control here," Jim assured him.

Cole nodded and turned toward the door.

"You'd best listen to what I'm tellin' you!" Yarborough bellowed. "I'm the only one who can keep you from gettin' a bullet in the back, 'cause Red Swann will come after you unless I tell him not to shoot you. And I'm ready to make a deal with you. It's your town, and I'll call Red off if you turn me and Troy loose." When there was still no response from Cole, he made one promise more. "And we'll ride outta here and never come back. How's that? You get to live and we won't bother this town no more."

Finally, Cole made a verbal response. "You're wastin' a lotta wind, Yarborough. What happens to you two ain't up to me. Matter of fact, I heard the town council was meetin' this mornin' to decide what to do with you. I doubt they'll decide to set you free."

Yarborough heard the last word as the door was closing behind Cole. Cole could still hear his cursing as he stepped up into the saddle. He was anxious to search for some evidence of Red's trail before it turned cold, but had to delay it until he made arrangements for his prisoners to be fed.

Arthur Campbell intercepted Cole when he saw him come into the hotel on his way to the dining room. "Cole," he called out. "Can I have a word with you?"

Cole stopped and waited for him.

"I don't know if you heard or not, but we've just come out of a meeting of the town council, and it has a lot to do with you."

"Is that so?" Cole replied. "How's that?"

"Well, we've got two dangerous criminals locked up in our jail and you're the man that put them there."

"Are you tellin' me you've got a problem with that?" Cole asked, frankly surprised. He thought the whole town would be glad to have the trouble-makers off their streets.

"No, no," Campbell was quick to reply. "No problem. What I wanted to tell you is the town can't survive without an effective sheriff. And the council voted unanimously to offer that job to you because we all agreed we aren't likely to find a man more qualified than you to fill that position."

Beyond surprised, Cole was astonished. He didn't know what to say. It was something he never had even the most remote thought about. His abrupt confiscation of the sheriff's office was done with no expectation beyond ridding the town of the outlaws holding it hostage. "Damn," he swore. "I ain't ever thought about bein' a peace officer."

"One of the things that came up in the council's discussion was the fact that you made it a point to arrest both of the men in jail now, instead of simply shooting them down like dogs," Campbell said. "That indicated a responsible officer of the law and not a hired gunman, like the men you put in jail. My boy, Sonny, just came from the jail a few minutes ago and he said he heard you tell Yarborough that a jury would decide what to do with him and the other one. Well, that jury has already decided and the verdict is death by hanging for the killing of John Henry Black and Harvey Settles. It's scheduled for tomorrow morning at eight o'clock." Cole showed little surprise, so Campbell emphasized the difference. "I know they're gonna end up dead, whether you shot them or not, but this way they got their trial, like it should be in a civilized territory. Like I said, we want you to take that job, so whaddaya say? Hell, you've already taken over the responsibilities."

"Well, I don't know," Cole hedged. "Like I told you, bein' a lawman is one thing that ain't ever entered my mind." He hesitated, then said, "And I've got one more man to run down before I'm through with this bunch. I feel I oughta tell you that I'm kinda hopin' he don't wanna come peacefully, if I do catch up with him."

"I understand," Campbell said, "and I feel like you'll do whatever you have to do and whatever's right. But the offer still stands. Take some time to think about it and then, when you're ready, tell me your decision."

"I'll surely do that," Cole replied, "and I appreciate the offer." He turned to leave. "I've gotta go talk to Maggie now to arrange to feed my prisoners, even if it ain't gonna be for more than one night and breakfast tomorrow."

"See there," Campbell chuckled. "You're already acting like a sheriff."

When informed of the necessity to provide meals for the two prisoners, Maggie was not surprised at all. She had assumed she would do so as soon as she heard there were prisoners, because she always had. "Arthur Campbell will see to it that I get paid," she said when Cole asked about it. "I get paid by the council, same as the sheriff gets paid, if we had one."

He didn't tell her that he had just been offered that job, because he wasn't sure he wanted it. While talking to Maggie, he heard some noise from the kitchen. Maggie noticed and told him Mary Lou had not come back from the doctor's office yet. "That's Beulah you hear banging around in the kitchen. She came in as soon as she heard two of those bastards were in jail and the other one lit out. Matter of fact, it looks like a lot of folks have come crawling out of their hiding places. For a while there, it was looking like a ghost town around here." Looking quickly over her shoulder to make sure she was not behind her, Maggie continued. "Even Carrie Green is here. I guess Arthur told you Gordon had come back to help out. Carrie's holed up in Mary Lou's room right now."

"I don't know if you women oughta be opening this dinin' room until we know for sure that Swann isn't still hangin' around."

"Well, we thought about that," Maggie said. "But you saw how many we fed this morning. Maybe we'll not stay open much longer and just find us a place to hole up till it's clear."

He left the dining room with his head filled with decisions needing to be made. It appeared that Red Swann had fled, but he couldn't be sure of that. The conscienceless miscreant might have a sense of loyalty to his partners and might be planning some attempt to free them. It didn't seem likely, but if it was the case, the possibility existed that a lot more people might get killed. Cole had to consider that, but how best to prevent it? The jail was pretty secure and built to defend against attack. Jim Low and John Beecher had volunteered to guard the prisoners overnight, which left Cole free to patrol the town in an attempt to stop any attack before it reached the jail.

He figured that he had only the rest of the day and that night to find Swann, if he was still there. Cole had searched every business and outbuilding in the town, making him pretty sure the outlaw was not in town, but he could be hiding almost anywhere outside of town, watching any activity around the jail. It was easy to assume that Swann had figured the smart thing to do was to run, but all his supplies and probably a lot of his extra ammunition were still in his hotel room.

Cole figured he would be hard-pressed to leave

without them. It would be pretty difficult for him to slip into the hotel to get his possessions without someone seeing him. After thinking it through several times, he decided he couldn't cover all possibilities. Figuring the first priority was to guard the condemned prisoners to make sure they met their appointment with the hangman's noose, he was satisfied he had that under control.

Laboring through the same possibilities that troubled Cole, Red Swann was weighing his options as the dawn broke on a new day. His gut told him to run like hell while the town was occupied with the two men they had captured. He had found a low ridge near the creek, about half a mile from town where he could keep his horse out of sight. He could see the back of the jail from there, and could get a closer look if he made his way on foot to a grassy mound a quarter of a mile closer. He had thought constantly during the night whether or not he wanted to risk a try to free Yarborough and Womack.

He had been leaning that way because of the possibility still remaining of running roughshod over the town as they had planned. But things had changed since the arrival of Cole Bonner. Red had ridden with Flint Yarborough for a few years, and it might not be right to desert him. Troy Womack, on the other hand, troubled Red not in the least. He never had much use for him or his brothers. It was Yarborough that caused even the brief deliberation as to what he should do.

Looking at the seemingly busy town, he decided it would be a foolish thing to try to break his partners out of that jail. "Sorry, Yarborough," he muttered, "I reckon this just ain't your lucky day."

With that decision made, he had a new problem to contend with. He was going to have to take off without his saddlebags and other possibles he had left in the hotel room. All he had were a horse and saddle, his weapons, and one cartridge belt. The thought of it reminded him that he had had nothing to eat since the day before. While he was thinking about that, he was distracted by a flurry of activity around the lone standing cottonwood next to the stable. Curious, he squinted to make out the cause of the activity until it struck him. Several men were rigging up a couple of ropes over one of the larger limbs of the tree.

They're fixing to have a hanging! They had evidently decided not to wait to turn Yarborough and Womack over to the U.S. marshal. *They're going to hang them right now!*

For a few minutes, Red remained kneeling in the grass, stunned with the realization that had he not had to visit the outhouse, he would have been invited to that lynching party with Yarborough and Troy. That was just pure luck, as was the fact that he got the jump on the little gray-haired fellow trying to ambush him when he came out of the outhouse. It told him that it was a sign from the devil, or whoever, that he'd best run while he had the chance. It was not easy to give up on his determination to have his vengeance for the treatment he had received from Cole Bonner. But maybe he would be smart to avoid the possibility of ending up like Yarborough and Troy. *Best I leave while I've got the chance*, he decided.

With that settled in his mind, he started to get up and make tracks, but another thought occurred to him. *I'll bet the whole town will be down there at the stable to watch Yarborough and Troy swing. It would be the perfect time to slip into the hotel and get my stuff.* The prospect brought a smug smile to his face. It would sure make his escape to wherever he decided to go a hell of a lot easier.

With that decision firmly made, he knelt back down to watch the preparations taking place at the big tree by the stables. He figured the best thing to do was to wait until the spectators started showing up for the hanging, maybe even until they brought Yarborough and Troy down to the stable. There should be plenty of time for him to slip into the hotel, get his belongings, and ride out the other end of town without anyone seeing him.

He had no idea what time it was, but he had to surmise that it was getting close to the hour of execution because a sizable crowd of gawkers had already gathered, and more were still coming.

Maybe I shouldn't wait any longer, he thought.

What if the hanging went faster than he expected and left him short of time to do what he planned? But he had a morbid curiosity to see ol' Yarborough when they stretched his neck. A moment after thinking it, he saw a wagon driving down toward the stable, and he was certain he saw Yarborough and Womack trussed up in the back of it. Red quickly changed his mind about watching the hanging and decided he'd better get while the getting was good.

Riding in from the opposite end of town, he could still see a few stragglers hurrying down toward the stables, but for the most part, the street was deserted. He rode his horse around behind the hotel and left it tied there at the back steps. Moving as quietly as he could manage, he entered the door to the back hallway and walked up the hall toward the back stairs. When he passed the splintered doorjamb at one of the bedrooms, it brought to mind the reason he had broken in before. And he couldn't help a feeling of disappointment for never having had the visit he had planned with Mary Lou.

Reaching the stairs to the second floor, he paused to listen for a moment. Hearing no sound that would indicate anyone was moving about upstairs, he proceeded up the steps and walked down the hall to the room he had shared with Yarborough. He still had the key in his pocket, so he didn't have to risk making noise when he entered. Inside, he discovered that the room had been cleaned and his and Yarborough's belongings were in one pile close to the door. *Waiting for somebody to come haul them off,* he thought, feeling lucky for having gotten there before that had happened.

With no time to waste, he pulled his saddlebags and his sack of personal items off the pile and took an extra moment to take a couple of Yarborough's possessions, as well. *He sure as hell ain't got no more use for them,* he thought as he stuck into his belt a bone-handled knife he had always admired. Then remembering, he picked Yarborough's heavy vest up and felt for the derringer he always carried in an inside pocket. The little pocket pistol was not there, but it prompted him to check his own vest to make sure his was where he usually carried it. He had adopted the habit after joining Yarborough but had never had occasion to use it. He felt pretty sure that whoever cleaned up the room had already made a thorough search for any money left in either man's clothes, but he went through Yarborough's extra shirt and trousers to be sure.

With that done, he went back out in the hall and tiptoed to the head of the front steps to take a quick look down at the lobby with a thought toward robbing the cashbox. Someone was manning the front desk, but it was only the owner's boy, Sonny. Red hesitated. The temptation was almost over-powering, but the risk of making too much noise made him think better of the idea. He turned about and hurried back down the hall to the back stairs.

When he reached the first floor again, he had to stop for a moment when he caught the aroma of fresh coffee drifting out the open kitchen door. It had been closed when he walked by before. Immediately alert, he dropped the sack he was carrying and drew his .44. He had heard nothing on his way upstairs and had assumed they had gone to watch the hanging like everyone else in town. Peering in the door, he saw no one in the kitchen, so he figured maybe Sonny Campbell had gone in the kitchen for coffee while he was upstairs going through Yarborough's things. That made sense. He holstered his pistol, picked up his sack again, though he found it difficult to forget his empty stomach. He briefly considered taking a few seconds to visit that pot of coffee he could smell, but decided against it and continued toward the outside door at the end of the hall.

Hurrying, he passed the room where he had damaged the door and was just before the second bedroom door when it suddenly opened. Startled, he and Mary Lou stopped cold when they confronted each other. Her immediate reaction was to slam the door, but Red, acting just as quickly, dropped his saddlebags and the sack and put a shoulder to the door. Just as Maggie's door had, Mary Lou's door gave way to his superior strength.

Bursting into the room, he didn't see her at first, then spotted her on the floor between the bed and the wall. He dived across the bed and caught her as she pulled a shotgun out from under it. "No, you don't," he warned as he grabbed the barrel of the shotgun, confident then that she was powerless against him. When she still fought to hold onto the weapon, he slapped her hard across her face until she could hold on no longer. "Now lookee there," he teased, "you got that pretty face to bleedin'."

He pulled her across the bed and threw the shotgun back onto the floor between the bed and the wall. "Now let me set you straight, Miss Honey-britches. If you don't behave yourself like a nice little lady, I'll cut your throat and say to hell with you." Lifting her up on her feet, he pinned her arms to her sides with one huge arm around her. With his free hand, he drew the bone-handled knife from his belt and pressed the blade against her throat to make sure she knew he meant business. "Who else is still here?" he demanded.

"Nobody," Mary Lou answered, her face still throbbing from his blows.

"Don't tell me no lie," he warned. "I saw that scrawny son of the owner's at the front desk. Now, who else is here?" He tightened the arm imprisoning her until she found it difficult to breathe. "And in case you're thinkin' 'bout hollerin' for help, you'd best know I'll shoot the little son of a bitch if he comes a-runnin'. Who else is here? Anybody in the kitchen or the dinin' room?"

"Nobody," she repeated. "I forgot about Sonny. Everybody else went down to the stables to watch your friends hang. Too bad you missed the party." She refused to be anything but defiant, even knowing she was helpless against his strength. She was rewarded for her curt remark with a slight penetration from his knife. Although it stung, she made no sound, a sudden tensing of her body the only indication that she felt it.

"You're a tough-talkin' little bitch, ain't you?" He sneered. "You know what you need? You need to be rode hard one time, and it don't look like to me that you've ever been. And I've knowed from the first that I'm the man to do it—made up my mind to do it."

She was immediately concerned. Up until that moment, she was counting on his desire to run before Cole and the other men caught up with him. Maybe, she feared, the crude ox didn't have enough brains to know he didn't have time to waste with her. "You'd better get away from here before they come back to get you."

"You're right," he agreed. "I ain't aimin' to waste no time here." He bent down with his mouth against her ear and whispered, "I'm takin' you with me, Honey-britches." With that, he started walking her back up the hall—much to her surprise—toward the kitchen door. Determined to resist, she tried to hold back, only to have her feet dragged along the floor. When he reached the open door to the kitchen, he paused to take a quick look inside. Seeing no one, he dragged her inside. "I ain't had no grub since yesterday mornin' and I can smell some bacon on the stove. I'll take some food with me." When he felt her struggle to free herself again, it only served to amuse him. "If you don't put up no more fight, I might even let you have some of it."

Still holding her tightly, he walked across the kitchen, when he spotted a pan of freshly baked biscuits on the table. He stuck his knife back under his belt and reached for a biscuit.

"Have some coffee with it," a voice behind him invited a split second before a full pot of hot coffee caught him flush against the side of his head.

Staggered, his open coat and shirt soaked with the scalding hot liquid, he had to release Mary Lou while he frantically grasped his shirt to pull it away from his skin. Roaring like a wounded bear, he turned to meet his attacker, but Maggie had already backed out of his reach. He lunged after her, but slid face forward on the floor after being slammed in the back of his head with a heavy iron skillet, wielded by Beulah.

Hot grease and bacon enough to serve a dozen diners was suspended in the air for a split second before landing on his prone body. Beulah set herself squarely, watching his response, ready with her skillet, and when he struggled to get to his knees, she landed another blow to the back of his head that laid him prostrate again.

Taking advantage of his immobility, Beulah's two fellow avengers did not hesitate. Mary Lou quickly reached down and pulled the .44 handgun from Swann's holster, while Maggie ran to retrieve her shotgun from behind the door.

"I ain't never seen coffee and bacon go to better use," she declared as she ran.

"Sure made a mess for me to clean up, though, didn't it?" Beulah observed. "Reckon I'd better put on another pot of coffee."

With time while their victim was still making no move to get up, Maggie turned her concern toward Mary Lou. "Are you all right, honey? You've got some blood on the side of your face."

"Yeah, I'm all right, thanks to you two," Mary Lou answered and put her fingers gingerly to her cheekbone. Smiling at Beulah, she said, "I'll help you mop up this mess after we decide what to do with Mr. Swann, here. I expect we better keep our guns on him till we do."

"Why don't we just shoot the son of a bitch?" Beulah asked. "If the men captured him, they'd just hang him with the other two. Save a lotta time and effort to put a bullet in him and be done with it."

"It wouldn't be any worse than shootin' a mad dog," a voice from the hallway door declared.

Startled, the three avengers turned to see Carrie standing there holding a shotgun. Of the four women, she had the most history with the loathsome beast and certainly no sympathy.

"I was wondering about you," Mary Lou said. "The last I remember, you were under the bed when I reached for that shotgun."

"I know," Carrie replied. "And I was so scared, I like to wet my bloomers, especially when he dragged you across the bed. I was afraid to move. But when he threw this shotgun back against the wall, I figured it was up to me to take it and come help you." She broke out a big grin. "But I see you didn't need me. I believe you three could take down a grizzly. I agree with Beulah, though, why don't we just shoot him and be done with it?"

"Maybe," Mary Lou replied. "But I think the mayor and his council are trying to act like a civilized community and give him a trial before they hang him."

"What good does that do?" Beulah asked. "Dead is dead, whether they give him a trial or not."

"Mary Lou's right," Maggie decided. "It ain't our business to execute anybody. We'll guard him till the men get back from the hanging. All right?"

Beulah shrugged. "I reckon. Seems like a waste of time to me, though."

Conscious of the conversation between the four

women to decide his fate, Swann did not move while he waited for his head to clear. Still dazed by the sudden assault, he was not sure he had control of his faculties. His head felt as if it was split open and his brains were hanging out the back, but he was gradually beginning to regain control of his senses. Knowing that he was in serious danger of not coming out of the situation alive, he gave no thoughts toward any mortification over having been completely overpowered by three women. It was no use blaming himself for believing Mary Lou when she'd said no one else was here. Instead, he tried to think hard on how to get out of there before anyone else returned to help them.

"He's moving!" Carrie exclaimed when Swann shifted his hands slightly.

All three women holding weapons immediately trained them on the prone man.

"Don't shoot!" Swann cried out. "I give up. I'm hurt bad. I think you done cracked my skull. I just wanna get up from here and set down in a chair. I'm done."

Looking at Maggie, Mary Lou felt sure she preferred that Swann stay where he was, facedown on the floor, until help arrived.

Before she decided to say as much, however, Maggie said, "All right, but you'd best move slow and easy, or I'll blow your brains out." She pulled a chair out from the kitchen table. "You can just sit right here."

With each move slow and deliberate, he got himself up on his knees before pausing in that position apparently to wait for his head to stop spinning. Then with great effort, he crawled over to the chair and pulled himself up onto it. After a few minutes, with his four women captors watching him intently, he spoke. "I think my head is busted. Can I just have a drink of water? I've got an awful thirst."

"Hell, no." Beulah answered immediately.

But Maggie shrugged indifferently and said. "I don't see no danger in giving him some water." When no one else objected, she said to Carrie, "Why don't you give him a cup of water, honey, but set that shotgun down by the cupboard before you do." She was wary of an attempt by him to get his hands on it, no matter the seemingly helpless state he presented.

Understanding Maggie's precaution, Carrie nodded, propped her shotgun safely out of his reach, and filled a cup of water from the bucket.

Wincing as if in severe pain, Swann lifted his head and murmured, "Thank you, Corina." Reaching for the cup of water, he suddenly grabbed her arm instead and jerked the surprised woman across his lap, at the same time pulling the derringer from his vest pocket. "Now, drop them damn guns or I'm gonna put a bullet in her head!"

The sharp report of the shot startled everyone in the kitchen, especially Swann when he rocked back in the chair and looked down to discover the hole in his shirt. Confused for a second, then realizing that he had been shot, he nevertheless attempted to go through with his threat. Before he could point the derringer at Carrie's head, a second shot slammed into his chest and he dropped the pocket gun to the floor. Not sure if she was dead or alive, Carrie rolled off of Swann's legs onto the floor as he slumped over sideways.

For a long moment, there was no other sound in the kitchen, save that of the cocking of a Henry rifle.

A moment later, the kitchen was filled with the screams of four excited women, crying out in relief. All heads turned toward the tall, sandy-haired man standing in the doorway from the hotel dining room. Unable to wait a second longer, Mary Lou ran to meet him.

He gently pushed her aside, his eyes still focused on the body slumped sideways in the kitchen chair. "Lemme make sure," he said and walked over to confirm that Swann was dead.

When he gave them an assuring nod, they all erupted into an eager report of the circumstances that had led up to the point of his arrival.

Fearing to think of what might have happened had Cole not shown up when he did, Mary Lou asked, "How did you know he would be here?"

"I didn't for sure," he answered. "But it struck me that he might wanna try to get his possessions back, and there wouldn't be a better time to do it than when most of the town was down at the stables. So I thought I'd better check."

"Well, praise the Lord you came when you did," Maggie exclaimed.

"Amen to that!" Beulah added.

Both women knew that one or more of them would have been killed had he not come—Carrie for sure, if they had tried to fight him.

Standing at his elbow, Mary Lou looked up and asked, "Weren't you afraid you might hit Carrie? He was bent over her so close, there wasn't much room to shoot. You must have been concerned about it."

"I reckon," he replied. "I'll tell you about it someday, but right now I expect I'd better drag him outta here. There's gonna be a whole passel of folks in here in a minute or two, after they heard those shots."

Before she could press him any further, Sonny Campbell, having waited till he was sure it was safe, spoke up from the hallway door. "There sure are. I can hear them coming already."

CHAPTER 15

Peace was once again restored to the promising town of Cheyenne where the Union Pacific Railroad crossed over Crow Creek. On the day following the shooting death of Red Swann and the hanging of Flint Yarborough and Troy Womack, there was still a feeling of uncertainty lingering in Cole Bonner's mind. After a good breakfast in the hotel dining room, where Maggie insisted he had earned a free meal, he was on his way to Doc Marion's office. Doc had told him that a new day might give him a much better chance at predicting Harley's recovery. Cole only hoped that the Lord saw fit to give Harley a little more time. His wounds were very serious, so he knew that was asking a lot.

Doc Marion met him at the door. "Morning, Cole. He's awake, but he's running a fever and he can't sit up yet. You can go on in and talk to him. Just don't stay too long. He'll tire out pretty quick."

He went into Doc's surgery and stopped short of the cot in the corner to see if Harley might be asleep.

"Is that you, Cole?" Harley suddenly rasped.

"Yeah, it's me," Cole answered and walked on over to his bedside. "How'd you know it was me?"

Speaking in a voice barely above a whisper, Harley said, "He shot me in the chest. He didn't shoot me in my ears."

Cole couldn't help laughing. "When Doc dug around in there for those bullets, I see he didn't take out any of that orneriness." He pulled a stool up beside the cot and sat down. "Doc said not to stay long, so how you doin', Thunder Mouse? You gonna whip this thing?"

"Damn right," Harley replied, although with noticeable weakness. "If Doc don't kill me with all his pokin' and washin'. I'd most likely get better a whole lot quicker if Old Walkin' Owl was doctorin' me."

"Maybe so," Cole allowed, "but I think Doc's pretty good at his trade."

Within a few minutes, Doc came in to administer a dose of laudanum. He gave Cole a nod.

Understanding it to be a signal, Cole said, "I'd best be goin' now. Got to go take care of my horses. I ain't been givin' them much attention for the last few days. But I'll be back after you've rested up some more."

"Cole," Harley said when his friend got up to leave.

Cole sat back down on the stool and leaned close.

"I want you to take me home," Harley said, "soon as I can set up."

Cole knew Harley meant Medicine Bear's village on the Laramie River. "I will, partner, just as soon as you're fit enough to go." He got up to leave then, thinking that Harley knew his time was short, no matter the prognosis Doc might come back with. "I'll be checkin' on you, so do what Doc tells you and rest up."

He was not really concerned that his horses weren't getting enough attention, but he went down to the stable to check on them and the horses that had belonged to the four outlaws. He only had two horses in Leon's stable, the bay he had been riding, and one packhorse to start with, but he had claims on the gray that Womack had owned plus one of the outlaws' packhorses. He was content to let Leon have the rest of them and spent most of the morning passing the time of day with Leon after they had settled their deal.

When the conversation died out, he went to the hotel dining room to see what Maggie and her girls had cooked up for the noon meal.

Mary Lou saw him when he walked in the door and guided him away from the long table where he was inclined to sit. "Sit down over here closer to the kitchen," she said as she led him to the table where Harley had been seated when Swann and Womack had walked into the dining room on that fateful day. "You'll get your coffee a lot quicker and it'll give me a chair to sit and talk when I can."

He sat down and in a few minutes she returned from the kitchen with a cup of coffee and a plate of food. "Did you see Harley this morning?" she asked and he told her that he had. She left him then and went to help Maggie serve the customers at the long table. It struck him that he was getting more than the customary attention and figured it to be because of his timely arrival the day before and the fact that he hadn't missed his mark with either shot.

When most everyone else was finished eating, he decided he might as well go talk to Arthur Campbell and get that over with.

Mary Lou stopped him just as he was getting up. "Sit back down. As soon as I take this tray of dishes back to the kitchen, I'm gonna have myself a cup of coffee. And I need somebody to talk to while I'm drinking it." When he hesitated, she asked, "Have you got someplace you've got to go to right now?"

"Nope," he answered. "I gotta go talk to Arthur Campbell for a minute, but that's all. Matter of fact, I'm just killin' time, waitin' around to see if Harley's gonna be fit enough to ride back up to Medicine Bear's camp on the Laramie."

That caught her attention right away. "Wait a minute. Let me take this tray back. You want some more coffee?"

"My insides are floatin' in it already," he replied, "but I reckon I've got room for a little bit more. Tell you what, though, let me go find Arthur before he decides to go somewhere. I'll be right back. That'll give you time to clear the tables and get your coffee."

"You'll be right back?" Mary Lou asked, and he said he would.

When he returned, Maggie and Mary Lou had cleared the tables of dishes and Beulah was busy washing the dirty ones. After a cheerful hello, Maggie disappeared into the kitchen, leaving little doubt that all the fuss over his cup of coffee with

Mary Lou was of more than casual importance. In keeping with the supposed reason for the visit, Maggie brought two cups of coffee and placed them on the table, then disappeared again. Cole wasn't sure he could handle any more, but he thanked her and took a sip.

Mary Lou didn't waste any time. "You said you were just waiting around until Harley was well enough to ride."

"That's right," he replied and took another little sip of coffee.

"Then you're gonna take him back with you to that Crow village."

"Yes, ma'am."

"Then I suppose you and Harley will be heading back up in the mountains come this spring. White Wolf and Thunder Mouse, following the elk and the deer." There was a hint of sarcasm in her tone.

"Reckon not. I ain't sure Harley will be able to go. I think he knows it, too." She started to say something, but paused, so he went on. "Besides, I can't go. I just told Arthur I'd take the job of sheriff here in Cheyenne."

She was too surprised to speak at first as it sank in. When she could, it was to chastise him. "Why, you son of a bitch. Why didn't you tell me that at first?"

"Didn't think you'd care one way or the other," he deadpanned. When she just shook her head, he continued. "Yep, I thought it was time for me to sink some roots somewhere, settle down, maybe have a son to carry on after his daddy is gone."

"Is that a fact?" Mary Lou replied, recovering

her usual attitude of indifference. "Got anybody in mind to have that son for you?"

"Well, tell you the truth, I was figurin' on seein' if you were interested."

She responded with a knowing nod. "Is that so? Well, I'm not interested in having a bastard boy or girl for any man."

"Reckon we'll have to get married then."

"Reckon we will," she mocked. "The sooner, the better."

"Suits me."

They sat for a few moments longer, just smiling at each other, both parties satisfied that things were finally working out the way fate intended.

"Well, I told the mayor I'd be right back. I had some important business I had to attend to."

They both got up from the table, and Mary Lou stepped up and gave him a quick kiss to seal the deal. "Same as a contract," she called after him as he walked out the door.

He signaled a confirmation as Maggie and Beulah came from the kitchen then, having listened just inside the kitchen door.

"Damned if that wasn't the most romantic proposal I believe I've ever heard," Maggie said sarcastically.

"I thought Ralph's proposal was about as romantic as buyin' a mule," Beulah commented. "But after hearin' you two go at it, I believe Ralph was et up with romance."

"It'll come," Mary Lou said with confidence. "The romance will come."

* * *

To everyone's surprise but Cole's, Harley rallied from his sickbed after two more days. Cole was well acquainted with the little man's will and determination, and he also knew that Harley was aware that the old man with the black hood and scythe was coming soon to take him. When Cole asked him how he knew, Harley said the old man had visited him a couple of times when he was asleep. Cole wasn't sure about things of that nature, but he saw no reason to doubt his friend. He couldn't help remembering the white wolf he, himself, had seen that somehow left no tracks in snow a foot deep on the riverbank.

When Harley said again he wanted to go home, Cole made preparations to take him. He suggested borrowing a wagon to transport Harley, but his stubborn friend insisted that he could sit in the saddle. He had no intention of returning to the village in the back of a wagon, he said.

Cole threw Harley's fancy Mexican saddle on his horse and helped him mount. When all was ready, a small party of friends gathered to say good-bye and wish him well. By then, everyone was of the opinion that it was the last they would see of Cole's cocky little friend.

Standing by Cole's side, Mary Lou placed her hand on his arm. "Don't go letting your wild blood get hot when you get back with your Indian friends. Promise me you'll start back as soon as Harley's settled in."

Still finding it hard to believe that she really wanted to be his wife, he grinned and nodded. "I promise. And don't you get to thinkin' you like it better when I'm not here."

She laughed. "You just be careful." He started to put his foot in the stirrup, but she stopped him. "I just remembered something you said in the dining room when you shot Red Swann. I asked you if you weren't afraid to take that shot with Carrie lying across that monster's lap. And you said you'd tell me about it later—but I forgot until now."

He shrugged, feeling some embarrassment for admitting a weakness, but she seemed to want to know. "Well," he admitted, "it was Carrie lyin' across his legs and I didn't have any doubt about taking the shot. If it had been you lyin' there, I mighta started thinkin' about how my whole life would end if I happened to miss. I ain't sure I wanna live without you."

In spite of his efforts to make his confession to Mary Lou only, Maggie and Beulah had managed to stand close enough in the kitchen door to overhear everything spoken between the young couple. A romantic sigh escaped from both of the two women as one, "Ahhhh. . . ." They turned and walked arm in arm back to the dining room, satisfied that at long last, everything was happening the way it was meant to happen.